Voices Carry

DIANE RINELLA

Copyright (C) 2015 Diane Rinella
Cover art copyright (C) 2015 Diane Rinella
Cover art and design by Heidi "Azurylipfe" Darras
http://azurylipfe.daportfolio.com/
with Diane Rinella

ISBN: 978-0692593844
ISBN-13: 978-0692593844

For the muse, the memories, and the energies surrounding me.

Acknowledgements

Voices Carry is deeply personal in ways few would understand. In fact, I can truthfully say writing it was emotionally turbulent. The leaps and bounds of growth it caused will take me decades to understand. But of all of the twists and turns my personal life took while writing *Voices Carry*, the core story, along with Brandon's love of music, never faltered.

I owe special thanks to Jared Wilke for doing one of our favorite things; drinking and talking about punk rock. Also, thanks to his wife, Shannon, for dealing with us. While the characters didn't turn out the way I planned, that conversation got my brain into the groove needed to create Saleena.

Special thanks to Darla Roybal and Jennifer Theriot for making sure I got this done while keeping my sanity in check. Lastly, and in no way least, about a zillion thank yous go out to my husband, Brian, who basically turned into a single parent while attempting to work on his own projects and without vocalizing the complaints I am sure he (rightfully) had. This one was a doozy!

Rock and Roll Machine

I am a rock and roll machine,
a product of my own revolution.
The road to success is dark,
but flames of my desire will light the path.
Are you the one who dares to stand in my way?
You may get destroyed, or I just might be saved.
~ Saleena Kale, 1977

I Can Remember

Brandon

Again my tears well, prickling my eyes with shards of heat and creating a barrier between me and the final photo of the woman who was to be my wife—the woman who left me love notes signed with her first name and my last, as if we had already married—the woman who had her life brutally taken, decades too soon.

Amber's brown hair cascades around her face in gentle waves, reminding me of an object of turn-of-the-century art—feminine and locked in time. Her brows arch so softly that even though they are not rainbow-hued, they tell my heart the eyes beneath them are treasures. I miss how those glorious green orbs warmed my heart like the sun. I would give damn near anything to get lost in them again.

The moment this photo was taken is forever etched into my mind. It may be a simple shot of her face, but I remember the wood paneling of the restaurant walls behind her, the white linen on the table between us, and the slice of carrot cake in front of her with the words "Happy 22nd Birthday" scripted around it in chocolate.

My fingers glide down the page, tenderly caressing Amber's image with as much love as if I were actually touching her cheek, and my tears pour. I wish I could feel those soft curves again—curves framing a smile that illuminated my world. A smile that helped me see the beauty of mankind.

God, Amber, it has been nearly a decade since you met with the angels, yet the tingle you bring to my heart still haunts me. The rose pressed into the page next to your photo makes me feel I've locked your ghost into this book. The day of your funeral, we all carried one with us—your mom and dad, your brother and sister, and I. It was something to focus our love into so when we dropped it into your grave our hearts went with you. I had thought of it as being your hand, and that I was walking with you through your transition into whatever beauty was ahead. I couldn't let go, not because I didn't want you to find happiness, but because we were robbed of what we deserved.

Someone once told me memories are akin to dreams—they have the ability to change and become something entirely different from what once was. No way, Amber, I would never betray you. My memories are precious. While I may not recall the reason you chose the dress you wore in this photo, or the color of the nail polish you had on, I will never forget how much you made me smile or how you again stole my heart, just like on the day we met. The memories of how your smile imprinted my soul, time and again, will never be allowed to lose their luster.

My fingers glide over the rose, and even though it is protected under a layer of plastic, the sorrow of losing my every dream emanates through. Amber said when it comes down to it, we are nothing but energy, and energy leaves an imprint for others to appreciate. For years I continued to feel Amber's spark. It eventually drifted away, and a part of me has been sick ever since.

But yet …

Recently I have felt something brewing around me. It reminds me of not long after Amber died, when I could swear she was in the room and offering comfort. It has been years, so why am I sensing her now? I'm not even sure I am. I can only assume it is my brain searching for a way to fill the void.

Knowing memories are all that is left of Amber is too much to bear. I lock her image in my mind before closing my eyes and shutting the book. Watching it get tucked away would be like burying her again.

New York Groove

Brandon

The sorrow of losing Amber has been carved into my soul and has forced me to accept that the tragedy I carry in my heart has become a part of me. In other words, I've learned to press on. Having the right elements in my life helps. To me, Warped Records is more therapeutic than Disneyland.

It's funny, Amber would love how Warped Records proudly displays treasures by brilliant artists, yet she would hate nearly every piece of music within its walls. With us, it wasn't that opposites attracted, but more that common passions brought out how our differences were like oil and water. Flutes and gentle melodies sent Amber's heart swooning so high my being still warms at the memory of watching her glow. I crave something harder. Something that turns me into a juvenile delinquent in all the best ways—crazed, ambitious, and with a slip of danger nagging at my hips. Rock and roll is not only a blast of passion that rips me away from the mundane and throttles me into magnificence, it is also the only thing that can get me out of a funk when happiness becomes elusive. Since losing Amber, that has happened a lot.

I pull into the lot as Dale is getting out of his car. Even though he should have left the office hours ago, he is still wearing a suit and looks like the Rat Pack-worshiping hepcat he is. With the simple exchange of "Hey" and pats on the arms, the weight of the dark cloud over my head seems to lighten. But the true sensation of breathing fresh air doesn't hit until we walk through the front door and the authentic sound of the new Sonics album flows into my ears. Hearing aging pioneers of garage rock still kicking ass sends my adrenaline charging.

From behind the counter, Shane greets Dale and I as if we are roommates—with a bop of his head—before returning his attention to a magazine. My curiosity over what has him so engaged nudges me to pop onto the counter and take a peek. Not only is it the same, nineteen seventy-seven issue of *Creem* I have seen him read numerous times; it's the same article about The Climax Blues Band. Sometimes it is hard to admit we music dorks are odd characters, but I can't even begin to imagine why he is so engaged over a band he refers to as a combination of blues, rock, and sap. Somehow though, these little quirks help me connect with him.

Dale catches sight of what Shane is *again* reading. "That's it. I'm tired of counting the grey hairs Shane has peeking through those curls. I'm daring to venture into one of the unsorted piles in the corner. Wish me luck." As he heads off, he calls back, "If I don't return in fifteen minutes, send an ambulance. Either a stack has fallen over and knocked me out, or I need mental help for spending so much time here."

For as neat as it looks, Warped Records is kind of a disaster. Records and CDs are all over the place—row upon row, pile upon pile. Regulars jokingly refer to the back room as Vinyl Heaven because once the door creaks open you know it is really Record Hell. Unless the music is in his genre, Shane is horrible about keeping this place organized. Thankfully our shared, and rather bizarre, affinity for power pop and seventies punk, along with a tender love for ladies who can rock your world with the strike of a chord, makes it easy for him to set aside whatever comes in that I will soon discover I need like air. Without that, shopping here would drive me mad.

Dale takes one look at the stacks and shakes his head before digging in. We met Dale when he came in looking for what he referred to as "old school, swanky music—similar to Sinatra and Martin, but more soulful and orchestral". When we put on a copy of my grandfather's favorite album, Ellington and Armstrong's *The Great Summit*, Dale's eyes enlivened, and his head rolled back to acknowledge heaven.

The friendship Dale and I share almost defies logic. Our differences are vast, especially when it comes to work habits. The thought of him selling custom software to large financial institutions may make my brain spin, but the stress in Dale's eyes has me fearing he will wind up on blood pressure medication before he is forty.

A chill runs up my spine, causing my stomach to turn as memories race back. Working too hard can take away everything, not only from you and the ones you love, but from total strangers as well. A stranger was more concerned over the company he worked for than himself, and it caused an accident that took away so much.

God, I hate how today everything twists into a reminder of tragedy. It has taken all I have not to cave to feeling the power of every smile I have ever seen is being sucked out of me. Yet right now ...

Somehow I feel enrobed in the comfort of a blanket, but it is not quite how it was when I used to think Amber was near. Why do I feel so strange?

The CD ends, and instead of silence filling the air, I am thrown off by a distant whisper. I don't remember hearing that on the end of the disk before.

The CD player clicks as it switches to the next disk, yet the voice that I am pretty sure is female continues. As it does, my newfound comfort continues to build. I know I shouldn't complain about feeling better, but am I hearing things? It seems to be coming from within the store, but there is no one here but us guys.

I lean toward the window and catch sight of a couple across the street. Either she is shouting or my hearing has gone super sonic. The voice gets drowned out when a CD spins and *New York Groove Plus* by The Sweet comes on. Shane must be in a new-albums-by-classic-bands mood.

Dale heads back, empty handed. Shane tosses the magazine aside, marches to the door, and flips the *open* sign to *closed*. "That's it. If you guys can't find anything to waste your money on, the night is doomed. Work has officially been canceled on the count of boredom. Who's up for a gallon of beer?"

Sure, I'll go anywhere and do pretty much anything so my heart doesn't dwell. "Where to?" I pop off of the counter, hoping for something new even though history tells me where we are headed.

"Pandora's Revisited?" Dale suggests.

"No way!" Shane's words remind me of a bark. "Bieber did a surprise karaoke appearance there last week. Their mojo is permanently scarred."

Yeah, just the thought of it already has me associating it with stale beer. "How about Jackson's?" I ask.

Dale waves that one off. "Nope. Last time I was there I ordered a pitcher of Sam Adams and they gave me Bud. If you can't trust your bartender ... " He shakes his head while looking to the ground in shame on behalf of the bar. I'm with him there.

Man, we can't keep going to the same place. "Let's head across town," I suggest. "Los Angeles has a bar on every block."

"Hey, how about The Whisky?" Dale asks.

Shane's jaw drops and tightens. It's hard not to chuckle at how he reminds me of a short, mortified Frankenstein's monster. "Are you crazy? It's tribute band night."

Our groans come out in sync. "Dare I ask whom is being slaughtered—I mean, *praised*?" I ask.

"It's a double whammy of Billy Joel and Elton John."

There is no winning with that one. Not only is our interest pretty low, why would anyone want to tinker with sacred ground?

With a communal shrug, we accept we are going to Mulligan's. No matter how much we swear we won't, we always wind up there, time and again—kind of like kids hearing the jangling tune of an ice cream truck.

Shane grabs his battered, gas station attendant jacket and we head for the door. Two steps shy of it, he raises an index finger and heads back behind the counter. "Hold on." He pulls out a small moving box so overflowing with audio reels that when he *plops* it on the counter, the reels start escaping. I have to scramble to keep them from spilling onto the floor. "Here," Shane says. "We got like, seven of these at an estate sale of some geezer who used to be a recording engineer up in Berkeley a thousand years ago."

"So like the seventies? Back when you were in grade school and my parents hadn't even met?" Many of the reels are loose, but some are not so neatly tucked into boxes with nearly illegible scribbling on them. The unwinding reel I hold has me both curious and apprehensive. Granted, I want something to put my head in another space but … What am I being given?

"I can't stomach going through them anymore. So far it has been Russian roulette between crappy punk and wannabe metal, but once in a while something interesting pops up. You'd think with all of the incredible stuff that came out of that area we'd luck into something, but so far zip. Make these disappear. If you find something priceless, don't tell me, and for God's sake, don't tell Rob I gave you those. He'll can me."

"How can Rob fire you? Don't you part own this place? Actually, I've never seen Rob. No one has. Rumor has it he only exists in your head."

"Oh, he's real. Trust me. He calls and yells at me enough to prove it."

After tossing the box into my trunk, the three of us head off to Mulligan's.

I hated college, yet I tried to relish in all of the things people love about it—the parties, the camaraderie, and the notion of having the world at my fingertips. But no matter what I did, the classes bored me out of my skull, and the party-lifestyle was too distracting. I pretty much had it when one day I returned to the dorms, sick as a dog with the stomach flu, and heard the guy down the hall getting it on with some girl. When I stammered out of the bathroom, I found the last thing I expected—my girlfriend slipping out his door.

Things continued to go downhill, and I was debating if college was where I needed to be when the sweet scent of lilies drifted across the lawn and filled my heart with hope. I swear I felt Amber's presence before I saw her—as if a great force told me to look in her direction. In a school filled with girls sporting low-necklines and form-fitting microskirts, much like my recent ex, seeing Amber in her well-fitted jeans and sweater that was just tight enough to make my mind wonder about what was underneath it was enchanting.

She took a seat on a bench, opened a book on art, and settled back with an expression saying she couldn't wait to see what mysteries were about to unfold. The sight damn near had me sprinting over not only for a better look, but also to talk to someone who was fascinated by something I struggled with. In a blink she got me to understand why some things grab people's attention, how color conveys a message, and how relative size and perspective can influence opinions. By the time we finished our conversation, I hadn't just met a woman I was falling for, I had gained the enthusiasm needed to succeed in the artistic side of my marketing classes.

Amber was so well versed in what she loved I always felt my passions were inferior. Despite our differences (such as she desired everything to be in pastels while I wanted to be knocked out by a rainbow), we shared our biggest goal— marriage, kids, and a picket fence—the epitome of *happily ever after*. The woman I planed to spend forever with helped me appreciate life, and missing the excitement she brought into it makes me feel broken. Shoot, everything about Amber makes me feel broken. Going to her grave used to sound comforting, but it always made me more miserable. Talking to her family kept me feeling connected to her, but then her parents confessed my being around was a reminder of death that caused the family to become at odds with each other. That's when I left my world in Detroit behind.

When I came to LA three years ago, Mulligan's had horseshoe-shaped booths with vinyl upholstery that matched the padded rim around the bar. Here in the back room sat a pool table and a dartboard. Despite honoring California's no smoking laws, the place looked dim and hazy, like something out of a movie from the fifties. I always expected Sammy Davis, Jr. or Frank Sinatra to saunter in and start singing.

If Amber hadn't got me to change the way I see the world, I probably wouldn't think it is a crime that someone modernized the place by making it look like something it isn't—from the Victorian era, down to the ornate wood bar and fake stained glass windows. Dale and I have said a zillion times that if we had the fortune of owning the place, we would have embraced the old décor and retro-dated everything right down to the glassware. If there is one thing Dale and I agree on, it is that class is timeless.

Actually, that and what he calls swanky, old music may be the *only* things we agree on.

Dale whips out his cell phone and starts typing. As much as I rib him about his work habits, I worry for the guy. "Dude, let up on the work. You're gonna have a stroke and not see thirty-seven."

"I'm not working. It's bad enough they are shipping me off to Saskatoon tomorrow for a few days."

"Canada? What's in Saskatoon?"

"Nothing but bottom of the barrel problems no one else wants to handle, but it is fun to say." Dale lets out a howl of "Saskatoooon!" He chuckles before snapping back into adulthood. "Anyway, I'm researching a new place to waste time with you nimrods. This way the next time I need alcohol to tolerate you two, I'll be prepared."

"Charming idea, *oh great bane of my existence*, but strip clubs are off the list."

"Of course they are, *Mother Theresa*. I would not dare mess with your eligibility for sainthood."

A petite, blonde-haired waitress in an alluringly low-cut T-shirt clears her throat and grabs our attention. Her cropped hair and how she raises her pencil bring about the notion of a pixie preparing to wave her wand. When she turns her head, I catch sight of the flower tucked behind her ear. My heart jumps into my throat. I haven't seen a rose in such a deep shade of pink since …

I swallow the pain burning up from my stomach. Dropping a rose into Amber's grave was intended to give us closure. My every dream was represented in that flower, and I couldn't let go of the last bit of it I had. Now it is pressed in the final page of a memory book, and I feel I am in the presence of a ghost.

The waitress pops on a smile and asks for our order. Unlike the voice of the woman she brings to mind, hers is a little abrasive. It snaps me back into the moment.

"Hi," Dale says. His smile is so charming even I almost find it irresistible. When it comes to style—actually, when it comes to pretty much anything—Shane and I are Dale's polar opposites. Shane is in his forties and looks like he always wears ratty jeans, Chucks, and a rock T-shirt because he does. He also has an air about him like he wishes it were nineteen eighty-three and The Clash were still recording, which is exactly how he feels. Even though my pants are less worn and my jacket is made of leather, our wardrobes reflect similar sentiment.

Dale is one of those guys that either creeps girls out or has them eating out of his palm. He is good looking—tall, toned, sewn into a designer suit, and wears the coolest, Jazz Era ties imaginable—but his being of Middle Eastern descent is a put-off to a lot of people. Even though his family has been in this country for generations, he won't tell anyone where his ancestors are from because he doesn't want to battle the stigma attached. It's a crap deal. It may also be why the waitress has suddenly found her note pad to be the most interesting thing in the world.

"Can we have a pitcher of Sam Adams and three chilled mugs?" Dale asks. "Oh, and a couple of orders of fries please." The waitress nods without looking up and then leaves.

"Damn! Check out the ass on her!" Dale says after she wiggles away. His smarmy grin tells me he wants the pixie to sprinkle fairy dust on him. Of course, I crane my head to see if I agree. Well, I am a man, and men are pigs, thus I am obligated to uphold the stereotype of my gender. Really, that's all I'm doing.

And yes, it is a nice ass—a nice ass in a microskirt that leaves little to the imagination. Did I catch a flash of yellow panties under it? No wonder why Dale commented on her ass. It's pretty much right in front of us. Is it odd that makes me uncomfortable?

Shane's bopping head signals he agrees with Dale's observation about the girl's anatomy. Since Shane's hands are tucked into his lap, and he's a little on the hunched side, he reminds me of a bobble head wobbling in the wrong direction. Experience tells me it is his way of saying he is as uncomfortable with the situation as I am.

"One of us needs to go for it," Dale says while staring at me. "You know how they say pixies are mischievous and magical. Imagine those qualities while she has you tied to the headboard."

I hate it when Dale's comments go off color but …

Okay, I am well aware how a woman dresses is never an invitation into her bed. However, am I wrong in thinking that flashing her underwear is a hint as to the type of relationship she wants? I don't want to be put in an uncomfortable position. If I can get Dale going in a friendly battle over something we both have some passion over, maybe he won't pressure me about the waitress. My attention goes to the hockey game on the TV behind the bar. "Why did I move to Los Angeles? If you don't like The Kings, you can cross over to the dark side and be a Ducks fan. Yay, a team named after something puked up by Disney. That's what a Red Wings' fan wants. Please! I should have moved to New York or Canada on principle."

Dale ignores my bashing and groans over my not giving a

crap regarding his comment about banging the waitress. It makes me snicker. Shane reclines in the booth, stretching out his legs and tossing his arm over the back. Instead of looking relaxed, he looks awkward. If these seats were not a little on the sticky side, I'd expect him to slide off. "Don't you think that if we want to check out the chicks, we should be in the front where all the action is?" he asks. I love this guy, but his lack of comfort with the idea and spotty experience in dating makes him sound like a little boy lost.

Dale's sigh is so heavy it's almost comical. "Yes, I absolutely know that is where I should be. But no, I'm with you two strait and narrow, goody goods. You know, there is nothing wrong with a one-night stand. However, for some crazy reason I choose to hang out with the worst wing men in history."

"Maybe we want something different," Shane says. I couldn't agree more.

A commercial for an upcoming episode of a TV show interrupts the game. A woman with long, deep auburn hair and bottle green eyes as bright as beacons appears on the screen. She's hot yet odd looking. Like, she's cute—some would say gorgeous—but something is off. Maybe it's the green eyes that are so bright they must be enhanced with contacts. It really seems her eyes should be blue.

Blue? No, not with that hair color. Hazel or brown, yes. Yet all I see are blue eyes that would be unnatural to her.

A montage of scenes forms, and each time I catch her little spikes jab, reminding me of a toddler who is repeatedly poking his finger at my torso. She's so familiar … Not familiar looking, but familiar *feeling*.

A promotional still with her image fills the screen, and I get locked into her eyes. Something inside my head ticks, and I am coated in the sensation of becoming disconnected—as if I am turning into someone other than whom I have known me to be for my thirty-one years. My butt is in the booth, yet my mind drifts, nearly floating away from Mulligan's and …

A white T-shirt cuts dead in front of my line of sight, yet

it isn't until the tray is set down that I realize our waitress is here and fully snap back to reality.

The waitress's hazel gems briefly catch sight of my chocolate browns before they give my nearly black hair, (I-wish-it-were-vintage) UXA T-shirt, black jeans, polished combat boots, and leather jacket a stealth scan. I get eye contact again when she gives me a chilled mug. A smile comes with it.

I shoot her a smile back, yet my eyes stay low. I'm still not sure what just happened with the sensation I got during the commercial. Also, this girl is cute. Cute girls make me nervous—and the flower tucked behind her ear isn't helping matters any. I've got to get my head back on.

The waitress is barely out of earshot before Dale reminds Shane and I that being selective is something he defines as unnecessary. "What would be so wrong with kissing her goodnight and then slipping out before she gets attached? If you rode that rocket once, you boys would be addicted."

Shane rests his head in his hands while looking hopeless. "And what is so wrong with wanting more?"

I'm with him. Truthfully though, even a tart for a night doesn't sound too bad. It's been a while.

"Nothing," Dale says. How earnest he sounds seems out of character. All this weirdness has me thinking someone slipped me a hallucinogen. "More is great," he continues, "but you guys do nothing to help you survive while waiting. What if you never find her? Are you willing to risk living a life of near celibacy? There is nothing wrong with sharing a night with someone if that's what she wants too."

I hate that he is right. Neither Shane nor I have had a date in months. I also hate that I can't find someone to share even a few kisses with. I've got to get away from this conversation. I don't need a simple change of subject; I need to flee. The men's room is the nearest haven, so I excuse myself.

I miss Amber—her smile, her laugh, her walk—everything about her. I'll never understand why her life was cut short. She left to get ice cream and …

Life is a chain of events leading to fate. One broken link and all of the pretty trinkets fall off.

On my way into the bathroom, I wave to Darla, my friend and co-worker. Her exasperated look cues me in that she is probably on the phone with her sister, who seems to be having all kinds of relationship problems. Darla waves to me while saying into the phone, "Escaping your situation only takes listening to your inner voice."

Yep, she's talking to Bailey. I guess I am not the only one who misses being happy. Maybe we should form a club.

The cool splash of water on my face finishes clearing my head. I can't keep living this way. Just because my fiancée died *nearly ten years ago* doesn't mean I need to lead a life of loneliness. Seriously, ten years is a long time, but it's not like I haven't been trying to move forward.

On my way back, the cute waitress zips past and slips me a piece of paper while only breaking stride to turn and make a gesture to call her. She spins back toward the bar and heads off, not noticing her flower has dropped to the floor. My reflexes nearly have me reaching for it, but I can't bear to look its way. Instead, my eyes go to the note, and my heart squeezes so hard I may fall over.

Amber.

The name of the pixie waitress is freaking Amber.

Weird things always keep me from moving on. Maybe my brain is finding excuses. Is this girl really poorly dressed, or did I imagine seeing her underwear as an excuse not to think about asking her out? Right now everything seems uncertain.

I tuck the number into my wallet. With the lame, yet truthful, reason of suddenly feeling ill, I excuse myself and head home.

The reels of tapes bounce when I drop the box on my living room floor. One falls out and rolls, unwinding a trail across the room until it *plops* onto the ground, reminding me of a soldier who has lost the battle. My heart breaks a little for the guy.

I plop down, and my normally comfy sofa seems to have lost all of its padding. I can't seem to find solace in anything. Anniversaries of monumental events of sorrow are something I do my best to forget. I need to think of something else— anything else.

My coffee table looks a little beat. I could head up the coast this weekend and hit some antique stores. This building is old—nineteen thirties old—and the entire far wall of the living room is made of built-in, walnut bookcases with decorative glass doors. I've done what I can to keep the décor appropriate to this place without breaking the bank, but maybe it is time to show it more respect.

The inside of my bedroom is a different story. Much like the contrast between the suit-covered, corporate tool I feel like at work and my casual, real-world self, this room is the other side of me. I like to keep people guessing where the line is drawn, which may be because there are times when I am not so sure myself. Concert posters are tacked to the walls. Some represent memories, such as Cavestomp! 2012—The Garage Rock Festacular, while others are from shows I wish I had been at, such as Badfinger when they played a school gym in nineteen seventy-three. How did that happen to a band championed by The Beatles? Sometimes the world doesn't make sense.

My back hits the bed, and despite how this room is usually where I feel most comfortable, I swear the walls are nagging at me. Amber would have loved this apartment, except for this room—especially if she opened the closet and got sight of my wardrobe, which consists of an array of rock T-shirts, some wickedly cool, semi-Goth dress shirts, and a few fifties lounge shirts. She'd be fine with all the straight jackets disguised as work suits though. When she died, the khakis, the sweaters, the button down shirts—everything about my wardrobe that didn't represent me—went to charity. People were so used to the repressed version of me that allowing my spirit to grow confused them. I'm happier with myself, yet I feel awful for the relief this new version brings.

How ironic is it our passions for art and music grew yet what we loved was vastly different? Amber was never crazy about my music, but she dealt with it, much like I did her … stuff.

Man, having tastes as different as we had makes you both learn to be politically correct and despise having to do it. Truthfully, I hated everything she listened to. Keeping my mouth shut got pretty difficult at times. In the end though, I took away a huge lesson: we love what we love, and what we love is worth cherishing.

I strip off my clothes and tuck myself into bed. If sleeping this mood off were the only way to kill it, I wouldn't mind if someone knocked me out for a month. I need my brain reset. I also need weird things to stop happening. Why couldn't Pixie Waitress have been named Wendy, or Barbara Ann, or Sheena? Anything else.

Sheena … What a cool name …

What would a girl with such a name be like?

The room is as quiet as the night can be long. It's almost too quiet for Los Angeles. My heart rate slows, and my thoughts slacken, putting me on the cusp between reality and slumber. The peace you feel when sleep is about to conquer your body is magic for the mind.

A whisper drifts in, sounding as if it is from another world.

"… hear me? … must be… somewhere."

Crazy. I don't think I'm asleep, let alone dreaming.

"… try this… a shot."

My eyes pop open. That was no dream! What the hell am I hearing? Am I awake, or do I only think I am? That was a woman's voice among static. It reminded me of an old radio broadcast, but it was also kinda ghostly. What the hell was it?

Okay, it might have been sudden and sounded as if it were in my head, but there has to be an explanation. Does one of the neighbors have a radio or TV on? The walls around here may not be thick, but I generally don't hear through them.

I pop up to get a better listen, yet all is so silent I question if my senses have shut off. Did I really dream that?

Seriously, I have to let up on myself today. There is a logical reason. Someone probably pulled into the parking lot outside with the radio blasting. Maybe one of the neighbor's cats stepped on a TV remote and shot up the volume. I can't let myself overthink this. If I do, my mind will start wandering to places I can't allow it to go.

After a few more minutes of dead silence I decide one of my theories must have been right. It is time for some much-deserved shut-eye.

In the dark of night, tiny lights surround me, but the glow of the dashboard is as bold as the morning sun. Suddenly, a horn honks so loudly it sends my heart racing. Headlights come from my right. If I keep going at this pace, the car will slam into me as it crosses my path. I hit the brake with my every muscle clenching to maintain the pressure.

The squeals of two sets of tires ring in my ears. Impact crunches, and the car skids left and spins out of control. It finally stops, yet my eyes stay locked on the road. God, please, I can't bear to see her. Just have her tap on my shoulder and tell me she is okay.

A chill swipes across my sweat-drenched face as I pop up in bed. "No! She'll die! I can't live with myself if she dies!"

The heave of my chest is so heavy it hurts. My eyes dart across the room, expecting to see that I am somewhere else.

Dear God, why now? All these years later, why am I dreaming of Amber's accident again? I wasn't even with her when it happened, so why am I now the driver?

Round And Round

Brandon

Thirty minutes into what should be a five-minute commute I've managed to battle my way to an exit so I can backroad it to work. Fatigue from a night filled with horrors has set in, and I'm wiped out to the point where I turn off the radio because listening feels exhausting. When I reach a stoplight, I set the parking brake and close my eyes so I can feel I have crawled into a hole.

Yawn!

There is no way I will avoid falling asleep at my desk today. Why couldn't I have felt this relaxed last night?

Music seeps into my head. My eyebrow slightly cocks as I recognize Mötley Crüe belting out "Angela". Someone must be blasting his stereo and sharing his love of hair bands with those around him. This is totally unfair. I'm not exactly a hair band fan, but man, those songs are catchy. This one is gonna stick with me all day.

"... not sure I am up to this," says a female voice.

I jerk, and my eyes pop open in a shot of panic. That was the same voice I heard last night. Again it sounded like it was inside my brain.

My head jerks around while searching for the source, yet I come up empty. I can't even hear Vince Neil singing anymore. What the hell is going on?

I roll down my window and wait—listening and knowing I soon have to hear the voice again, and this time coming from an identifiable source. Instead the only difference is the sound of passing cars amplifies, and I catch the rattle of a jackhammer in the distance.

Okay, there has to be a simple explanation. Some guy must

have had his radio up and turned it down during a commercial. That's totally normal.

Yeah, what about the TV I thought I heard last night? Is a cat stepping on a remote normal? Sure, it is possible but—

Oh man, I'm so wiped out that I must hear my exhaustion talking.

Honk!

My body flails as the guy behind me gives a not-so-gentle nudge to tell me the light has changed. I race to the next light so I can stop and listen again.

I wait and …

Nothing. All seems normal.

I close my eyes and tell my brain to dump all thoughts so it can reach a state of Zen. Again music slips in. The thought of it being in my head causes my skin to prickle.

Stay calm. It's only music. If you were going to make up hearing things, you would never pick "Round and Round" by Ratt. Someone around here is sharing his love of hair bands with the world. Hair bands may rile you in general, but they are not a reason to freak out. Relax a bit and—

"Long day ahead."

"Aah!"

My body jerks, and I have to slam on the brake before my car rolls into the one in front of it. That was the same voice as last night! What the hell is going on? Whom am I hearing, and why does she sound like she is in my head? Once more, why do I hear Ratt playing? Is the music attached to the voice? It has to be.

Hooonk!

The guy behind me lays on his horn, which again sends my body jerking. I also gasp to the point where air locks in my lungs. My hand flies to my chest and presses as if trying to keep my heart from beating out of my body. Dear God, what the hell is happening?

Again the guy honks, and it's all I can do to pull myself together to get to the next light.

Why did my inner voice have a sex change? Was that

Amber? Has she been gone so long that I don't remember how she sounded? How could I forget her voice? There isn't much that could be sadder.

I open my car door, and all is fine until my feet hit the ground and my knees start to buckle.

I'm tired, and a little freaked out. But I am only freaked out because I am tired. Simple.

Within a few steps I've gained my stride and am on a mission for coffee.

Walking into Endeara Candies is akin to being tossed into an alternate universe. If anything about me shows I am crazy, it is working here. I swear the head of Human Resources has some kind of X-ray vision into people's heads and makes hiring decisions based on how wacky they are. We all show up in suits and uniforms, looking like we went through cookie cutters, but outside of here we are as goofy as trail mix made with Captain Crunch and diamonds.

Darla greets me as soon as I swing open the lobby door. "Welcome to Wednesday!" she calls from her desk. It's said half seriously and half sarcastically. She is the perfect example of the contrast here. In the real world she dresses like the colorful, classy, and free-spirited soul she is, but here she looks professional, sans the long locks that are dyed the same colors as a peacock's tail. I am dying to spike them up into a fan. God that would be gorgeous!

"How's life in the hellhole?" I ask while trying to cover how shaky my voice is. I swear to God I'm so jittery my spleen is quaking.

"Here." She hands me a zip bag of … grey jellybeans?

"Since when do we make *grey* jellybeans?"

"Since some of the guys worked late last night to get caught up on an order, were done sooner than expected, and decided to experiment. This is the result, and I got the joy of tasting them this morning. That's how life in the hellhole is."

"What flavor is grey? Coconut?" What the hell. I'm game. Thinking I am hearing a voice already implies I am insane. I might as well prove the theory by eating some of the stuff we make here. Then again, supposedly if you think you are insane, you can't be.

"Coconut would stand closer to reason than reality. Before you try those, I am reminding you we have a lot of diversity here at Endeara Candies. Also, I suspect alcohol may have been consumed during that little experiment."

Against all sensibility I pop one into my mouth. My teeth break the coating, and "Holy shit!" The thing is so hot my eyes are gonna shoot out of their sockets. Darla hands me the trashcan so I can spit the thing out. "What was that? Habanero or something? They should make those red and in the shape of a flame thrower."

"Habanero would have been too sane. Those guys experimented with Ghost Pepper, hence they thought grey would be spooky."

I let out a huff of heat. "Gah! I think I might die! And here I thought you were my friend."

"I am, which is why I gave you a diversion from whatever is on your mind. Here." She hands me a chocolate bar that looks so good I am about to salivate. It's a nice thought, but what I need is to raid the First Aid kit and drink some Burn Gel.

"We don't make stuff this good here," I say.

"Exactly. No one should eat the crap we make. Traitorous chocolate is the only way to go. So, you okay?"

Her look of sisterly concern makes it clear she isn't asking in regard to the near death experience from the Ghost Pepper.

Crap. What I am going through is nothing. Well, it has to be nothing because … because it can't be the alternative. For the last few years I have gotten through the rough times by forcing myself to move forward. I'm going to say I am okay and move on. I am certain that by using mind over matter all will be dandy.

As soon as my mouth drops open to form the words, I know Darla will see through anything I tell her. That gets reinforced when I pause to think of a new approach and the look in her eyes tells me she's feeling every jitter along with me. God, how the hell is it that anyone else in the universe can mess with you and it's all fun and games, yet with Darla you know the more she does it, the more she cares?

I can't tell her I fear I am losing my mind.

Maybe if I get it off of my chest, hearing how stupid this all is will make it go away. After all, if I can't talk about it, I must really believe I am crazy. If I talk about it, that will show I know it is just my mind being out of whack, and I can conquer it. "When I was at Mulligan's last night, I met this waitress—"

Darla smacks her hand onto the desk. "Stop right there. Any story beginning with, 'When I was at Mulligan's' has a ninety percent chance of ending horribly. Let me guess, the new waitress, *who happens to be named Amber*, slipped you her number and it is messing with your head."

Oh, thank God. See, this all makes sense. I'm also guessing by how Darla is closing her eyes and fighting a cringe that not calling was a wise decision. "Yes, and before you say another word, no, I did not call her, nor do I plan to." Darla's eyes pop back open, and she sweeps her palm in a motion for me to carry on. I'll roll with it so I can keep seeing how crazy it is to think I am losing my mind. Regardless, I lower my voice because no one else needs to know I think I am losing it. "After that, I had the strangest dream. Well, it wasn't exactly a dream. It seemed real to the point where I felt I heard it."

She returns the hushed tone. "Are you saying you're dreaming of bimbo waitress or just her voice? Either is gross."

"That's the thing. It's not the waitress's voice I'm hearing. That grated on me. What I am hearing sounds sweeter."

"This *dream*, was the voice in control?"

My head jerks back as if her words have smacked me. "God, no."

"Is it abusive?"

Is she crazy? I shake my head. "Not in the least."

"What's it saying to you?"

I must be slow because it is now sinking in that she is doing her own version of a sanity check. I'm taking how she still seems unfazed as a good sign. "I can only make out bits and pieces, similar to hearing a weak radio signal. Here is the thing. It's been almost ten years to the day since Amber died. Do you think this voice is only my brain messing with me, or am I truly certifiable?"

She touches my arm, and her voice returns to a normal volume. "There are a lot of people around here I know are nuts. You, Brandon Wayne, are not one of them."

This is great! See, normal as can be. "I don't even know why am asking you this, but do you have any idea what could be going on?"

"Well, you are asking me because my real name is Lucy and you owe me five cents." My head cocks. She's lost me. "Okay, when people don't get Peanuts' jokes, then I think they are crazy. Seriously, cut yourself some slack. You've been up against a lot over the last few years. Losing Amber, returning to school so you could graduate, moving across the country, leaving your family, changing your friends—those are all huge events." Darla lightly squeezes my arm. I didn't realize her hand was still there. "People who have lost loved ones have been known to hear voices, so it could be a result of missing her. It also could be your brain trying to put itself in a better space. Or it could be survivor guilt. When tragedy strikes, we often find ways to blame ourselves because it is the only way to express our hurt."

The fact I can't catch on to a simple Peanuts' joke is proof my mind is not in the right place. I'm not crazy; I'm tired and being way too hard on myself, which explains last night's dream. It also must be the reason I am hearing things. "You're right. Her death isn't my fault—not a single aspect of it."

Something in her forced slip of a smile causes my heart to ache. She takes a moment to consider her wording. "Have you ever noticed how quick you are to point out how you are not to blame? We've talked about Amber a zillion times, and never once have we found anything that could put you at fault, yet you seem to feel that way anyway."

I do know every decision leading to Amber's death was

her own. If it were my fault, I'd have reason for this despair. Maybe I would even take myself out. Instead, I'm left wallowing and not knowing which way is up. If I didn't know better, I would think my feelings are disguising something deeper. "Yeah, I need to move on."

"Great idea. Just don't do it with the waitress at Mulligan's. I'm telling you, that girl is bad news." Darla's phone rings. She looks at the caller ID and sighs.

"Bailey again?"

Her eyes stay on the phone. "Yeah, she is having a hard time accepting how much she is being taken advantage of. At least she is aware that being a nice person isn't doing her any favors right now. You know, sometimes it is hard for me to be the one people turn to, especially when they often hope I will help them make light of a situation. I've run out of steam on this one."

I wish I knew how to help Bailey on Darla's behalf and give them both a break. I hate that all I can think to do is give Darla a smile and a heart-felt tone I hope conveys how much I appreciate her. "Thanks, Lucy. I owe you a nickel."

She gives me a smile and answers the call with forced cheer. "Hey, good morning, or is it afternoon there yet?" As I head off to the elevator, Darla takes a moment to listen before sounding resigned to Bailey's misery. "Anytime I'm in this chair I am open for business. What's wrong?" Right as I enter, I hear Darla ask with hesitation, "Are you really sure you want me to say it?" As I turn to hit the button, I catch the sadness in her eyes—despite how she catches a breath and forces out words that sound as if she is making light of another person's pain. "I told you so." Her eyes rise to meet mine, and her words confirm the reason why she suspected Bailey called. "Let me guess—Carlos is cheating." By the time the elevator doors close, her forced demeanor is long gone. The concern radiating in her eyes makes me wish I had siblings.

There is no comfort in knowing I am not the only one suffering from matters of the heart.

It'll Be Alright

Brandon

Tabloids litter the coffee table in my dentist's waiting room. The world's fascination with celebrities truly amazes me. You would think living in Los Angeles would make people immune to star lust and thus tabloids wouldn't sell within a hundred mile radius, yet they're inescapable.

And to think that on my way to work yesterday I feared I was crazy. To me, how people lust after celebrities and follow their every move is kinda nuts.

I dig through stacks of tabloids while hoping to find something else. Shoot, I'd read one of Shane's ancient issues of *Creem* or even, God forbid, *The New Yorker* over a tabloid. Unfortunately, my only choices are *People, Star,* and—

I turn my head at the sight of *Parents* before moving on to the next stack as if the current one were diseased. One time I saw a woman who reminded me so much of Amber that when she stepped away from the stroller she was pushing, I had to look inside. The green eyes of the cooing, little girl reminded me of Amber's while the deep shade of her hair matched mine. I knelt to say hello, and her smile touched me so deeply that, for a moment, I let myself imagine the hell Amber endured never touched us. The little girl giggled, and the beauty caused tears to run down my face. Walking away from her was as painful as leaving Amber's grave right after we set her in it.

This is too much. All this wallowing has to end.

I'm quick to grab an issue of *Star.* If I am going to lap up celebrity gossip, I might as well go for the king of the rags.

Two pages in, I feel someone has dropped me on an alien planet. Vibrant pictures of people I don't know are paired with headlines in bold, yellow letters—a look designed to bring forth my optimism and convey these are friends I am happy to see. I've never understood what causes people to be fascinated with others because they appear on TV. Yet when I turn the page, a photo of a girl with brilliant, green eyes that sparkle with life puts my heart into my throat and causes me to take pause. Isn't this the girl I saw on the TV at Mulligan's? Again she is stealing my breath like the glow of heaven.

The headline drops weight into my gut. *"Kason Alert! Katherine Miller at Toronto hotspot with boyfriend, Jason Day."*

Jason Day? She's with him? The thought makes the world seem empty.

Yeah, there is no way that is gonna last. Give up on it now, honey. You need someone who's not a total ass.

Wow, what happened to my head? And where did that dickwad thought come from? Thanks to nightmares, I had another rough time last night, but that is no excuse to be a jerk. Also, how is it this woman grabbed my emotions?

Oh no. Please don't tell me I have a celebrity crush. I'd rather be certifiably crazy than have one of those.

Instead of tossing down the magazine, I let Katherine's eyes draw me in. Maybe I've now crossed over into fantasizing, but something in my soul tells me my suspicion she hasn't found what she is seeking is real. I also can't help but think she loves to dance in the kitchen, she lives for long walks on the beach, and she would take peanut butter and jelly sandwiches any day over lobster.

I rattle my head and snap out of my dream world. This is ridiculous. Why am I projecting ideals on to a woman I have never met?

Maybe I am not projecting. Maybe it says something about those things in this article, and my eyes latched on to words that painted a picture. After all, everything in these rags is marketing. Since I am a marketing guy, I need to read this and see how they hooked me.

Yeah, that is crap. I have a crush on a celebrity even though there is nothing about this woman that makes her my type. Then again, it's been so long since I have had anything more than a few dates with a woman I am no longer sure what my type is.

The article tells the sighting happened at Harblano's right after "Kason" participated in a marathon for Rays Of Love, a non-profit benefitting the families of victims of violent crimes. Jason founded it in memory of his brother, Ray, who died in a convenience store robbery five years ago.

Oh, dear God.

My stomach squeezes as my mind rewinds to getting out of the passenger seat of my friend's car, my hands trembling, my feet unsteady, and my head in a fog. How was I going to tell Amber's parents the police were at my door, saying their little girl had been taken from this earth by someone who thought texting about work was more important than staying safe and keeping Amber alive?

I feel for Jason. I feel for anyone who buries a loved one, especially one as young as Amber who had so much ahead of her.

My eyes become weighted with sorrow, and I have to focus on catching a deep breath in order to stop the tears from forming. Losing someone you love in such a violent way messes you up. I need to think about something else quickly—anything but where my mind is headed over thoughts of young people dying.

I close the magazine with plans to grab another one, and an issue of *Parents* locks me in a stare down, reminding me how much Amber and I lost. With a hearty sigh I toss the issue of *Star* over it.

My stomach rumbles. Harblano's sounds like a damn tasty Cuban restaurant. I need to grab lunch the second I am done with this appointment. Are they a chain? Maybe there is one on my way back to the office.

I look it up on my phone and find it's a gourmet burger joint. My stomach grumbles again over how good it sounds. Google maps shows they only have one location, not far from Majestic Studios. Is that where Katherine films? I type

"*Vampires Undercover shooting location*" into my browser and—

God! What am I doing? Two nights ago I started hearing voices and having nightmares, yesterday I freaked out over hearing a voice while in my car, and now I not only have a crush on a celebrity, I am stalking her? This isn't like me—not by a long shot. Am I just overtired, or am I more of a mess over Amber than I realize? For God's sake, it's been ten years. I've gotten depressed before, but I've never had my brain go into overload.

Ten years … A guy can only blame the universe for not putting the right woman in front of him for so long. Dale is right. I'm too uptight. There comes a point in everyone's life where he needs to bend the rules and open his mind. This might be that time. A date, even a trampy one, would do me a world of good.

I pull Pixie Waitress's number out of my wallet and start dialing. If she gives her number to every guy like Darla implied, and was really showing off her neon yellow undies, she's probably only interested in one thing. Right now, anything that can get me over this hurdle is fine by me.

My dialing halts. It's hard to ignore how clearly her name is written on this paper. It also makes me feel a little sick.

I'll give her a pet name so I won't have to think of her as being Amber. Apparently Brian Jones of The Rolling Stones gave the same pet name to every girl so he didn't have to bother remembering real ones. I'll call her Cream Puff or some other nauseating thing. Girls enjoy that, right?

Hell, it doesn't matter if she enjoys it. It's only for a night.

Actually, with how long it's been, it will only be a few minutes. The poor girl. I already feel horrible about being Racer X, and I haven't finished dialing.

Abruptly I stop. What if she's really a nice girl? People have often gotten the wrong impression of me.

I start dialing again, typing in the number as fast as I can, even though the rational side of me is screaming to stop. It may have a point.

I'll do this right. I won't expect a thing other than to treat her to a decent meal just as I would any other first date. Whatever else happens, happens.

But after entering the last digit, my thumb hovers over the call button. This goes against how Amber changed me into the person I am. Going out with a woman I am not interested in, especially only with the intent of jumping a hurdle, is disrespectful to all of us.

A dental assistant steps out and calls my name. With a sigh of relief, I crumple the paper and toss it into the wastebasket. I may need to move on, but I'm not the kind of guy who can do it with anyone. In both her life and in her death, Amber made me become true to who I am. I need to stand by that.

Voices Green And Purple

Brandon

When I decided to pursue a career in marketing, I dreamed of creating multi-million dollar campaigns so brilliant that corporations paid me tens of thousands in bonuses. I also fantasized their paraphernalia would turn into collectables that begged people to fork over hundreds of dollars for the sake of nostalgia. Then I came to work at Endeara Candies and literally got a taste of reality.

My palate is not refined—not by a long shot—yet even I know this candy is bottom of the barrel. It's what old people buy for their great grandkids because it is cheap and reminds them of the stuff they had as children—back when ingredients were simple and real. I'm convinced our customers never eat our products because if they tried, Endeara would go bankrupt. Thus, it is my job to insure that even if our customers do bite in, they are so overwhelmed by our slick marketing they think they taste what they should.

I pop an orange gumdrop into my mouth to see where the experience takes me. While I know it won't taste like Florida's finest, I expect it to taste like oranges, or at least a reasonable facsimile. The second my teeth break into it the taste of ham and cigarettes makes me gag so hard I fear I am about to hack out a lung.

Gah, clove! Who went into my desk and switched out my fruit gumdrops for spice drops?

Dammit, Darla!

My office phone rings with a call from Dale. I'm barely able to stop coughing enough to answer it. Three nights ago he said work was about to ship him off to what we think of as the middle of nowhere. This should be interesting.

I pop him onto speakerphone. "Hey, man. How's Saskatoooon?" He's right. The name is fun to say.

He laughs. "Saskawho? I've been the victim of a last-minute detour to Toronto. You know, part of the place the film industry refers to as Hollywood North. It is almost as synthetic as the real deal, if you know what I mean."

Judging by the tone of his voice I am not quite sure if Dale has spent the last few days drooling over hot chicks or cringing over silicone. "Why are they keeping you locked away in Canada?" I grab another spice drop in hope of killing the vileness in my mouth. Green spice drops should be mint or some acceptable replica.

"Because I solved their problems in Saskatoon with lightning speed. Now they love me so much there is talk of keeping me here with a big, fat raise and an easy chair."

"Dreamer!" I pop the spice drop in my mouth and chew. Gah!

I cough so hard I nearly spew the thing across the room. Artificial lime? Thanks, Darla, for mixing spice drops with my gumdrops.

"You okay, bro?"

"Yeah, a *friend* played Russian roulette with my candy stash." I hold the bag to the light and scrutinize the creatures that tried to kill me. Gumdrops and spice drops are supposed to be sized differently. These aren't. How did she pull this one off? The bag gets tossed. Besides, after all the drilling the dentist did yesterday, I should lay off of the sugar.

"Darla strikes again, huh? With the stuff they make there, that has got to be toxic! Hey, hold on a sec."

The ambient noise from his end of the line disappears. I lean back, put my feet up, and close my eyes.

Hold music creeps in. Warrant's "Cherry Pie"? That's an odd choice. My foot starts pounding out the rhythm of the bass drum. The song becomes an anthem, beating itself into my head and making me rally behind it. This is totally gonna be stuck in my head all day.

"So far, today has been promising."

No!

I bolt up in my chair, gripping its arms with white knuckles while my heart tries to gallop out of my chest. That voice came over the phone! It wasn't any voice either! My words sprint out, cracking as they go. "Dale, you there? Who's with you?"

Ambient noise returns, followed by Dale's voice, "Hold on another sec." I'm definitely not on hold now, yet I still hear Warrant. This is exactly what happened in the car two days ago with Mötley Crüe.

"Anyway," Dale says, "I was thinking maybe …"

"Sometimes this job can be so boring."

My lungs struggle for air. There she is again, and she sounds as clear and loud as Dale does. I'm tempted to throw down the phone and run, but all I can do is sit here, frozen and gripping the chair.

Haze begins to coat my inner vision. Pixels form and merge. At first the image is black with a smattering of light peering through, and then browns and creams work their way in, leading to full color, yet it is all buried under fog. My jaw clenches. What the hell is going on?

The haze clears, and although my heart won't stop racing, something tells me I am safe, regardless of how I have a hard time believing it.

The image before me is of a female arm reaching toward a coffee table and a copy of *Neon Angel*, the autobiography of Cherie Currie of The Runaways. Next to it is a stereo with an iPod attached. Is that where Warrant is coming from?

"I find myself waiting around, wasting so much time. At least I'm becoming well read." She chuckles. "If you can call this well read. At least I finally have a chance to look into some of the things that interest me."

Dale's voice slips in. "I think I'm headed to great places."

Everything sounds jumbled to the point where I'm not sure who said what. I don't want to risk disturbing the vision by asking Dale to stop talking. I also fear that if I speak, I'm so far over the edge my voice won't work.

The view slips to a dark brown carpet, and although I am

still gripping my chair, I seem to be walking; yet I can't tell where. All I catch are glimpses of what I'm pretty sure are pictures hanging on the wall of a fairly small space. Is this a trailer?

We pass through a door and the music fades, but the sound of heels clicking on tile echo into the mix. The acoustics also change, and I catch sight of a bathroom sink.

"Anyway, I need to head off. We're getting ready to …"

Was that Dale? I'm not sure anymore.

Sweat builds on my brow as my view turns to a mirror. My ability to breathe is strained when I see the woman wearing jeans and a T-shirt with a design I can't make out. Her skin is fair and freckled. Her eyes seem hazel or maybe brown. I can't tell the color of her clipped-up hair, but it seems dark red. Who is this woman whose voice keeps infiltrating my mind? And why am I suddenly seeing through her eyes? It's almost as if I am her, yet I know I am not.

I'm not, right?

No. I'm Brandon Wayne. I'm sitting at work in Los Angeles, California. I'm thirty-one years old. I'm on the phone with Dale who is in Canada.

I force my view downward and see what I know is real— my hands gripping my chair.

"Yo! Brandon, you there?"

The sudden volume of Dale's voice causes me to flinch and gasp. My brain fully snaps back into my surroundings and the reality of sitting behind a metal desk. The sterile walls of my office that I have covered with colorful concert posters pop to life with such intensity that I start smacking my hands on the desk to make sure it is solid. A montage of thoughts flows through my head. I was eating toxic gumdrops at a place where we are required to dress professionally, yet no one bats an eye at Darla's peacock hair and my choice of décor. My reality is almost as strange as my make-believe.

That *was* make-believe, wasn't it? I feel trapped within my own mind. Am I really here?

"Brandon!" Dale yells. "Did you choke on one of those

gumdrops?"

I run my fingers through my hair, and pat myself down. Yes, I still have a body. Wait, am I still—

A peek into my pants brings relief. Thank God the gift He gave me is still there.

"Brandon!" Dale yells.

"Yes! Yes! Sorry!" I brace myself against the desk. "Someone distracted me with work. What did you say?" Dammit, my voice cracked.

"I won't be able to meet up this weekend as planned. Hell, with the way things are going, I may ask you to break into my apartment and send me some stuff."

"N-No problem." What just happened? *Why* did it happen? My words sound as disoriented as my head feels. "Where did you say you were again?"

"Tor-on-tow, Can-a-da," he says so slowly he practically spells it out. "I may need you to get some stuff from my place and send it to me. Man, what is with you?"

I shake my head again, further clearing it. Right. Dale is away on business. "Sorry, let me know what you need. I still have the spare key from when you lost the last one."

He laughs. "You mean from the time some girl at a club stole it, and you helped me get the landlord up at three in the morning to prove to the locksmith I lived there. I was certain if I couldn't get the guy to change the locks, an axe murderer would slay me. Lesson learned. Catch you later."

This is all so ... so what? I don't even know. So unlike me? I'm no stranger to missing Amber, and then a celebrity crush was bad enough. Why has yet another woman of mystery entered my life? I need to get a grip.

I start to take a seat but jerk back before my butt hits the chair. It's gonna be a while before I sit there again.

I pace while trying to make sense of everything. There has to be a reason for this. I am not crazy!

Am I?

Okay, enough with the thoughts of insanity. I must know that woman somehow.

I try to think of women I have met—girls I went to high school with, ones I met in college, the ladies here at work, and those I saw while sitting in traffic. Nothing. None of them look like the woman in my vision. This has to do with Amber's anniversary. It has to.

No, if it did, I would see Amber, and she certainly would not be reading a book written by a rock star. There has to be another explanation.

My eyes drop to the gumdrops on my desk, the ones that long ago only contained simple ingredients. Maybe it is the chemicals.

Someone poisoned the candy! I have to get down to the plant.

I dash off and get all the way to the elevator before realizing I've heard the voice without having eaten any of our products.

Okay, good. I didn't turn into a screaming idiot. At least I have some rationality left.

I return to my office and finish gathering myself but again stop shy of touching the chair. Instead, I grab my coat and head out. We're all supposed to meet at Mulligan's soon anyway. I could use a damn drink, or maybe eighty of them!

Paranoia Is Freedom

Brandon

My hand quakes as the cool bottle of beer touches my lips. Given what I experienced earlier, along with what I am gathering the courage to do now, it's amazing this is only my first drink. Into the browser on my phone I type "hearing voices" while fighting the urge to add the word schizophrenia for fear of what I might learn.

After a gulp of air and another swig, I glance down at the search results and click on a page that sounds authoritative. Still it takes a little more air before I can face what is written.

"At some point in their lives, most people hear voices that have no apparent physical source. If you have thought someone called your name, only to turn and see that no one was there, you have heard voices."

Man, I know a lot of people that has happened to. Thing is, the voice I am hearing seems to be in my head, not around me. The phone call today with Dale was the exception.

I would be able to move on with only this information if I were only hearing my name called. In fact, I haven't heard my name at all. Is that good or bad?

"A good example of this is getting a song stuck in your head, also known as 'having an earworm.' Something triggered the song, and you feel it is constantly playing, no matter what you do."

If getting a song stuck in your head means you are crazy, Shane, myself, and millions of others should have been locked up at birth.

I take another swig of beer. Maybe it is the alcohol, but I am starting to feel a speck of comfort. Still, what about the damn vision that still has my insides vibrating?

"Hearing voices can be a sign of severe mental illness. However, many psychics claim to hear voices as well as receive visions as a type of

foreshadowing. Additionally, research shows people who have lost a loved one often hear voices during times of duress, right after a funeral, or on monumental occasions involving the deceased."

I swallow hard, close my eyes, and set down the phone. I could allow myself to think I am experiencing memories of Amber if I could recall her saying what I am hearing. Not only can't I, none of it is in her voice.

Amber believed that we are composed of energy, and we leave an imprint wherever we go and on whatever we touch. Maybe the energy she left behind is messing with my mind. That doesn't make sense though, because not only had she never been to Los Angeles, I don't have any of her possessions in my car, nor do I have any at work. I can't see how she could be tied to this.

I start to reach for another swig but go for the phone instead. It is time to brave researching the "s" word via a bona fide medical journal.

"Schizophrenia is a disorder that tends to run in families. It may also be triggered by viral infections or highly stressful situations."

Viral infections? That's scary. There is no mental illness in my family that I am aware of. Also, Amber's death may be depressing, but it doesn't have me any more stressed now than before.

"Warning signs of schizophrenia include hearing or seeing something that isn't there (Check.), *feeling as if you are being watched* (No, but I have felt something brewing around me. Does that count?)*, nonsensical speaking or writing* (People still seem to understand me, I think.), *feeling indifferent about important situations* (Lord, I wish. If I were indifferent about this, and you can't get much more important than mental health, I would not be researching it.), *weak work or academic performance* (Hey, it's not my fault our products suck and are thus hard to market.), *poor hygiene* (I showered this morning and am wearing clean clothes.), *withdraw from social situations* (I'm sitting in Mulligan's, waiting for co-workers.), *inability to sleep* (Yes, but I am having nightmares about an auto accident. My lack of sleep is not without reason. However, those dreams are stressing the crap

out of me. Maybe I have found the reason after all.), *odd behavior* (Define odd.), *and/or a preoccupation with religion* (Umm ... No).

The only thing I am getting from this is that at some point, everyone thinks he hears something, which I happen to be pretty good at right now. Stress can be a huge factor, but I wasn't stressed until I started having nightmares, which came after hearing the voice the first time. Nightmares are a normal part of life. Also, the only thing mentioned regarding visions implied I could be psychic. Wouldn't that be a twist?

When I had that experience today, I knew who and where I was. I could think independently and exercise free will. Those must be huge indicators that I am not nuts.

Enough. I am going with the stress angle. Time to put my attention elsewhere, such as the Red Wings' game on TV. A man should have his priorities. See, I am not indifferent about important things.

I look up as The Capitals nail one into the Red Wings' net. Crap! My eyes cringe shut. I should call Dad. His rant right now must be epic. It may have happened decades ago, but he still talks about how The Capitals were once so bad that fans wore bags over their heads. Knowing that, every time they score against us the world seems lame.

The game pauses for a commercial, and a green M&M in white boots wiggles her way across the screen. Now *there* was a brilliant marketing idea. Of course, the product doesn't totally suck either. It's hard to sell a product you don't believe in. In fact, it can be downright depressing.

Hey, maybe my wallowing can help. People eat when they are depressed—regardless of how the food tastes. God, this is so perfect. Could I really get away with selling our crap candy based on the buyer's lack of self-worth?

That brilliance warrants a second beer, so I signal the waitress for another. This is sweet. I may be on the verge on creating the greatest campaign ever, all while totally sane.

Speaking of waitresses ... I eye the room in search of the pixie. I should apologize for not calling and at least thank her for the number. I'll go up front and see if—

"Listen scum, I've just about had it with you."

Every bit of my body tightens and locks—my grip on the beer, my stomach, everything. That was *the* voice, and I heard it *through my ears!* This time I am absolutely certain it was not in my head.

My eyes slowly rise and scan the room while daring myself to find the source. Come on, God, let me see it. Whatever it is, I can face it. I just need to know what I am up against.

"You don't want to piss me off!" comes from behind the bar.

No, from the TV!

My eyes lock on Katherine Miller—the same actress that keeps grabbing my attention. I huff out relief at solving one part of the mystery, but that is not all I feel. Emotions sweep through me, sending my heart soaring into the air and then spiraling down into my gut.

"You'd be amazed what happens when I get angry."

Yes, that is the voice! But how can it come from her? The woman I saw while on the phone with Dale today had hazel eyes, not to mention freckles—tons and tons of freckles.

She also didn't have any makeup on. The bone structure is the same, so is the body and her posture. Colored contacts, matted skin, zero freckles—she's hardly recognizable. Why do they cover her natural beauty? It seems unjust. Now she looks so … manufactured—so Hollywood.

Am I really sure …

"One word of advice—run!"

Yes. That is, beyond a doubt, the same voice that has been haunting me. Someone is trying to tell me this woman holds something special for me.

"Thank God you're here already." Darla's voice causes my head to snap in her direction. "Now I can cower with you and not have to deal with a bunch of losers until the rest of the cool kids get here."

She plops down across from me and steals a sip of my beer. A fresh bottle? When did that get here?

Even though the commercial has ended, my eyes go back

to the TV in hopes of catching a glimpse of the woman who puts me in a tailspin.

"Hey, Brandon." Darla double snaps her fingers. "You with us?"

"That's the voice," I utter, still captivated by the TV.

"Huh?"

"The voice I heard the other night—it belongs to the woman in the commercial." Man, I sound crazy. I need to backpedal a bit. "Remember how I heard a voice? I figured out it was coming from the neighbor's TV."

Darla's eyes go to the screen where commentators discuss the embarrassing goal the Red Wings handed over before the commercial break. "Brandon, that's not an ad." She not only sounds concerned, she looks it.

"A moment ago they played ads for another station."

Her eyes narrow. "What about when you heard it in the car?"

Yep, she's convinced I am losing it. "A commercial from another radio. You know how annoying it is when people blast ads." I shrug and smile. "Go ahead, it's okay for you to think I am crazy."

She chuckles. "Man, you are easy to mess with. Besides, you would be amazed what it takes to make me think someone has lost it." A chime comes from Darla's purse. When she sees who sent the text, she looks like her heart has been broken.

"Is Bailey okay?"

"Not really. She's not in physical danger, but the mental abuse is sinking in. It is going to get worse when I tell her what I learned yesterday. You know how I turned in my notice because Rox over in payroll is starting a dating service and I am going to work for her? While I was doing research, I found Bailey's boyfriend on a dating site. The profile was created long after he moved in, too. This guy is the biggest piece of scum ever to walk the earth." Darla drops her head, rubbing it like the whole mess makes her feel helpless when it comes to offering true help. "I'm sorry," she says. "I need to go call her. She's been waiting on some information all day."

I wish her luck as she heads off. "Hey," I call out, "please be sure she knows we are not all scum. Some of us would do anything to find a good woman to treat with respect."

Darla forces a smile before walking off while dialing. Meanwhile, my eyes go back to the TV in hopes of seeing the woman who makes my heart damn near stop.

Katherine

Bailey's brush is about to hit my lips when Darla's ringtone sends her jerking. She's been scattered to the point where I felt her hand quaking while applying my eyeliner. This mess with Carlos is really getting to her.

She closes her eyes and centers herself before apologizing. Is she kidding? I tell her I am the least of her worries and insist she takes the call. Bailey snatches up the phone and answers, "Hey. What did you find out?"

As words flow through, Bailey hangs her head, hiding the tears forming in her hickory-brown eyes behind long, wavy black locks. Carlos has been mooching off of her for months. Last night, when Darla told her she found his profile on a dating site, Bailey called me, sounding destroyed. She deserves so much better.

"I know he's not worth it," she tells Darla, "but I don't believe in being an ass because he is. Thanks for the info. Sorry to interrupt your Friday night out. I'll call you later."

Right there is the problem. In the years I've known Bailey I've known a woman who always gives people another chance, even if it is at her expense. It takes a lot of strength to risk being someone's doormat because you try to take the high road. I touch her arm, hoping the compassion will help ease her stress. "You okay?"

"My problems sound like a screenplay for a TV movie on a fifth-rate network." She turns to hand me a tissue. Either she doesn't want to face anyone or she is so frazzled she has forgotten I've already removed the remnants of my old lipstick. I clean my lips anyway.

"He closed the profile?" I ask.

"You mean the one he *claimed* was generated when he worked in Internet securities and ran test cases for a client? Yeah, and Darla is on the lookout for others." Her hand scrapes through her hair. "God, Katherine, Carlos is such a slick liar. He even got me thinking the profile could have been related to his old job, especially since I can't figure out how he is paying for it. Seriously, how long does it take to find a job? Even being a bottle washer would help pay the bills. I know it looks bad, but what if he isn't cheating? I mean—" She swallows back a sob. "How could someone do that to me? Am I not worthy of loyalty?" Before I can pop up to give her a hug she tosses her hands in the air. "Oh, I can't take this anymore! Talk to me about something else—anything else— like that new movie. Did they figure out when you will leave this place and head off to the real Hollywood?"

I force a smile while wishing there were something I could do to help her. Also, as of the last few days I'm not nearly as excited as I should be about an opportunity I have been dying for. I'm still not sure I understand the reasons why, and that makes it hard to talk about. "No, but soon—at least that is what I keep telling myself. We've finished the test fittings and makeup design, so I am pretty much ready to rock. I am sick of my schedule getting twisted around. First it happened because of Jason doing a side project. Now they have to flip everything on its head for me. At least the producers are supportive, to an extent. They want me to get more exposure, but they also don't want me to do so well that I strike gold and bail."

"Yeah, throwing off the balance by losing a key player would probably kill the show." Bailey takes a good, long look at the lipstick she holds. It's the same one she always uses given the night scene we are about to shoot, yet she seems uncertain. This sudden lack of confidence is yet another thing that makes me worry for her.

She decides her choice is the right one, but when I raise my chin for her to apply it, she shakes her head and exchanges it for some foundation. My blasted freckles won't stay hidden for love or money.

Bailey's Lucite purse sits on the makeup counter and gives me a great way to change the subject. She has the best taste in vintage fashion. Every day she has at least one thing with her as a reminder of the era she loves, be it an old purse, a compact, or jewelry. "Have I ever told you how much I appreciate your sense of style? That ancient purse is to die for."

She snickers at my attitude while touching up my foundation. "The forties weren't before the birth of Christ, you know?"

"Made ya smile." The comment makes her grin turn bold. "I hate how we toss away cool things because they are no longer trendy. I'm seriously jealous of your stuff." Bailey reaches for the lipstick, and I tilt my head back. Suddenly, my stomach flips, and I swallow hard. "You okay?" Bailey asks.

No, I'm not so sure I am, and I don't get why I've spent the last few hours trying to hide how I am almost as edgy as Bailey is. Rapidly I nod and blurt out the first thing that comes to mind. "Yeah. For some reason the tension of the day is hitting my stomach."

Next it is Bailey's turn to try to wisecrack my head into a better space. "You're not feeling sick because you have to do yet another love scene with Evan, are you? This show has the most ridiculously overplayed love triangle in history."

"Gah!" I squirm so much I must remind her of a dying fish. Pretending you have a secret thing for a guy you can't stand sucks.

"Seriously, Katherine, you and Jason work way too hard. With all of the extra stuff you each take on, it is a wonder you ever see each other at all. How do you carry on a relationship that way?"

"I often wonder that myself." The question hits a chord I suspect is tied into how I am feeling today. I work too hard, and sometimes I think it is killing me. The thing is, I have an obligation to keep going. "If I don't drive my career, no one else will. I gave up a lot to get where I am, and I can't stop now. I am the one who controls my destiny." Bailey takes a step back. At first I mistake her look for somehow being offended, but through her tone and reflection I can tell I happened to hit the nail on the head for her.

"You know, I've controlled my own destiny all right, but not in the way I wanted. Cosmetology school led to an interest in theatrical and performance makeup, but my career wasn't supposed to stop there. I had aspirations of taking business classes. I planned to open a school where the students paid their tuition by working for Indie filmmakers who would in turn pay the school a modest fee. Now I am pushing forty, and the career of my dreams and the family I always wanted are as elusive as ever, all because that is what I have allowed. Why have I limited myself?"

Bailey's alarm goes off, reminding her she is due on set soon. "You know," she says, "this may help me ditch Carlos. It is time to stop wondering what is wrong with him and start thinking about my needs."

Reluctantly I stand to leave. I can't help but worry for Bailey. I wish we had more time to talk about this.

In an effort to lighten her mood I make a show of turning my head so I can hug her without fear of messing up my makeup. About a month ago, a brief encounter with Jason basically destroyed all of her work, and the memory of how the director flipped out over the time it took to fix it is still fresh in all of our minds. At least what I am doing has her grinning again. "Are you sure you are okay?" I ask. "You've got me worried. Why don't you stay with Jason and me? He won't mind. Hell, he's never home anyway."

"Thanks, but no. I'm not in any danger. I promise if the situation changes, I will be on your doorstep without giving it a thought." I raise a brow. As if she is reading my mind, Bailey races to reassure me. "Really, I *promise*."

With her kit and extra blotting paper in her hands, we head our separate ways.

The cool of the night feels glorious. I really needed some

fresh air.

Why didn't I open up to Bailey? I know she has a lot going on, but she is also my closest friend. She'd want to be here for me. Also, they say talking to your hairdresser is great medicine. If that is true, trusting your makeup artist when you are about to be filmed for worldwide television makes her as medicinal as penicillin.

Over the last few days, something has been freaking me out to the point of jitters. I keep telling myself it is merely stress over my career, but that feels like the brush off for something bigger. It must be the fear of things going south with that upcoming movie. The old adage of *there are no small parts, just small actors* massively applies. The size of the role is minor, but my scenes drive the plot. Nailing this has the power to put my career on a rocketship.

By the time I reach Stage 19 my heart beats normally, but my blood feels hot and racing. My stomach twists when one of the secondary players dashes past. Now I think I see the real nature of the problem. That girl is only nineteen, yet she already has her foot in the door. The ten years I have on her may only mean I am glued into everyone's brains as a second-rate network hack. If I don't pull off that movie role, *Vampires Undercover* may be my swan song.

I can't allow it. I turned my back on someone precious so I could have a career. I have to be successful—even if I am not sure I want it anymore—else I'll be a more horrible person than I already am.

Footsteps dash up behind me. I turn to catch sight of The Smile, that famous grin that has won the hearts of millions. With it comes soulful, brown eyes and sun-lightened hair nearly everything female longs to run her fingers through, yet I'm the lucky stiff who gets to know the man who comes with them for more than his looks. How jealous would the female population be if they learned with Jason Day, the fantasy can't hold a candle to the reality?

He goes in for a hug, and I'm quick to jerk back. "Oh no, you are not going to get me in trouble again for messing up my makeup." He baulks and slides his arms around my waist. He's pretty hard to resist.

"Am I allowed to do this?" He kisses me on the top of my head. "And people think being an actor is easy. If they only knew."

"What are you doing over here? Shouldn't you be home by now?"

"A major equipment setback threw everything off. I've already sent someone home for my bags, so I can go straight to the airport when we are done. Now while that may suck, this screw up did give me a chance to sneak off and get a couple of calls in, along with getting to kiss your head. That alone is worth all the annoying delays in the world, not to mention I'm pretty sure I am going to have some amazing news soon."

Jason's eyes lock into mine, making me feel as if I am the most precious package in the world. "Everything I want is coming to fruition," he says with a hope-filled voice, "and I get to have it happen with you by my side." He risks Bailey's wrath with a tender touch to my chin and raises my lips to meet his. How they scarcely make contact makes me want to surrender all the more. "I'll see you Thursday." He dashes off. With a pump of his fists in the air he screams, "Perfect! Life is perfect!"

Four days apart … Though we have done it a million times before, it's still going to feel like forever. He's right though. Things are happening, and I should share in his enthusiasm. I need to flip my mood and enjoy the moment. For better or for worse, a massive change lies ahead. My bones are buzzing over it.

Brandon

What is it about Katherine Miller that sends my heart soaring? Am I experiencing intense fantasies as a cover for the pain over losing Amber, or is there something more? Then again, I've never had a true celebrity crush before. Are they always this encompassing? No wonder why tabloids are so popular.

Tonight at Mulligan's my friends joked and laughed while the TV held me captive in hopes of another commercial. Several times the need for more understanding sent me slipping off to read about Katherine on my phone. I even followed her on social media. If I need someone to help me get over Amber, why her? And why does she make my heart flutter like the wings of a hummingbird? I got so tied up in the mystery that I broke the speed limit to get home, pulled out my laptop, and started up Netflix On Demand.

Vampires Undercover is already in its fourth season. Netflix has the first three, so I'm telling myself I have the time it takes to watch sixty-six episodes to figure out what is going on inside my brain before allowing my panic to further grow. This show sounds like *21 Jump Street* meets *True Blood*. I'm hopeful that by the fifth episode I will be so sick of it that Katherine Miller will never cross my mind again. The odds have to be good, because under normal conditions I would have no interest in watching a show about teenagers—played by actors pushing thirty and sometimes forty—who bust their own for killing instead of drinking synthetic blood. Watching it couldn't be more out of character.

Wait; isn't acting out of character a sign of mental illness?

Shut up, Brandon.

The names of the actors appear in a font that implies dripping blood. This already reminds me of the B-rated films I loved so much as a kid. Is that why this is happening? I want to regress to a time before tragedy struck? It's not exactly a terrible theory. It's also a reasonable one.

The thought of B-rated vampires with red, glowing eyes brings back the giddiness of being nine. Now I'm practically sitting at attention while tapping on my beer and wondering what I'm in for.

Hey, lying to myself about being excited over cheesy vampires is way better than admitting I am going mental over a celebrity.

Jason Day appears, wasting the space on my screen. I should have made popcorn to throw at him. Why does this guy bring out the nasty in me?

Because you have a crush on his girlfriend, you moron.

No, the guy gives off a bad vibe. Jealousy has nothing to do with the creepiness he emits.

Yeah, you keep telling yourself that.

"Well, gentlemen, what do we have here?"

Although I expect it, hearing the voice that has haunted me for days causes my heart to feel it is shooting up my throat with the intention of choking me. But then Katherine steps on screen and …

Seeing her causes the notion of a memory to nag at the base of my neck. Experiencing déjà vu is like having a word on the tip of your tongue. You are certain you know it, yet it won't come to you. If it takes long enough to remember, you start to question if it even exists.

This same type of feeling puts an inkling in my soul, telling me Katherine looks so different from in my vision because standing out is what she strives to do. An attractive cover gets attention while a plain one gets overlooked. Why is it I feel I understand this because I know her? More so, why does she put longing in my heart? It is like she is a love I lost long ago and have been searching to find.

This is seriously crazy. Longing in my heart? A lost love? Reminds me of someone I do miss. Missing Amber is fine, but projecting someone into her place so I can forget the ache in my soul will never be okay.

Sorrow hits my throat when I pull out Amber's memory book and turn to the last photo taken of her. Dreams of what we could have had fill my mind, making me mourn my lost future. Yet when I turn to see Katherine's image on my laptop, I feel tossed into another dimension. The depth of my being whispers that something beyond the realm of now is before me.

My feelings for them are not the same. Two different

women, two very different sets of emotions, all of which I associate with love. I pause the episode so my eyes can lock on the woman who seems to be messing with my head.

I know you, Katherine Miller. None of this makes any sense, but I know you. What will it take to find out how?

Searching For Something

Katherine

A rare, late call time should have put me in heaven. Why can't I sleep in every day like I did today? And why do I still feel so crappy? Then again, it is Monday and I last worked on Saturday night, leading well into Sunday morning. All these crazy hours are doing a number on me.

The clock inside Bailey's empty trailer says I'm even earlier than I thought. Her chair looks so comfortable that I practically fall into it and lean as far back as it will go. I've half a mind to catch a nap. Maybe that would settle my stomach.

Yeah, but going to sleep early last night meant I didn't review today's lines. It also meant I reneged on the promise I made my acting coach and didn't do my character study for the film. I can't blow that part. I've never been one to bear my soul like my character does, so apparently learning to speak from my heart is key. It does seem to be getting me somewhere. Still, I'm not sure I believe in soul mates let alone buy into the concept of talking to one who isn't there while hoping he will hear. However, it is probably this character's last resort before throwing herself off of a cliff. Desperation makes people do funny things.

My yawn is so deep I don't think my mouth could go any wider. I hate that I don't sleep soundly when Jason is gone. At least he'll be back late tonight, which in some ways is bad. Short trips and tight schedules are exhausting. Why do we do this to ourselves?

Because busy actors are successful actors, so sleeping alone is a sign that we are on the right career paths.

I sigh at the thought that used to be comforting. A few months ago something reminded me I have more than one goal, and it's one with a ticking clock. When I woke this morning, Jason's empty pillow made me long for something I fear I may never have—a true partner. I don't just want someone with the same goals; I want someone who is on the same team. Reaching out to the person who can fill the void in my soul was supposed to be character study, not a life lesson. But each time I do it my character resonates deeper, yanking out more of myself. The actor's reality behind the character's motivation may always slip in, but this time it's messing with my head and nagging that Jason will never give me the partnership I need.

That's not a fair thought. Jason may be so gung ho that two years ago he insisted on creating a three-year plan to work our tails off and make the A list before settling down, but I agreed. However, if he wants a family as much as I do, why was it a few months back he was so damned freaked out by an unplanned pregnancy he was on needles and pins until I miscarried? Can't success and family co-exist now?

God, I am so sick of being uncertain. It makes all I have seem useless and puts my heart into a void. The only good that can come of it is being a primer for my exercise, which I should be working on. I settle deeper into the chair and try to get a grip on the questions that make my heart hurt. Some of the words from the script slip in, and while the concepts seem alien to me, my own situation brings them to life.

What does it take to become at peace with myself? Would you understand if I told you something inside me feels ancient? I've never been able to talk to anyone about that.

Hollowness grows inside me. How have I managed to hide from the fact the script reflects heartache I wasn't aware I could relate to? There is more to me than I have ever understood, and I have spent my life casting it aside instead of exploring it. Why do I shortchange myself?

How do I explore the feeling something important is out there and I may never find it? Do I leave everything behind so I can search the globe? How do you Google that? I don't know if it's a career, a person, or an aspect of myself. What would you do?

An air of peace rolls over me, quelling my nerves and

covering my body like a blanket. Have I grown as an actress and taken this exercise to another level? I hope somewhere in the pit of silence I will hear a message—a thought surfacing from the back of my brain or a word from God. Instead, I am overwhelmed by the sensation someone wants to appreciate who I am—someone I have never met. True comfort can exist for me, and that person holds the key. Logic tells me it is madness. Illogic tells my heart I am being lured into an affair. But my soul feels surrounded by peace, causing my breathing to slow and my lids to turn heavy. I find myself sending a silent message of love to the man I know must exist.

From outside the trailer I hear Bailey talking on the phone. I wouldn't mind if she stayed outside a few minutes longer. I seem to have found bliss. The second she steps inside I'm sure we will start gabbing as usual, and I will lose this beautiful connection to the universe.

Brandon

After pulling into Endeara's lot, I park and shut off the car. What is it about Katherine Miller? Why was it that all weekend long something inside me screamed I know her? And I mean all weekend. Come Sunday morning I came to realize I had spent thirty-six hours watching Vampires Undercover.

Thirty-six hours of watching that ridiculous show.

Thirty-six hours of eating food that had been stashed in my freezer since the coming of Christ.

Thirty-six hours with little sleep other than the occasional nod off.

I wanted someone to kill me. I also smelled as if someone had. After a bath and a nap, I went on to slip in eight more episodes before I passed out, hard. I'm almost grateful it is Monday so I was forced to leave the house. There was no way I was calling in sick, not after reading about how schizophrenics mess up at work and avoid social situations.

The moment I open the door I hear Darla say into the phone, "I'm so relieved to hear you are finally going to take action against that loser. From the way this conversation started, you had me a bit scared."

Poor Bailey. If she is anything like her sister, she deserves better.

I make my way across the lobby while wishing I had spent the weekend coming up with a new angle on that damn gumdrop campaign. There has to be a way to market something that is deemed to be food yet is totally inedible.

Yeah, whatever. I'm well aware I am going to spend my day watching TV on my computer. That damn show has me so hooked I'm not even sure I care about Katherine Miller anymore, which is pretty awesome. Maybe that's why I didn't hear a peep out of the voice all weekend.

"I agree," Darla says into the phone even though she looks dead at me. Fire flares in her eyes. "Finding an iPad with secret email and bank accounts proving both infidelity and that Carlos has squandered tens of thousands of dollars while not contributing a penny to your household should be the last straw."

I stop dead in my tracks with my jaw dropped. She has got to be kidding. Bailey had better bail on that douche. I've half a mind to find out where she lives and drag her away myself. That's crap!

I start to head off but not before uttering, "What an ass!"

Darla covers the mouthpiece. "No shit," she says back. She looks like she wants to rip the guy's balls off. Someone should.

I'm not even a step away when an odd sensation softens my heart. I feel as if … as if peace has rolled over me, quelling my nerves and covering my body like a blanket. Maybe it is compassion for Bailey, or maybe not having a voice jump out at me for a few days has brought relief.

Darla hangs up the phone, and all seems normal again. Losing my sudden bliss may have something to do with the pissed-off look on Darla's face. "Yep! You heard it right! That asshat not only cheated, rather epically, he also bled her dry while gallivanting around town like Mr. Moneybags!"

"Please tell me she is dumping him."

"Damn right she is! If she doesn't—" Suddenly, all three of Darla's phone lines light up. "Welcome to Monday!"

"Indeed." I fake tipping a hat to her before heading off to my office.

Let's see, a one-hour network TV show contains fourteen minutes of commercial messages plus eight minutes of in-show branding for a total of twenty-two minutes of marketing content. Thus, after a weekend of watching forty-four episodes of *Vampires Undercover,* I have absorbed nearly thirty-four hours of this horrific show that has sucked me in as if I were a fourteen-year-old girl. Although it being on Netflix got me to bypass ten hours of commercials, I was still the victim of nearly six hours of marketing. Therefore, I spent this weekend studying the current trends.

That's crap. I put bags under my eyes and rotted my brain on poorly written television, not to mention loving every minute of staring at a woman who puts my senses into a spin.

I don't get it. I've had celebrity crushes before—Debbie Harry of Blondie circa nineteen seventy-eight, Joan Jett and Cherie Currie of The Runaways circa always, Brody Dalle of The Distillers gets serious honorable mention. Past crushes may have made my head fluttery, and they have definitely put my hand into my pants with trips to fantasyland, but they have never convinced me I know someone, let alone that she is a person I could love.

Man this is creepy, but there is something more here. I just know it.

Groggy head in hand, my *Vampires Undercover* marathon resumes. I can't focus on anything but this obsession, regardless of how lame it makes me feel, so I might as well surrender to not getting any work done today and making up for it later. I've got sixteen more hours of lapping up brain-smothering hell before I will have to track down the current season online. I can't let this madness go that far. After all, what could possibly happen after that? It's not as if we will ever cross paths. She's a well-guarded celebrity who lives thousands of miles away. Katherine's fame is a carrot dangling in front of my face that makes me feel I'm a hopeless donkey.

Does the situation have to be hopeless? Maybe I could go to Canada and track her down. Everyone has to eat, right? I already read about one burger place she goes to. There have to be other places near the studio as well. I could go and hope to run into her.

No, the odds are too low. If I research places she has been known to frequent, I could probably narrow down where she lives. There has to be a grocery store or—

Oh no! Stop right there.

Brandon Wayne, you have now reached the point of crazy talk.

But what if someone is telling me this is the person I'm supposed to be with, yet I ignore it?

Yeah, right.

A yawn roars out of me. Having scarcely slept over the weekend is doing me in.

My head dips as I start to drift off. I whip it up and snap back to attention. The last thing I want is to be caught sleeping while watching this. Lord knows no one here would ever let me live it down.

Katherine's eyes suck me in. I try to imagine them without the colored contacts and lighting that makes them sparkle like diamonds. I swear to God they should be blue, but that would look so—*yawn*—wrong.

The camera goes in for a tight close up when Katherine tries to compel a victim to forget the horror he endured. Funny, I don't see contact ridges. They must get removed in post-production. How much CG do they use on—

My head dips, and I try to shake off the need to sleep before it dips again …

Darkness closes in around my vision, and the image of blue eyes, bleached hair, and pale skin—all glowing under the rays of the sun— come into view. Just the sight of the girl heading my way brings about euphoria.

The heels on her boots are so high it is a wonder she can walk straight. Her formfitting, black tank top and miniskirt command respect by revealing enough to show off what she's got without screaming tramp. Her smoky eye shadow is accented with a smidgen of blue, violating the rules. She's only supposed to use black—like a black bar across her face.

No, she does that at night. During the day she upholds the image that makes people think she is an underground fashion model—tough but elegant and with the sweetest air about her. She's breathtaking. I want to wrap my arms around her, not just to hold her but to also claim her as my own.

"Hi, honey," she says with a wave.

God, that voice is so gentle.

Her ankle twists when she steps on some bark, and she stops to check her shoe. Beside her is a fire hydrant painted to look like a Minuteman.

A Minuteman? Like in the Revolutionary War?

Laughter comes from behind. The scent of lighter fluid wafts up my nose, and warmth runs up my back as flames in the barbecue behind me flare. It's a contrast to the cool drink in my hand. We're all drinking beer out of cans with retro logos. Mine has a pull-off ring tab and a seam along the side that reminds me of welded steel.

A teenaged girl in blue satin shorts and rainbow socks, roller skates in my direction. Her hair is sandy brown and curly, reminding me of Barbara Streisand's on the cover of Superman. *Her bright blue eyeshadow sparkles in the sun as she skates past.*

"Brandon?"

The girl beside me wears a red satin jacket and tight, white pants with a rainbow coming up the back of the legs and arching across her butt. Another is in a sundress and a macramé necklace with yellow beads forming the center of jute daisies.

"Bran-don?"

Macramé?

What's up with the seventies' fashions? Wait, this isn't a retro can. It's actually made of steel.

"Hey! Wayne!" Darla's volume practically scares me half to death and sends my arms flailing. "Your phone is still off from the weekend. You have an appointment downstairs."

I race to turn on my phone. Dear God, please don't let her see what I am watching. I need to shut that off. I've got to stop losing my head.

Darla closes in, and I can't turn my monitor off fast enough.

"Please tell me you are not watching that show."

Busted! Play it cool. Make her only think she saw what she did. "What show?"

"That horrific vampire show with the super hot guys who run around in towels and girls who are painstakingly made up to look like Barbie dolls."

"How do you know there are super hot guys if it's not worth watching?" Look who's busted now.

"Nobody is perfect."

"Really, Darla?"

"I refuse to divulge any information other than those guys are hot, and I'm human. I assume you have the same excuse where the women are concerned."

Busted, again. "I am doing research. This show is aimed at teenagers, and I need to broaden our demographic." Hey, that was pretty good, fast thinking.

She tips her head back and laughs. "Riiiight!"

"Who in this room has a degree in marketing and needs to work on product placement with a small budget? We can't exactly afford to get into a summer blockbuster, so a less expensive, highly targeted audience is the way to go."

Her lips clamp. Did I get her? That did sound legit.

Darla turns smug. "If it is research, why do you have your iPod set up so the headphone cord looks like it is attached to it instead of your monitor?"

"Hey, we've already established that no one sane wants to admit they watch this show."

She's not even fazed. "Checkmate. You coming down for your appointment, or shall I send him up?"

"I'll be down in a second." I can't believe the stupid thing I'm about to do, but as much as she can tease people, Darla seems to have the answers when they are most elusive. "Hey, if you were afraid you were losing your mind, but didn't really think you were crazy, yet it is possible you were, what would you do?"

Her mouth rounds in confusion. She then rattles her head. "Wow. That sentence was all over the place. Self-doubt is a pretty good sign you are not funny farm bound but …" Her eyebrow cocks. "Brandon, you don't look or sound as if you have slept much lately. What's going on?"

I shake my head. I can't go there. "Never mind. It's just insomnia."

"Brann-donn?" She crosses her arms and waits.

Her eyes narrow, and I start to feel uncomfortable, not because she is scrutinizing me, but because she has my number. "Let me guess," she says. "This has to do with the voice you heard."

"Ugh." I scrape my hand through my hair. I knew I didn't fool her on Friday night but … God, I am really stepping into this. "This sounds totally wacky, but I can't help but feel someone is trying to send me a message."

"You mean from beyond?"

I nod. God, my life is just plain nuts.

Darla takes a seat on the corner of my desk, and the woman whom I am used to being a jokester becomes beyond a doubt serious. "If there's anything I've learned, it's the world is a mysterious place. Have you considered talking to someone experienced in these things?"

"You mean like a shrink?"

"No, someone who knows about the interworking of the universe, like a psychic. A shrink will only look at what is in front of you. A psychic will give you all the angles."

The thought had crossed my mind, but I'm not sure how much I believe in that stuff.

"I'm going out on a limb here," she continues. "You're the first to admit your situation with Amber had a lasting affect even though you claim you don't blame yourself. If that is true, why are you always so quick to bring up that you are not guilty? Guilt is a human thing, but hearing voices is unworldly.

Since you are suffering from both, why not talk to someone who can see your situation in its entirety?"

The word unworldly is disturbing yet so accurate. Darla may have hit the nail on the head. I try to cover how freaked out I am by crossing my arms and joking it off. "How is it Darla, the advice queen, knows about psychics?"

She squares off by taking the same stance. "The same way your friend does."

"What friend?"

"The one you are always at Mulligan's with."

"Shane?"

"No, the one who pretends he's all that but knows he isn't. He idolizes you, you know?"

"Dale? How do you know—"

"I had an appointment right after him once. He saw me get out of my car and scampered behind a bush."

My head rattles. "Wow! What would Dale be doing with a psychic?"

Darla heads for the door. "If I could figure out what any man does, I would not be helping Rox start a dating service. Instead, we would make a fortune on the lecture circuit."

"Hold on. What do you mean, he idolizes me?"

"Come on, Brandon, wake up to reality. I'll tell your appointment you'll be right with him."

My brain is spiraling. All that stuff about Dale is weird, but Darla gave me a bowl of food for thought. Are my images of Katherine real, or are they fantasies brought on by guilt? Does that blonde girl I dreamed of tie into this? Speaking of blondes, what about Pixie Waitress's disappearing act? Darla knows who she is but … I don't know what is real anymore.

Before she slips away, I call out to Darla, "Hey, do you know what happened to that waitress from Mulligan's?"

"Don't even think it, Wayne. Besides, I heard she went back to Modesto after they fired her for skankin' up the place."

Good, more confirmation that she was real. That's one less concern. Darla is right. I need outside help who won't think I am crazy. If that fails, I'll seek help from someone who does.

Dream Police

Brandon

While I had no clue what to expect when calling a psychic, there is no way my experience was normal. Initially, the guy who answered told me Jennifer was booked for the next few weeks. However, when he heard Darla referred me, and Dale had been there before, he worked a consultation into today's schedule. That was odd enough, but then he added, "Don't worry, man. It's free."

A free consultation? I thought psychics robbed people at every corner. Welcome to Los Angeles, where the guy who hears voices is the normal one.

Forty minutes later I exit the freeway in El Segundo and turn into the driveway of a house tucked behind a 7-Eleven. The high pitch of the roof, the beds of blooming pansies lining the walkway, and the perfectly manicured rose bushes next to the door, make me feel I am approaching a fairy tale cottage.

The guy who greets me is probably in his late thirties. His casual style of long, frizzy brown hair, no shirt and no shoes, actually helps me relax. Then again, even though the air is clear, it is possible I am loosening up because of residual smoke. That stellar beam in his eyes has me suspecting he's baked. I'm kind of jealous.

"Hi, I have an appointment with Jennifer."

"Yeah, man, come on in." With a sweeping motion, he welcomes me into an issue of *Better Homes and Gardens*. It's kind of jarring. I expected something mysterious and, from the looks of this guy, commune-like. This seems where the over-compensated ex-wife of an accountant would live.

A lady with kinky, blonde hair that nearly reaches her waist comes out to greet me. Once I get a good look at her my heart starts pumping so fast I might meet my maker prematurely. Is that—

No, it can't be.

"Hi, I'm Jennifer," she says. "You must be Brandon." She motions for me to take a seat in the dining room where she pours me a glass of red wine. "Here, take a few sips, but don't drink it all. Sorry, it's straight out of the bottle. No doctoring."

Against everything Mom ever told me about taking candy from strangers I sit and sip. I don't know much about wine, but it tastes fine—I think.

Jennifer turns up the brightness on the chandelier and takes a seat across from me. Holy shit, she really does look like Stevie Nicks!

Jennifer is about sixty. How old is Stevie now? Supposedly she is pagan, though she denies being a witch. You don't need to be a witch to be psychic, do you? I try to appear nonchalant while eyeing the place for her Grammy collection.

Jennifer leans in and locks her eyes on mine. Would it be rude of me to ask her to sing? Maybe Stevie has a twin. Seriously, her appearance is freaking me out more than the way she is staring at me, and that's pretty intense.

"Take another sip," she says. Her insistence is casual but persuasive. I fight to keep my shrug internal. I don't want her to think I'm rude, but what's up with the wine? Nothing about this experience seems normal.

Once I comply, Jennifer pulls out a pad of paper. "Dump the rest onto this. If it goes over, no big deal."

This time I actually do shrug. When I toss the contents of my glass, it *splats* onto the paper without wasting a drop. Jennifer goes back to staring into my eyes. "Now what?" I ask.

"Give it a minute. Meanwhile, tell me why you're here."

"If you are psychic, shouldn't you—" She cuts me off with a death glare. "Sorry."

She nods to the wine that has dried in a mass of spirals. "Exactly what I thought, Jonathan."

"My name is Brandon."

"Jonathan," she says, firmly. She rethinks it. "No, Johnny."

Man, this is weird. "Brandon."

"Yes, but Brandon is here because of Johnny and Saleena."

Who the hell are Johnny and Saleena? There is a John in the plant at work. Maybe he is spiking the gumdrops, and I am hallucinating.

Jennifer tilts her head. If she were a puppy, I'd expect her ears to be pointed as well. "Katherine," she says. My body stiffens and turns cold. "Hold on a moment." Her heels click as she heads down the hall, punctuating the panic racing through me. How the hell did she know? I am not surprised she guessed I was here because of a woman, but to call Katherine by name?

Jennifer returns and hands me a single Tarot card—The Fool. She's probably calling me out for thinking that hearing a voice could possibly mean anything other than I should be locked up.

"Go home and meditate on this. If outside thoughts keep you from concentrating, tell them they will hold your attention in due time. Focus only on the card until it becomes a mere blur and your mind is released. If you can't do it, stare at it until you fall asleep."

My insides are shaking so much that all I can do is stare at her with an open mouth. I finally snap out of it enough to take the card. The shirtless man strolls up and opens the front door. "Can you return during lunch tomorrow?" Jennifer waits for my nod before ushering me out. "Wonderful. My calling Katherine by name should be enough to convince you your money will not be spent in vain. My fee will be fifty dollars. Be prepared to stay half an hour, and please remember to return my card." She points her finger at me. "Don't bend it."

When I step outside, the world looks normal, yet my insides feel as if I have landed on an alien planet. What the hell just happened? Only fifty dollars? I was expecting so much more. This must be the beginning of the swindle.

The darkness of night covers my apartment. A beam of light comes through the crack in the curtains and lands on The Fool card sitting in my hand. On the card, a dog is at the feet of a man holding both a rose and a vagabond's bag. He looks like he is about to dance over the edge of a cliff and into the water. I would expect the dog to warn the idiot of impending doom. Instead they are about to dive into stupidity together.

I don't tend to notice ambient noise when I am in bed. Now that I am supposed to focus, a plane passing overhead distracts me, and the refrigerator won't shut up.

This is dumb. I reach for my iPod. What makes for good, new-agey, meditation music? Certainly nothing I own. In fact, nothing in here looks right for the mood I need.

After hitting shuffle and skipping over three songs, Blue Oyster Cult's "Don't Fear the Reaper" kicks in. Is it amusement or nerves that cause me to chuckle aloud? I'm entertained by not only the sentiment but also over the singer's alias. How the name Buck Dharma implies kicking righteousness in the ass seems appropriate.

Silken vocals, sustained notes that bring on the sensation of gliding, and the insistence there is nothing to fear in visiting the other side, have a soothing affect and make me wonder where all this will lead. By the time I reach the instrumental break and guitars are soaring, my peripheral vision is blurred. The Fool's image morphs into a frame of film.

Guitars wail as a movie plays in reverse—the clouds on the card become distant, the rose transforms from a blossom into a bud, the tide recedes, and The Fool backs away from the cliff, through a field and ... and onto a stage? His colorful outfit is replaced by black leather pants and an abused, white T-shirt. His hair stays blonde, but it grows long and straight while he forms the curves of a woman. The satchel and rose morph into a guitar.

The girl I saw in the park now has a black bar painted across her eyes. She's singing her heart out and stealing mine along with those in the crowd. God, how I love a hot female singer.

The room is packed even though there are only about a hundred of us, and the stage is so close to the ground anyone could step on it. Everything is so compact the whole scene—the band, the audience, even the brick walls themselves—feel like one entity. And it's dark, maybe even a little evil feeling—the true hallmarks of punk rock decadence. The people around us have spiked hair and are dressed in T-shirts, ripped jeans, Converse high-tops, and leather jackets. One guy has a safety pin in his cheek. The clothes, the bad acoustics, the smell of seafood and curry, the popcorn-covered floor, the air weighed down with smoke and whisky—everything reeks of being a spectacle in the purest sense of rock and roll.

The band finishes, and the crowd loses their minds. I bolt backstage while screaming something about being their manager, not that anyone seems to care who goes where. The hot blonde stretches her arms around me, and my heart warms at the touch of Saleena's kiss. I want to treasure her forever—but all goes black.

The Fool returns. He and the dog each take a single step forward, and the vibrant petals on his rose turn dark.

A new vision creeps in—one of keys in one hand and my other on the handle of a car door. I open it for Saleena, and then head to the driver's side. My steps stagger, and a wave of concern hits, yet I'm also happy to the point where I can't stop laughing.

The tires screech as I accelerate, but the car doesn't move. We laugh at my failure to release the parking brake. I get it right the second time.

Cars and lights flash past as we head up a steep hill. Are they stopped, or am I speeding to the point where perception is distorted? My head screams to slow down, but the other me keeps racing up a hill in this metropolis with skyscrapers and turn-of-the-century buildings. The light ahead turns yellow, and I gun it. The engine revs but not as hard as expected.

As we near the intersection, another car heads across. To no avail, the real me tries to get the driver me to swerve. Tires screech, and a scream penetrates the air. The impact on my right causes me to throw my arm over my eyes. Warmth splatters and drips into my mouth—red, metallic-tasting warmth.

My God.
I can't look, and I don't have to because I know.
I ...
I killed her.
I killed Saleena, the girl who was in the car with me.

The Fool reappears and takes another step forward. The petals on his rose wither and scatter onto the ground. Light creeps in, and I find myself sitting in a room that is illuminated by a single candle. Its flicker is reflected off of an engagement ring that has one mere chip of a diamond. My right hand feels weighted by metal.

No! This couldn't have happened.

My current and former hearts race as I raise the gun.

I can't do this. I can't think anymore. This has to stop now!

Cool steel trembles against my temple. I cock back the—

"No!" I jump up in bed—sweating out of every pore, my chest aching from pants, and my stomach ready to hurl.

I killed a girl. I robbed someone of her life, and then took my own.

Shivers of reality crawl across my arms, traveling up my neck and down my back. All my unexplained guilt over Amber's death hasn't been for her at all.

You Never Had It Better

Katherine

Blaring music jerks me awake and sends my heart into a sprint. The volume on this alarm clock nearly gives me a heart attack each morning, but if I don't wake with a jolt, I'll hit snooze until noon.

Why does four in the morning come so early? Scratch that. The real question is; why do I have such a bad taste in my mouth? I feel hung over, yet last night I didn't have so much as a sip of wine.

The heat that keeps making guest appearances in my blood stream returns when I sit. It seems to have brought its friend who prickles my nerve endings. My body is acting like it did when …

Oh no.

Bolting out of bed puts my stomach on a swing. This can't be! When is my period due? My pills ended a day ago, but I screwed up at the beginning of the month and missed one. That usually makes my period start early.

Oh no!

Calm down. Every now and then you skip a period.

Yeah, but it's never accompanied by fire in your veins or a twisty stomach!

I race to get dressed. I don't have long to get to the drugstore and still make call time.

"No, no, no! No, no, no!"

My foot taps frantically on my trailer's floor. Jason has been super blunt about not being ready—so much even holding the test stick feels deceitful. I didn't consciously screw

68

up my pills. Or did I? I blew it a few months ago too, and the same thing happened. A few days after getting a second pink line, pain kicked in and my period started. Did I subconsciously screw up again in hopes of a better outcome?

No, with my fluctuating schedule, it's difficult to keep anything on track. Lack of sleep sometimes makes me forget, too. Jason and I are so damn pigheaded about our goals you'd think we would play it safe and double up on protection.

The clock says I have another minute to go, but I hold the test stick up to the light anyway. No second line is in sight, yet I know where this is going.

Jason was caught so off guard last time he was nearly mute until the miscarriage happened. This time around he is probably going to wonder what the hell I am up to. Do I tell him when he gets home tonight, or do I try to come up with a way to soften the blow? Shoot, does it even matter?

Burning creeps up my throat. Oh God, here come the jitters again.

If this turns out to be a false alarm, I am going to insist Jason start wearing a condom. This can't happen. It absolutely cannot!

I put the stick on the coffee table and step into the early morning darkness outside my trailer. I can't face two lines, but I also don't know if I can hold it together if there is only one. I don't dare admit part of me wants this to be true, and that how Jason feels won't affect the outcome. Given the choice, I would take this baby over Jason in a heartbeat because not a day …

I inhale sharply and steady myself to face what I constantly try to push out of my mind.

Because not a day passes where I don't wonder what happened to my little girl.

My eyes burn at the memory of being in the hospital. Fire flared through me, yet I was so exhausted from pushing I couldn't think to fan myself. When I overheard the doctor say the baby checked out fine, I thought sweeter words had never been uttered. But my elation crashed as I watched a nurse carry my little angel out of the room after me having caught only enough of a glimpse to know she had dark hair.

Despite the fatigue and drug-induced haze that kept me feeling tied to the bed, I bolted up and screamed for them to stop. When I signed the adoption papers, it made sense I would not get to see my baby, but the magnitude of what I had done was rolling over me. Watching the nurse shelter my darling, as if I were a threatening stranger, sent my heart plummeting. Somebody had to help me. I begged another nurse to let me know the joy of holding my baby, but the viciousness of her tone as she said, "Contact is against the rules!" smeared what was left of my heart into Hell.

I went through nine months of love for that child—nine months of prayers, nine months of doing everything I felt was in her best interest—and never got to see her precious face. I helped create that face, and I loved every moment of nurturing it as it grew inside me.

Adoption may be a beautiful thing, but do they have to make the act of giving up your child so painful? Why couldn't they give me even the briefest moment to welcome my daughter into the world? To grant me the ability to give her one tiny pearl of wisdom about how the world can be a tough place, but we are blessed with the ability to make choices. Telling her the choice I made was the one I felt was best for her was all I wanted, and I was robbed of the opportunity. I'm so grateful I thought to scream that I love her so she could carry the thought with her. That and hearing her cry were the only contact we had outside the womb.

Reality creeps in, and I try to smack down knowing I gave away a precious gift for selfish reasons. Every day I tell myself I did what was best for her, but the truth is I did what was best for me. I gave away a person so I could take a crapshoot at a career that may crash and burn with a cheesy TV show. I have always felt that if I could take back signing those papers, I would in a heartbeat. When my miscarriage happened, it seemed God was punishing me for being selfish. I didn't mean to do the wrong thing. I would never make that mistake again.

Tears trickle down my face and onto the coffee table as I brave picking up the stick. My hand trembles so much that although the second pink line is as bold as the first, there appears to be only one. My stomach flips. The need to puke almost overcomes me, but the joy that brings a smile across my face makes me not care. This is incredible.

The sobs come hard and fast. I didn't let myself see it last time, but this time I do. I've been given a gift. This is why something inside me feels it is changing. Not only is a miracle happening, God is giving me a second chance. I can't right my wrong, but I do feel forgiven by a greater power.

God, I didn't intend for this to happen, but I promise I won't let you down.

Brandon

The overstuffed chairs in Jennifer's living room are even more comfortable than they look. If that Fool card sitting on the tea table between us didn't seem to be mocking me, I'd almost be relaxed.

The guy from yesterday, again barefoot and shirtless, carries out a tray with a couple of glasses and two bottles of wine. "Red or white," he asks.

"Red, I guess?" Red is the color of blood. Does that make red wine the one of death and white the one of life?

Jennifer touches my arm. "Relax, honey. This one is to drink. Pick what you enjoy."

"Red then. Definitely red." Hell, I'm still not sure I said the right thing.

The shirtless guy does the honors of pouring. Jennifer leans back in her chair, crosses her legs at the ankles, and takes a sip of her white wine. I follow suit. "Did you find what you were looking for?" she asks.

Lord, I sure found something. Whatever it was still has me quaking.

DIANE RINELLA

Sweat builds under my collar as I describe the dream. The impact of the images affects me nearly as much now as they did last night, causing me to gulp my wine.

Shirtless guy returns with a plate of chocolates. "Thanks, honey," Jennifer says before reaching for a piece, and I'm quick to join her. I need something to focus on other than what may have been a blast from the past.

"Now, what would you like to know about Saleena?" she asks.

"The girl who was in the car with me?" I ask hesitantly, seeking confirmation. Jennifer nods, and my insides shudder. I'd rather forget about Saleena for obvious reasons. "She's not why I'm here. I keep hearing a voice. Sometimes it's during the day, but it is mostly at night. It has kept me awake for so long I'm not really sure I am hearing it anymore."

"She's the voice," Jennifer says.

Shaking my head shows her I disagree. This woman may have gotten me to flash back to a past life, but she is way off base now. "Sorry, but no. I know who the voice is." I can't believe I'm sharing this. Then again, what am I afraid of? A psychic thinking I'm crazy? That in itself is nuts. "I had a different vision before—one I am pretty sure is recent—and I saw the source of the voice."

"Trust me, it's her." Jennifer's tone is insistent, yet she stays relaxed and takes another sip of wine.

"That doesn't make any sense. You see, not only does the voice from last night not match, I know who the source is. Wait, don't you need cards or something for this?"

Jennifer gives me a smile that politely says crutches are not something she finds necessary. "The voice you are hearing now belongs to the same soul you knew before. She's been reaching out to you for a little over a week. Depending on your state of mind or how scattered your attention is, you may not always hear her, though it is possible you have noticed her in other ways."

"You mean, feeling as if someone is thinking of me?"

"Yes, or via some other sensation, such as a buzz or an air

of peace rolling over you."

I don't know what is freaking me out more; hearing a voice and getting visions or how spot on Jennifer is.

"I told you to think of yourself as Johnny because you and Saleena were once a couple, as you probably have been many times before."

"Before? You mean in other lives?" That would sure explain why Katherine looks so odd to me. It's not that she doesn't look like herself, it's that she doesn't look like the person I remember.

"Most definitely. Have you considered that your guilt over what happened with Saleena explains how you unjustifiably harbor it for your ex? How long ago did she die?"

"It was about—" My thought freezes so I can process what Jennifer is saying. I never told her about Amber, did I? So much is going on I am not sure of anything anymore. "How do you know about Amber?"

"It is etched into your eyes." Jennifer's touch to my arm both grabs my attention and, much to my surprise, calms my nerves a tad. Her gentle tone reminds me more of a maternal figure than the rock star I keep thinking she is. Right now I wouldn't mind crawling home to Mommy, but she'd probably tuck her little boy in his bed after giving him milk and cookies and tell him to sleep it off. Sleep and I are not friends. "Brandon, it is okay to accept there is someone else out there who is far better suited for you than Amber was and your souls have never let go."

What? This isn't why I am here. "If Saleena is someone else now, how does she know to contact me? Also, what I saw took place in the seventies. That wasn't very long ago. I thought reincarnation, if it even happens, took at least a few decades, if not hundreds of years."

"Oh, it happens. Keep in mind that humans are the only creatures who know the concept of time. To all other beings, as well as spirits, time is immaterial. Think about how your lives were cut short. If we come back when we are ready, all this tells me you two are eager to finish business."

Shirtless guy carries in a paper plate with two pieces of cheese. Great, I missed breakfast and am starved. Maybe eating lunch will make all of this magically seem logical. I reach for a piece, and Jennifer yanks the plate away and carries it off. "This isn't for eating. Hold on."

Muttering seeps in from down the hall. When she returns, Jennifer hands me a stick of what I am pretty sure is dried sage. "Draw a circle on one piece and an x on the other."

I do as she says while wondering how I got myself into this madness. All this has to be wrong, yet it is so obviously right. The pieces fit—maybe even too well ...

Can this be a scam? How could she get this kind of information about me?

"Take that home and leave it on your counter tonight. Whichever piece molds first will tell you what to do next. If it is the one with the circle, follow your heart—whatever that means to you. If it is the one with the x, leave the vision behind and never think of it again. Let the mold pave your path to happiness."

Is she serious?

This has to be a set up. Dale and Darla must be in cahoots. They know just enough to make it happen, too.

No, Darla may play pranks, but she would never take part in head games. Besides, I've never told anyone Amber's devout passions and desire to plan everything to the letter repressed my spirit. That one has been tough to admit to myself.

With the cheese plate in my hand, Jennifer sends me on my way.

Destination Unknown

Katherine

How Jason went from relaxed to flopping around in bed like a fish out of water makes me wonder if my stress is contagious. Does he see through the claim that my queasy stomach is brought on by a bout of food poisoning? Actually, his tension is probably related to my not being responsive to his desires. What is it with men and their constant need for sex? He walked through the door after midnight, and we have to be up at four. You'd think he'd want some sleep.

Then again …

My eyes take in the beauty of how the sheet conceals just enough to make it look as if he is posing for the cover of Playgirl. Dear Lord, those sleek muscles. I wouldn't exactly mind …

But at the sight of his face, my interest dwindles. My inner voice nags that I've wound up with the wrong person—just as it did Monday in Bailey's trailer. I want the comfort I found there again, yet I haven't been able to bring myself to try to find it. I can't face accepting there is someone else out there who is better suited for me.

Ugh! Why do I keep slipping into odd thoughts? This pregnancy is doing a number on me. Between feeling sick while wanting to jump Jason's bones, and the madness that keeps twisting my head into thinking Jason is all wrong for me, I'm practically straight-jacket bound. This is going to be one long, first trimester.

Should I come out and tell Jason I am pregnant? Last time he freaked so much he made me feel like an idiot. It's been months, yet I can still hear the panic in his voice. *"You must have read the test wrong. You do know there are supposed to be two lines, right?"* Jason went so far into denial over our plans getting derailed he even said if the baby weren't his, he would understand. He may have been freaking out, but the wounds I got when he wielded those words continue to sting. Still, when it comes to pregnancies, my hurt runs much deeper than any pain Jason ever caused.

I sniffle back the tears brought on by memories of the man who fathered my daughter and how he literally walked out the door after hearing the news. Three weeks later he came back long enough to let me think we would make a go of it before he turned around and bailed on us for good. I prayed he would have a change of heart. After all, how could he walk away without taking even the tiniest amount of responsibility? The magnitude of his betrayal continues to warp my mind. By the time I accepted he was gone it was too late for an abortion. Thank God it worked out the way it did. Considering how giving a baby up for adoption has torn at me, what kind of mess would I be if I had chosen that route?

The tears slink down. I discreetly dab them, but sniffling back the pain grabs Jason's attention. A tuff of his buttered toast-colored hair slips over his eyes as he settles in. "You okay?" The concern conveyed by the tension in his brow is sweet. This is one of the many things I love about him. "Maybe that upset stomach means you have the flu. Can I get you something?"

I snuggle into his chest while keeping my head tilted down. "I'm fine, thanks."

He pulls me in, and for as comforting as it is, somehow it all feels wrong. "It's too bad we have to get up so early. The one thing I hate about this job is calling out sick is not an option." As if on cue to Jason's words, my head starts throbbing. "I hope you knock this thing out before you leave. I'll miss you, you know?"

My heart sags. I'll miss him too—at least I think I will. The time I have spent physically alone while living in my head has been pretty enlightening—way more than I want to admit. How is it talking to a fabricated person is more satisfying than talking to Jason? The hormones must have something to do with it. "It's only for a few days."

"Still … I hate you being gone. Every time it happens a part of me fears you won't come back."

"Why would you feel that way?" This is encouraging. Maybe my miscarriage gave him a change of heart, and he will be cool with the news after all.

"Because if my plan fails, now is the best time in my life. I wish there were a way to know I am on track and not about to stall out. Every move in this business is a crapshoot, but it's the only way to get what I want."

Yeah, what he wants is why I am freaked out over my news. It's only fair to tell him. "You know, there are other things we both want."

He laughs. "Yes, I am well aware. We've got to cross over into movies before this atrocity of a show is canned. Once producers have you locked in their minds as one character, you are screwed for at least five years while they forget about you. The second I get anywhere near the A-list I'm bailing out of here."

His unexpected words cause my mind to jump in an entirely different direction. "What? Are you kidding? You can't do that! You're the reason why women watch this crap. If you bail, we are all out of work."

He snickers. Not a drop of arrogance is anywhere near it, but there sure is a lot of ignorance. "Nah, this show has three stars. If one goes, the others pick up the pace until a younger, hotter replacement is brought in. Fans are not as fickle as you think. Look at *Two and a Half Men*. Charlie Sheen left, they nabbed Ashton Kutcher, and boom! Ratings gold. My leaving would probably lengthen the run of the show. That would give you more time to move up another rung or two on the proverbial ladder."

Is he crazy? What they pulled off with *Two and a Half Men* was a huge long shot. They also had Big Three Network money behind them, not to mention Charlie Sheen pissed off so many people the audience wanted to see the show thrive without him. Jason has to know that. Lastly, what star as big as Ashton Kutcher would jump onto this wonky ship?

"In fact ..." He cocks his eyebrows and gives me a wicked smile that has his hickory brown eyes gleaming. My stomach does a loop-de-loop, and a wave of heat smacks me. I'm pretty sure the hormones have nothing to do with it. "Looks as if our upcoming hiatus will have me busier than planned. Apparently I am a shoo-in for the lead in the next Christopher Nolan movie—provided I am willing to sign on for the sequels. Holding off on renewing my contract for next season was wise."

My eyes go to full circles while my voice goes as nuclear as the bomb he just dropped. I don't know if I am more upset about how this will affect our child or how Jason is oblivious to his importance regarding the careers of everyone on this God-forsaken show. "What! You know the rest of us already signed. You made it sound like you just hadn't gotten around to it yet."

Jason's expression sinks. I swear I can sense the sagging of his gut. Does he really believe what he did was above board? "I had every intention of signing if the movie didn't work out. Why cause unnecessary drama by saying something before I knew what was happening?"

I get where he is coming from, but we are supposed to be a team—not just he and I, but all of us—cast and crew. No wonder why I am seeking comfort Jason can't provide. God, my life is jacked!

Maybe it is the stress. Maybe I can't deal with not getting what I need from Jason, or maybe I am just plain crazy, but my heart craves the feeling of compassion I get when reaching out during my acting exercise. *"You wouldn't do this to me, would you? We would be partners, and even if our needs were different, we would talk this over as a team. Neither of us would ever make life-altering decisions without the other."*

Oh God, what am I doing? Why is my brain talking to someone who isn't here, especially when I am having a conversation with someone who is?

Jason brushes the hair from my face, and those heart-stealing eyes lock on me in a way that has me feeling adored, despite the fact I also want to grab a spoon and scoop them out. The side of Jason I love to the end of the universe and back is dead in front of me. It's also pissing me off for loving him the way I do.

"Katherine, my only concern is for us. It may make the most sense to stay in a guest star capacity, since it will give me an excuse to come home more often. However, since I'll be dealing with a movie franchise, it would be wise to nab another role as fast as possible, so I don't get locked into yet another character. We need to keep spreading our wings. Then, in about five or six years, we can start the family we've always talked about."

"Five or six years? We agreed on three, which are about to expire. Jason, you do know no woman has forever, right? Things start getting risky when the mid-thirties are in sight."

"It'll be fine. Women have babies well into their forties nowadays. Besides, there are other ways."

I bolt up and stare down at him. I also have to swallow the contents of my stomach. On second thought, let them come up! Let them spray all over him! This is unfair. "My desires have value too. I made a huge mistake once by choosing a career over a person. I owe it to her to be successful, but I also need to see my other dreams realized." Desperation begins to ring in my voice. The doctor has told me time and again the occasional missed period means nothing, especially with my wonky schedule. Still, I can't escape the fears that rattle my gut. Now they nearly choke me, causing my words to sound cracked. "You and I are supposed to be partners. We had an agreement. For all I know it may already be too late."

Jason swallows hard. I haven't a doubt something I said hit a chord. "Heyyy," he says with a tone aimed at soothing me. He sits to meet me eye-to-eye. Although my heart may soften, the pain it harbors refuses to fade. "There was beauty in what you did. Remember those people sent you a letter saying you had given them a miracle? We need you to get your head in a better space, and see the fortune you have."

For as hard as he is trying, he's not helping matters. "So my fortune makes it okay to trash my feelings?"

"No. Not at all. But, honey, I am not ready for a family. Someday we will have one, but not now."

Now how the hell am I supposed to tell him I am pregnant? *"I could tell you, couldn't I? You would be happy."*

Why do I keep slipping like that? How different are my needs that I have to make up someone to satisfy me?

Jason curls me into his chest. His heart races as if he has dodged a bullet. Maybe he already suspects and thinks denial made it all go away before, so it can do it again. "Get some sleep, honey," he says. "All will be better in the morning."

Little does he know, that is when I have an appointment to officially confirm this pregnancy. He does have a point though. This may be a jazzed up mess, but I won't lose sight of what is important. Yesterday I said that given the choice I would take this baby over Jason, and nothing will make me think differently.

One Way Or Another

Brandon

God, how did I get into this situation? A few days ago I was an average guy with a messed up past. Now I'm a creepy stalker who follows a celebrity on social media. Learning I killed someone in a past life seemed to be the icing on the cake, but no. Now that I find myself sitting alone in my darkened bedroom and staring at a Ouija board I fear how much deeper into insanity I can go.

Today things got even weirder. Emotional jabs kept telling me something was wrong with someone I love. I'm not sure I can fully buy into what Jennifer said, but maybe if I can see it for myself, I can accept it—hence my trip to the *botanicals* shop. I have got to take matters into my own hands.

This Ouija board is straight out-of-the-box. Doesn't it need some type of spell cast on it before use? They must do that at the factory.

Oh, that's crazy! Everything about this is crazy!

That damn cheese is starting to smell; yet both pieces look perfect. I should be more patient. It was only yesterday Jennifer told me to hold off for guidance.

Has it really only been a day? That happened Wednesday, right? Yeah, okay, I went to work today and then bought all this mystical crap. Well, it is practically dawn, so it is now Friday.

God, that means it has been ten, insomnia-filled nights since this madness started. No wonder why I am edgy.

With my hands on the planchette, I concentrate on Saleena's blonde hair, her sparkling blue eyes, and her voice that was as sweet as candy—all while trying to forget the horror of her blood splattering across me. Life was so much easier when I was only weirded out over hearing Katherine's voice. Who would have thought I would long for that madness again?

If Saleena was reincarnated into Katherine, can I still contact her? Can her soul be in two places at the same time? If so, can I contact my former self?

I toss myself back and smack my head against the side of the bed. Death is way too complicated.

Maybe I should try a different way. Tarot cards don't require a spirit, do they?

Oh, whom am I kidding? All I did was look at the book, and I got confused.

Dude, you need to get a grip. Do something or bag it.

I stand and spray the cards onto the floor, creating a mosaic of confusion. I'm pretty sure I've broken some sacred law and have doomed myself by being disrespectful to these pieces of paper. Still, I snag a coin from my pocket, close my eyes, and flick it in the air. When it *thunks*, I slip an eye open. The quarter landed on an angel pouring liquid between two chalices—Temperance.

That figures. I don't need a book to know I bought all this stuff only for it to tell me the same thing Jennifer did. This all needs to work itself out.

Temperance is the last image I see before tossing and turning myself to sleep. Three hours later, my alarm clock sends noise ripping through my head, jolting me awake. I was out hard. If I dreamed, I don't remember a second of it.

When my feet hit the floor, they land on something cool and pliable—Tarot cards. God, this room looks like a psychic threw up in it.

"Coffee," I mumble while scrubbing my hand through my hair and stammering into the living room. The open curtains allow the sun to bathe the room in a golden glow that brings a sense of peace. Jennifer said my next action is to either follow my head or my heart. Following my heart would mean tracking down Katherine. Following my head means forgetting the whole thing. The question is simple: Am I in, or am I out? I don't need to decide now. All I need is to enjoy looking at the flowers and trees outside and accept that, one way or another, everything will balance out.

Ooh, Blondie! Music is another thing I need. Music and coffee. Coffee sounds brilliant. "One Way Or Another" rocks its way into my brain, and I start bopping my way into the kitchen. I'll do the right thing in due time—which will probably be growing tired of the situation and letting it die. It's all a matter of—

Shock hits my veins, turning my blood into a Slurpee that causes my fear to build as it crawls through me. I must be having visions again because what sits on the kitchen counter can't be real. The cheese from Jennifer draws me toward it like a siren of the sea. "Dear God," I utter. The piece with the x etched into it looks fresh as a daisy; the other is buried under a mountain of mold—thick, furry, unmistakable mold.

If this is telling me to follow my heart, why am I suddenly inclined to run away, change my identity, and forget Brandon Wayne existed? My passport is current. I have a modest savings account. Maybe it is time I saw Zimbabwe, Togo, or some other place no one would think to look for me.

Slowly, I approach the sign I hoped so hard for. This can't be real. Last night this cheese looked as normal as can be, and then boom, penicillin city. I stare at it and utter in disbelief, "Follow my heart ..."

Music fills my mind as the gentle tones of a wire brush skating across a drum seeps into the air. A flute tinkles in, causing my lungs to steal all the air they can. Dear God, help me because I have no clue what is happening.

My fear builds at the sound of a new voice. Frank Sinatra starts singing "Anything Goes", and prickles crawl up my skin. Suddenly, reality kicks me in the head, and I dash for my cell phone that nearly freaked me into a coffin. "Hello!"

"Rise and shine, sleepyhead!" Dale says. "How's the weather in sunny California?"

I look out the window even though I know perfectly well what it is like. "Su—Su—Sunny."

"Hey, man, you okay? I didn't wake you, did I?"

"No, believe me, I am *wide*-awake." I am awake, right? My name is Brandon Wayne. I live in Los Angeles, and I am pretty sure I am awake. I also need to keep functioning like a normal person for fear if I don't, men in lab coats will show up at my door, give me a nice, white jacket, and haul me off to a farm. "Why do you sound so chipper?"

At least I still seem to be able to process things, because based solely on his chuckle, I know where this is going. Dale has two laughs—a normal one and a maniacal one that surfaces when he has something he can't wait to share. "I had quite the night!"

I can only begin to imagine. In fact, I'd rather not. Merely knowing Dale often brings images of drunken debauchery to mind.

"Man, I have to tell you about what is going on around here! Life has been in-sane!"

My eyes lock onto the cheese. That volume of mold doesn't make a lick of sense. How did it bloom to life on one piece, yet there isn't a speck on the other?

"I can't believe this latest script. This show may be kind of lame, but this script is ridiculous."

My eyes widen and lock; yet I somehow have the foresight to drop the phone enough to conceal my gasp. Katherine is back.

Okay, Jennifer said Katherine is reaching out, and I have nothing to fear. She even said I could find comfort when this happens. Lastly, a mountain of mold is telling me to follow my heart. The next logical step is to give acceptance a shot and listen. Maybe then I can find enough information to prove Jennifer right or enough to show how certifiable I have become and it is now time for medical help.

As I raise the phone, I dare not look to my hand for fear the sight of it trembling will cause me to chicken out. I will show strength. I will listen and dare the voice to show me what is real. Whatever it is, I can and will face it.

My quaking hand causes the phone to rattle against my ear.

With a calming breath, I insist on allowing myself to cave to whatever I find—real or imagined.

My head gets fuzzy, causing fear to build.

I will not be afraid. I will move forward.

Haze coats my mind, and an image of Katherine, fully dolled up and walking through a room, seeps in. How is it I can see her now when before I saw through her eyes?

She tosses the script onto a counter in front of a mirror surrounded with bright lights. A makeup table? Of course. I'm seeing a mirror image. Everything has an explanation.

"If I were not such a professional, I wouldn't bother learning my lines. My gut tells me that when the producers get wind of this, they're going to redline so much of the script I'll have to learn a new one."

God, Katherine, I see it now. Though your body has changed, Saleena is reflected in how you carry yourself. I remember so much about who you were—your laugh, your walk, your scent that reminded me of wild flowers. How did I ever forget?

The comfort of discovering a long-lost treasure builds. When it comes to this woman, there is nothing to fear. I only need to accept there is more to life than what we normally see.

Steps approach. Reflected in the mirror I catch a glimpse of another woman. This one has long, dark hair and deep brown eyes. She looks hauntingly familiar. Katherine's head turns and …

"Brandon?"

And I lose contact.

Who was that? How was it she looked familiar, yet I'm certain I don't know her?

"Brandon!" Dale yells. "Did I lose you? Damn cell phone."

Despite my sense of calm, I need to grab air in order to force out words. I can't help but feel rattled. "No," huffs out. "I'm here. Must be a bad connection."

"Anyway … "

Why is it I can sense her randomly, yet I only get a visual when I'm on the phone with Dale?

"… which means they are keeping me here for another week," Dale says.

Is she with him? When it comes to women the man does seem to get around. "Hey, are you alone or are you holding court with some girl?"

"I'm painfully alone in my room."

Then how …

Dale and Katherine are both in Toronto. I need to get to my laptop and pull up a map.

Does it seem at all reasonable that Dale's vicinity to her is letting me get these visions through the cell towers? No, but hell, nothing about any of this is reasonable, including how my gut tells me it is time to accept this insanity as reality. "Hey, where exactly in Toronto are you?"

"Downtown at the Sheraton. Why?"

That's not far from where Katherine films. "How about I fly out first thing tomorrow and hang with you Saturday night and all day Sunday? You can dump me at the airport on Monday morning." But I'll fly back on Tuesday, after some private exploring. Meanwhile, I'll uncover anything the media has posted about where Katherine hangs out.

"What? Brandon Wayne wants to get out of his little world and spread his wings? Don't toy with me, man!"

"What do you say?"

"Fathers of Toronto, lock up your daughters!"

Dear God, help me. Hanging out with Dale may be nuttier than trying to track a voice in my head.

"This is going to be one crazy weekend!"

Dale may be right, but if this is crazy, so be it. Actually, my decision is perfectly logical. I can choose to believe I am crazy because I am hearing voices, or I can see myself as one of the sanest people on the planet because I accept there is more to the world than can be seen. Maybe those who refuse to look beyond here and now are the crazy ones. If Jennifer is right, this isn't a matter of listening to my heart; it's a matter of listening to my soul.

I say goodbye to Dale, and then pop on to Facebook to

read Katherine's latest post, *"I've been waiting to tell all of you something big, but have to keep it a secret a little longer. Stay tuned!"*

Big things are definitely happening because I am daring to embrace madness. Katherine has no idea how bizarre her life is about to get. Despite my resolve, my hands jitter while I comment on her post, *"Better things are coming than we can ever imagine. I am certain of it!"*

Katherine
Is it weird that I like the décor of my gynecologist's office? That is weird, right? The bathroom has the wildest, nineteen sixties, bronze wallpaper with calorie charts and cartoons of people of varying weights. It's so dated and dorky it is awesome.

It is freaky how being in that room makes me feel like I am a kid again. I was born in the eighties, so the paper was outdated by the time I was old enough to remember anything similar. I must only feel that way because of the cartoons.

My feet swing back and forth over the edge of the exam table, and I take in the dated charm of blue and silver wallpaper that was probably made when the stuff in the bathroom was. Jason would hate it. Why do some people think respecting the past is a crime?

God, it's so nice not to feel stressed. The new determination I found when I came to terms with my desires last night has me feeling the best I have in days. I will make this situation work, with or without Jason. The producers can find a way to shoot around my pregnancy. If they write me out of the show, I'll find another one.

The door creaks open, and Doctor Florin sticks his head in. He's probably in his forties, but his round face and glowing skin always make me think of a little boy. The way his eyes hide behind large glasses and comically flick back and forth drives the thought home. "Is it safe? The paparazzi didn't follow you, did they? I missed a spot while shaving, and I'm afraid it will make the tabloids." I can't help but chuckle. "So, how is my favorite starlet?"

"Fantastic. How is my favorite doctor? Gone on any great hiking adventures lately?"

"Every weekend without fail." His voice trails off as he flips through my chart. For as jovial as he is, the way he leans against the counter with his weight oddly shifted has me nervous. "The nurse says you suspect you are pregnant. Have you taken a test?"

"Yep. Two of them."

"And you got clear results?" His eyes seem to ask the question twice as strongly as his words do.

My jitters come back. Something is definitely wrong. Still, I won't let my positive attitude falter. "Double, bright pink lines. I've been queasy enough to know they are right."

The trepidation he uses while setting down my chart causes my stomach to tighten. It's not the same physical sick of the last few days. This tightness extends up into my heart. "Katherine…" Oh no. His voice is so tender. This can't be good. "The tests we use are pretty sensitive. Unfortunately, yours showed as negative."

The tightness releases and drops my heart onto the floor. His test has to be wrong. My body could not have failed me again. My voice drips with the desperation that tears at me. "Doc, I've been feeling the hormones in my blood for days. How can the test not show them?"

Judging by his pressed lips, more tact is coming. "I'm sorry. I don't know what to tell you other than the situation you saw has changed." I can see he is searching for a different answer—something truthful to leave me with hope. But no matter what he says, it is clear that karma is having its laugh. I am about to miscarry again.

"Doc, I know you have said not to worry about the occasional missed period, but this is the second time this has happened recently. Something is wrong somewhere. I just know it." Actually, I don't know it; I fear it because then I threw away far more than I ever bargained for.

Doctor Florin pulls up a seat, and I brace myself for our heart-to-heart. How many times have I prayed we would never have another one of these? "Last we talked about this, you only missed about one period a year. Has that changed? Missed periods are often the result of stress and traveling. You are no stranger to either of those."

"It happens about every ten months or so but … Can't you run a test or something?" I swear I am being punished, and I need something to show if karma is messing with me at will or if it has done a permanent whammy on my system.

Doctor Florin forces a crooked smile. "Well, we have checked you for PCOS and Aherman's Syndrome. Everything is in order, but it can't hurt to run those tests again, can it? I'll have the nurse make out a slip for a blood draw."

Who am I kidding? I know exactly what those tests are going to say.

The test he took today was flawed. It has to be.

I wish the Doc a good day and head home. Tomorrow morning the life inside me will show he is perfectly fine, and I will be right back in this office, holding a test stick. That has to happen because if this pregnancy fails, I have a bigger reality to face.

My jaw clenches. Memories from months before play in my brain as what must be the talons of a demon stealing my joy poke at me from inside and rip. My nails dig into the arm of the sofa, and I double over.

This pain is nothing. What causes my suffering is the emotional havoc rattling in my brain. Cramps can happen in early pregnancy. This pain will stop, and tomorrow I will see that second pink line again, plain as day. Drinking some tea will help me feel better. However, so would knowing I could turn to Jason. I wish I had a hand to hold right now.

When I stand, the talons dig again, and warmth trickles inside me. I squeeze out tears that burn like the flames of Hell.

My baby is dead, and there wasn't a damn thing I could do to save him.

This is my fate. I had my chance years ago, and I blew it. If Jason is right about me having done the right thing, why has it caused so much sadness? If I did wrong by my daughter and this is penance, why have two innocent souls suffered? Hell isn't a place where bad people go when they die. Hell resides within me.

A gusher flows inside. It sends me racing to the bathroom and forces me to accept I am about to face the color of sorrow. Another dream, another precious face, destroyed by my hands.

Although a Vicodin-induced fog spins in my brain, I am well aware the hand I envision holding isn't here. I wish I could drown out my inner voice that keeps smashing my face into reality. Facing what I am up against is difficult enough, but I'm not ready to face Jason and probably never will be. All I can handle is lying here on the bedroom floor, mourning for another life I never got the joy of knowing and hoping Jason will give me the understanding I need in my time of failure.

The front door opens, and I close my eyes to hide from reality. Their burn intensifies, but I'd rather suffer through the pain than face Jason. I'm not ready to accept I am losing yet another angel let alone the karma I fear has sealed my fate with infertility. How do I tell Jason I may never be able to give him the family we dream of? I feel as if I have spent years misleading him and will now rot in my deceit.

Suddenly, his footsteps race toward me. When he reaches the threshold, he stops dead with his widened eyes on the bottle of pills in my hand. The last time I saw him my biggest concern was how our future would unfold. Now my head pounds, my eyes burn, I'm buzzing from painkillers, and I have the worst cramps of my life. I don't want to face any of this, yet I've no choice but to tell him my fears. I hope he will be my partner in misery and not the man who bolts because I may not be able to give him what he wants.

He kneels and caresses my hair away from my face. Panic causes his voice to race. "Honey, what's wrong?"

I'm at a loss where to start, so I let the truth come out best as my hazy mind manages. "After what happened last time, I was scared to learn the truth. Then we had that talk last night and—"

Pain shoots across my gut and up my back, causing me to grip my midsection with a whimper. Jason catches sight of the bottle of pills and rips them from my hand. "I'm calling an ambulance. How many of these have you had?" He reaches to his back pocket for his cell phone, and I place my hand out to stop him.

"Only one." I don't feel I can fill my lungs. Lord help us, because I have no idea how to say any of this. "I'm not a mess because of the pills. I'm having another miscarriage."

Jason's eyes drop, and although mine divert as well I can tell he swallows emotion. I can barely bring myself to peer up and catch sight of him dropping back on his heels. His eyes squeeze shut, and I can't help but feel they are mirroring the tightness in his heart. The pain in my gut seems insignificant compared to the guilt that plagues me for not telling him about the pregnancy last night, yet it still tears at me.

"God, Jason, isn't it bad enough a baby is dying inside me? Why does this have to hurt so much?" My tears turn to sobs, making me feel all the more hopeless. After this, how could I possibly ever smile again? "I don't understand. I'm not even thirty."

Reality is punctuated by another cramp, and my teeth bear down and grit. Poor Jason can only sit there while looking like he wishes he could help. "I've blown it. This is karma saying I will never get another chance." Jason is so focused on me he doesn't seem to notice the tears falling from his eyes. He places a tender kiss of mourning on my belly before lying next to me. How can he be so sweet when I've let him down in so many ways? "I need to see a specialist. I have to know what is going on."

"Honey," he says through stammered breath, "let's step back a little and get through this."

He's probably right, but my fears have the best of me. "I need answers. What if there is a problem and waiting to find out means I've waited too long?"

The tenderness in his eyes almost makes me feel as if everything will be all right, but I need more than what he can give. "Let's get you into bed," he says. "You'll feel better once the pain stops." I sit and reach for the phone. "What are you doing?"

"Finding a specialist."

"Katherine, stop. You are taking this too hard." Swiftly he grabs my hand. His eyes are wide and focused as if facing fear.

"No, I am calling."

I start to pull away, and his grip tightens. For a moment our eyes are locked. Suddenly Jason diverts his to the carpet. "There's something I need to tell you." His gaze returns to mine, and the feeling this is something I definitely don't want to hear nearly strangles me. "This is not going to go over well," he whispers, "but I can't let you think this is your fault." His chest swells as he faces me. He closes his eyes on his unsteady exhale. "While I can't promise nothing is wrong with you, I am probably the reason for the miscarriage."

My brain sobers in a flash.

"I've been afraid to tell you this but … When my brother was killed in that holdup, his wife was pregnant. She lost the baby a few weeks later."

Those poor people. Why did they have to suffer so much? Jason rarely speaks of the event that gutted his family. At the mention of Ray everyone goes into a tailspin for weeks.

Jason's eyes turn dull. "Seven months after Ray died, Lydia saw that just because she had to accept the lost of her husband and unborn son there was no reason the entire dream needed to die. Since Ray and I share the same genetic makeup, she asked me to be a sperm donor.

"I wasn't even thrown by it. We were all so distraught over what we had lost that letting Ray's family grow, even in an unorthodox manner, seemed right. It wasn't long until I got devastating news. Not only is my sperm count nearly non-existent, the little I have are weak." The courage Jason found to tell his story caves to his sorrow, and his voice begins to crack. "We made three attempts at insemination before giving up. Lydia persuaded the doctor to try IVF. Only one out of twelve eggs fertilized. We were thrilled when it implanted but …" With a prolonged inhale, he grabs for more bravery. "Her story matches yours. The miscarriages are my fault."

My senses, my heart, my mind—they all lock. I feel lost—so incredibly gone. A moment ago I was wallowing in sorrow and now … shock.

Memories flood my mind. I cried for nights after my last miscarriage while fearing I was the cause. All that stuff with Lydia happened before Jason and I met. How has he failed to mention his infertility each and every time we talked of having a family? What about the times we said we would adopt *after* we had one of our own? "You bastard!" I yank my hands away and step back. "Here I thought I was the one letting you down. How could you hold that back? You saw me nearly destroyed during my last miscarriage. What the hell kind of person are you, and what gives you the right to withhold such information from the woman you claim you are going to have a family with?"

I feel for Jason. I can't discount how he lost a brother and a nephew, and then how he made a decision to support his sister-in-law in such a monumental way only for their hearts to be shattered. Still, how could he betray me?

Everything from my throat to my gut tightens, including my hands that are now clenched. "What else have you been hiding? No wonder why you acted so strangely the last time this happened. That comment about me having an affair was not made out of panic but out of thinking I did, because how else could I be pregnant. What the hell kind of relationship do we have?"

"Katherine, I am so sorry. Please understand how hard it is for me to talk about Ray. I've had to live with the feeling I failed him on his last wish."

I open my mouth to let him have it, but the power of his words overcome me.

Jason looks to God. His trembling chin and eyes that seek understanding make me feel foolish for my anger. How his eyes request forgiveness, coupled with the gentleness of his actions when he reaches for my hands, breaks my heart all the more. "Katherine," he says with the tenderness of a whisper, "think about how you felt a moment ago. Now try to see what you feared is real for me. You are right. I should have been strong enough to tell you."

A wave of misery hits, not only from the miscarriage, but also from Jason's emotional baggage. I still want to tell him what an insensitive jerk he is for leading me on, but I also know facing that your body is denying you the privilege of happiness hurts like hell.

The talons in my gut dig deeper, causing me to whimper and squeeze my left hand, seeking the support of a person who isn't there. I need someone to tell me all is going to be fine, but it also needs to come from someone I can trust. Right now I trust a person I am fabricating more than I trust Jason Day. Proof of that is how I have come to realize this entire time I have envisioned someone holding my hand and supporting me through this. Now I get why I have felt so confused when talking to someone who doesn't exist. My head was telling me to face what I must have sensed all along—Jason will never be able to give me the support I need.

I have to get out of here for a few days and clear my head. Most of all, I need to find myself. I may have to drop this for now and focus on my health, but I've got big decisions to make about my future.

... And I Will Be With You

Katherine

The sound of Glen Miller's orchestra wafts out of Bailey's trailer, and the soothing tune helps me gain a moment of peace. The comfort is short lived as the laughter that bursts from inside her trailer causes me to turn and walk away. Facing happy people when I am sad seems to make everything five times as rough. I grab a seat on the concrete and rub my gut. The bulk of the pain is gone, but the memories haunt. Having a person die inside me has shredded part of my soul.

My cell phone buzzes with a text from Jason. *"How are you? Can I do anything? I am so sorry. I love you."*

Again the tears well. I love him too, but that doesn't change how I am questioning our relationship. First he neglected to tell me he may leave the show, and now I have learned the truth about his fertility. How dare he trap my heart in a web of lies?

I can't think about this anymore. If I don't get my mind on something else, I will never make it through the day.

I check for texts and emails—anything to grab my attention. I'm so desperate to find an encouraging thought somewhere that I tread into dangerous territory—reading the comments on my latest Facebook post. Sometimes I find ego boosts while other times I find people who are flat-out mean for no apparent reason. Doing this is a fool's game. Depression must make me masochistic.

Much to my surprise, among the speculating comments regarding my earlier post about good news being on the way and fawning observations about my body, a sweet message stands out, *"Better things are coming than we can ever imagine. I am certain of it!"*

The message hits my soul like a bonfire of hope sent by a

greater power. Brandon Wayne, your optimism is probably what will get me through this day. You are right. I need to stay positive. What good thing haven't I taken a moment to enjoy?

Well, I do have fans. For whatever crazy reason they love this show, so I'll pass my optimism on to them. *"About to wrap another episode. You're gonna love what happens! Time to celebrate by doing something special for myself. Any suggestions?"*

A bit of weight pops off of my shoulders when I post the message. Thank you, Brandon, for helping me find the sun.

Brandon
Optimism.

Today I am, and will stay, filled with optimism.

Though the woman at the airline terminal seems to be looking everywhere but at the people in front of her, I smile when I hand her my boarding pass. The machine beeps, and instead of moving forward as others have, I stay and wish her a nice day. It takes a moment, but eventually my stillness grabs her attention, and she chuckles. "You have a great day, too!"

Optimism—sometimes I think we can change the world with it.

There is a spring in my step as I enter the gate. I'm not crazy. Staying home and wallowing would be crazy. Acting when something needs my attention is sane as can be.

Stepping onto the plane brings about a sigh of peace. One needs to embrace chaos in order to truly live. Let life begin.

Listening to The Mr. T. Experience's "… And I Will Be With You" through my iPod may help optimism stay with me, but it doesn't keep my nerves at bay. What if I stumble across Katherine at a bad time? What if my leads turn up empty? If I do find her, what can I possibly say?

Still, I have to remember that I am embracing a new world—taking a road others dare not travel. Every moment of this experience—the food I was too nervous to eat, the movie I couldn't focus on, even the sight of houses below as we now descend—are treasures to be embraced.

My eyes close off the world, and I smile with the comfort that only being true to you can bring. I must be close to her, because Katherine's sweet voice floats into my mind almost instantly. I can't help but gasp due to the natural anxiety that accompanies suddenly hearing her. Regardless, Jennifer is right—listening to Katherine is soothing. *"I need a vacation so desperately. I wish you were real so we could run away together."*

"I am real, Katherine, and I'm on my way. I fear something is wrong with you. My body has been buzzing with it."

Why is the image of houses below returning to my mind? Could one be hers? I need to remember she may live under the flight path. One clue could change my entire future.

Pressure builds in my head, starting at the base of my neck and growing to the crown. I become uneasy as I realize this is not the usual discomfort I feel while flying. It sounds like my blood is rushing through my ears.

The pressure releases with a little *pop* and rebuilds. My body stiffens in response. I seem to be hearing the inner workings of my heart in my head. Is it fear? Anxiety?

With a couple of hard swallows, the pressure equalizes and I let out a hearty breath of relief. Nothing similar has ever happened before.

I glance around and become unsettled by how the other passengers appear to have felt nothing unusual. With the exception of the affect that had on my nerves, I feel normal again. This airport must require a funny descent or something.

When I step outside of the gate I am flooded by a new sensation—tingles. Why am I experiencing all of these physical changes? Can they mean I am near her? If I can see her image through a phone call, this proximity should allow it too. Shoot, if I really try, maybe now she can hear me.

Is that possible? That would solve everything. I need to

give it a shot before I hook up with Dale and all hell breaks loose.

The only place I can grab a moment of privacy is inside a men's room stall. My ears fill with the sounds of running water, air dryers, and flushing toilets. Even when I plug my ears, I'm distracted when the guy in the next stall coughs.

Finally, I'm able to tune everything out and focus. *"Katherine, can you hear me? It's Brandon, the one you have been talking to."*

Not a single, female voice enters my head—not even from outside. My tension softens at the memories of the comfort she can bring. What a beautiful person she must be to have this influence.

My mind suddenly snaps to attention, feeling as if someone has cleared his throat and is preparing me to hear something isn't right somewhere.

"Katherine?"

Minutes pass without a word from her.

She may be working now or doing one of the many things that occupy a person's mind. Still, I can't shake the weird feeling something is off.

Optimism, I remind myself.

I'll try again in an hour. Somehow this will all work out.

I pop open Facebook while waiting for Dale. How it sucks people into data mining is brilliant. Go ahead and take the quiz about what type of fashionista you are because now someone knows what ads to litter your news feed with. Also, thanks to cross-domain tracking, those cookies you got will follow you to other sites. There will be no escape until you clean your cache, which most people rarely do. Chances are that by then you will have bought the product. Cha-ching!

Ironically, ruthless data mining is one of the reasons why I hate Facebook. Between that and how I can't market gumdrops, I'm beginning to see how much I suck at my job. Schizophrenia has nothing to do with my incompetence. I'm sane as can be.

Katherine hasn't updated her status since yesterday. Again I try to push away the interference the world brings and reach out to her. Instead of finding focus, the weird feeling that something is off crawls up the back of my neck. I pull my jacket around me even though I don't feel cold.

My phone chimes with a text from Dale. *"Just off freeway. There in 5."*

Something about receiving that text causes my phone to slam me with messages. Random texts pop up, along with a Twitter notification. Katherine tweeted not long after my flight from Los Angeles left.

"A whole two days off? Heading back home to see my family! Excited!"

No! She can't be headed to Seattle! Was the sense I got that something was wrong with her related to going home? When she said she was going to do something special I thought she meant getting a massage. I could not have possibly guessed from her last post that—

I yell to God, out loud, for everyone to hear, "You have got to be kidding! Seriously? A little warning would have been nice!"

That image of houses I saw when we were getting ready to land wasn't a flashback; it was her view! We just missed each other. Again Amber's words about us being composed of energy and how we leave an imprint for others to appreciate comes to mind. This weird sensation I've gotten since landing is Katherine's residual energy telling me she was here and left. Oh, this is crap! Pure, unadulterated, unfair crap! Why is the universe jacking with me so much?

Enough is enough! I'm having Dale take us to the nearest bar so I can soak my head in a gallon of whisky.

Where I Am Today

Brandon

For God's sake, it is Saturday night.

Dale takes yet another work-related call, and I nearly reach across the table and rip the phone out of his hand. "Is this how you treat your dates? No wonder why you don't have a girl friend."

He actually takes a second to cover the mouthpiece and whisper, "Well, it is rather dark in here. Kind of romantic, don't you think?" He winks and air kisses me.

"Gah!" He may laugh, but I damn near squirm out of my seat.

As much as it sucks that I can't pursue the real reason why I'm here, my poor timing was probably the universe's way of saving me from getting arrested for stalking. For better or for worse, flying across the country and trying to live life Dale's way will definitely put my mind in a different space.

See, optimism is the way to go. Dale and I are friends for a reason. In our own way, we are peas in a pod—misfits, if you will.

God only knows what debauchery I'm in for. I've managed to avoid nights like this with him. The closest I've come to participating in one of his escapades was being designated driver for his cousin's bachelor party. That was months ago, and I think those guys may still be hung over.

"What are you in the mood for tonight?" Dale asks.

"Whatever. You're in charge."

His chin juts back. Judging by his expression, he's wondering what's up. Thankfully, when times get tough, guys don't talk. We pat each other on the back and push onward. I'm here to get shoved. Maybe there is some credence in what

Jennifer says, but it is also entirely possible my brain fakes visions while I'm on the phone with Dale because he is the one who can shove me into changing. It's time I step back and see what could be the big picture, regardless of how I feel about what it may be.

Dale clasps his hands together. "Okay, after we finish here, we'll head down the block. There's a little restaurant with some of the cutest waitresses." As he continues on about our options, the flicker of the TV across the room steals my thoughts.

Seeing Katherine on there would be salt in my wounds. When I booked this trip, I knew there was no guarantee of running into her. But to have forced myself to make peace with my inner demons, and then come all this way, only to immediately learn my hopes won't be fulfilled, drags my heart through the mud. Regardless of how I think what I am hearing is real, regardless of being convinced I can feel her energy, and certainly despite psychic guidance, I can't live this way any longer. I have to move forward.

My words race out to interrupt Dale. "If you're only out to hook up, why not head straight to the place where the odds are most in our favor?"

Dale's eyes widen and lock long enough to process what is going on. His tone is steadfast, yet something about the glow of happiness that paints its way across him seems dim. "That's my man! I didn't know you had it in ya!"

I don't. I don't even know how I'm going to fake being like Dale.

Ache creeps into my jaw. I stretch my neck and drop open my mouth to release some of the tightness that has built. Thinking about what could happen tonight, compared to what I really want, has me grinding my teeth. Yet with a forced grin, I tap my beer against Dale's and polish it off, then flag down the waitress for another round.

"Hey, I know it's just beer, but you gotta pace yourself."

No, I'd rather be numb. "Pick a place so we can go load up."

Dale's eyes narrow as if he is trying to extract my story without asking. "I've never seen you *load up*. You know, for all the time we've spent in bars, you've never been close to wasted. That's another thing I didn't know you had in you. In fact, I'm rather skeptical now."

"Well, there's a first for everything." He's right. I often say I am going to tie one on, only to stop after my second or third beer. It doesn't matter if I'm in a bar, at a party, or in my home. Something inside me says enough. I'm optimistic that tonight will be different.

"Where are we headed?" I ask. "Pick the place where you've had the best luck, and that's where we'll go." Translation: Let's get this hell over with.

My second beer arrives. I get the very last drop out of the first before handing the waitress the bottle.

"Let's head over to the Gold Club."

I toast, "To the Gold Club," and take a swig while his suggestion sinks in. "Hold on. Is that a strip joint?"

"Yep. A strip joint with a buffet, so we can go straight there."

"Food? You pick up girls in a strip joint? I thought the only girls you could pick up there were hookers, yet I know you refuse to pay for it."

Dale crosses his arms, and I get a glance I'm not sure how to read. Does he want to lay into me, or is this whole strip club thing a test to see where my head is? "I thought you were only out for a good time. And yes, food. The place is aimed at businessmen. You'd be surprised by the number of deals that go down there."

My eyebrow cocks.

"*Legitimate* deals. What I shell out at those places I get back triple in commission."

No wonder why salesmen come off as sleazy. "I may be open to a lot of things, but if I'm going to hook up with someone, I hope she has some kind of interest in me other than my pocketbook. Besides, I don't get why guys are willing to get hard-ons while their *business partners* watch. How often do you wait for your client while he is *in the bathroom*?"

"Okay, Wayne. Cut the crap. What's going on?"

"I'm here for a good time, remember?"

He leans in, and I get a finger pointed at me. Busted. "Yeah, *you* may be here, but where is the real Brandon Wayne? I've never seen him even remotely interested in picking up someone. Besides, you, whoever you may be, have both a tone and body language that is more geared towards kicking someone's ass than it is partying."

Now that he's mentioned it, I notice I am not tapping my foot; I'm stomping it. We haven't left the hotel, and I'm already acting like public enemy number one. Subconsciously, I've given myself an attitude that is destined to doom me before I start.

Enough crap. Enough making excuses for what is going on. Not only do I need to surrender to who I am, I want to. Acting this way has me disappointed in myself. "I hate this. I hate acting the macho man so much it is turning me into an absolute jerk. None of this is why I came here."

Dale shakes his head and looks around, totally clueless. "Why did you come here?"

"Because every day I wake up alone and either go to work or hang out with you and Shane. I need something different, but the different I want isn't this." If I had a towel in my hand, I'd toss it down in surrender. Life isn't turning out the way I want, and that fact may be making me so delusional I have created something as hard to let go of as Amber is. Hearing voices, feeling sensations, buying into what a psychic says—regardless of how accurate it seems—and forcing optimism so I can accept all of this as real and stay out of the nut house, is fucking terrifying!

Facing the different dimensions of my reality brings up a lot of emotions guys aren't supposed to express—at least not to each other. That notion is crap! "I can't stop thinking about how my life would be if Amber hadn't died. We had the date we were going to get married. We knew exactly when we would start having kids. Together we had goals, and alone I've got diddly squat. I should be singing my kid to sleep. Instead, I'm in a bar with a guy who lives a completely different lifestyle than the one I want."

I wish I could let loose. I also can't help thinking letting loose has problems of its own. It goes back to what I discovered with the past life regression. I killed someone because I was drunk and driving, and then shot myself in the head because I hurt her. I get it now. The reason I don't get wasted is because my head is still jacked up from the last time.

I'm also being an ass, and Dale doesn't deserve it. When it comes down to it, he's a good guy; else I never would have let him into my life. "I'm sorry, man. I just want life to work out. I need to get past the image of what could've been and create a new reality. The thing is I don't want some ordinary girl; I want someone who is ideal. Is that so wrong?"

Dale's eyes stay low as he subtly shakes his head. He probably wishes he could ship me off on the next plane. I would not blame him if he did. However, of all the things he could say, he softly confesses the last thing I would expect. "No, it's not wrong at all." Dale swallows hard, and then looks as if he is covering how much he shares my sentiment by taking a swig from his beer. Did I hit a chord?

He sets down his bottle with caution. Brief eye contact that sends his gaze back to the table and a hint of a shrug tell me to carry on with releasing whatever emotions are spiraling in me. I'm taking him up on it too, because I'm starting to realize one of the reasons I came here is one I never saw coming— and it has little to do with me. Dale and I may not be so different after all.

"I want what I was supposed to have. I want a woman to face each day with me as a team. I don't want to help her up the stairs after she's had a baby; I want to wait on her hand and foot because she has already done so much. When the baby cries, I want to drag myself up with her and change the kid's diaper. While she's feeding him, I'll make cocoa to help us get back to sleep. When morning comes, I'll be in charge of the coffee and toast while she makes the eggs." My shattered dreams nearly tie a knot in my throat, intensifying the pain in my words. "It was all within reach, and someone took it away."

I wish I could find it in me to shut up before I turn into a sobbing mess, but I need to vent. As much as the truth shreds my soul, I can't shortchange myself any longer. "When I interviewed for my job, my boss asked what life's big picture meant to me. Instead of keeping my answer professional, I conceded to telling her how, despite the pain of losing the person I thought was destined to make my life complete, I dare to dream for my future. Imagine how much hope it gave me when she said when I need flexibility, she will have my back. Everyone at Endeara is family, and family helps you build your dreams."

I can't keep the fire of the heartache burning in my eyes at bay any longer, and I let my tears hit the table without concern over what anyone thinks. The only thing that matters is I now understand myself more than ever. I'm Brandon Wayne, and I dare to be optimistic about hearing voices and things that should frighten me not because a psychic said it was okay, but for the sole reason of wanting something better. Unfortunately, because of how others may see my actions, there is only so much I can share. "The truth is, I took a job marketing a product I hate, and I don't care about partying and getting laid, because I dare to seek happiness. That's who I really am. Besides, what is my ideal woman going to think of a bunch of notches on my bedpost?"

Dale's eyes have been locked on his beer this entire time. I've always wondered why I put up with a womanizer who hyper-focuses on making money. Now the reasons behind our friendship are no longer evasive. The longing I sense in his heart is confirmed when his eyes rise to meet mine. "You're right. I get it." Those eyes go straight back to his beer, yet his emotions still face me. "I really get it. This lifestyle is for the birds. Hell, even they shouldn't go through this." He shakes his head and takes a swig. As the light hits his eyes, the gleam of moisture becomes apparent.

Dale has commented in passing that if he ever ran across his soul mate, he'd be thrilled. I always took it as him trying to make Shane and I feel less like outcasts. Shane is as tired of being alone as I am. He hides behind that counter because nearly every time he has reached out, he's gotten hurt. That doesn't only go with him for women; it goes for him with friends of both sexes. When Shane takes a risk and reaches out to you, you're special. Now I am learning Dale is in the same boat. I see it etched in his watery eyes that won't look at me.

And come to think of it, he was pretty reserved when we were at that bachelor party. "It's my cousin's big night, not mine," he said in response to my wondering why he was only providing the bills and not stuffing them. Now the incident makes me wonder if he is concealing loneliness behind an image, especially after that comment about business deals. Is that why he convinces himself he wants to be in those places? To make sales? How much value does the almighty dollar hold?

Dale taps a couple of screens on his phone before tossing the thing in front of me with a movie app open. "Pick something. Apparently you are my date tonight, so I'll treat you to dinner and a movie."

Here is where our big opportunity to talk like damaged souls crashes. Darla would get me to finish dumping, make me find humor in my situation, and then give me a pep talk about how it's all going to work out. Men just find a stopping point and move on. We don't really get to know each other, and it's a huge mistake.

Knowing Dale has a love for vintage everything, I pick going to an old, single-screen place. What's playing at The Kingsway doesn't matter, but escaping reality does.

True to his word about me being his date, Dale tosses down enough to cover our tab, and we head off.

Katherine

Although I've accidentally arrived at a time when no one else is home, memories greet me—beautiful memories of Mom and I dancing in the kitchen while Dad played his guitar. Memories of giggles from when I was little and chased the cats around the living room. I can see my sparkling, red shoes as if they are still on my feet. All of these wonderful things keep this Seattle home filled with love, light, and warmth no matter how bleak the world outside gets. I want that in my life again.

Whenever I need to rediscover myself, I come here while leaving the colored contacts and concealer behind. It is great when I go natural in LA and don't get recognized, but it is freaky how I can look like the girl who grew up here yet no one remembers I am her.

I was tired of blending in with half-dead grass, so the summer I turned sixteen, I used every penny of my birthday money on revamping myself. After dyeing my hair Intense Red Auburn, soaking it in hair gloss reminded me of fire under moonlight. I tried bleaching the freckles I always hated. Since I could not stand how my hazel eyes looked as if someone splattered chocolate in them, I covered them with bottle green-colored contacts. Getting attention from boys wasn't enough. I kept up my transformation until I reached the true mark of glamour—which was when the other girls started hating me. Since then I have considered normality to be a wild extreme.

My room hasn't changed since I moved to LA in pursuit of what some call unobtainable. It was here I resolved to change my appearance. Here I decided I wanted to be a rock star, found I couldn't carry a tune to save mankind, and figured I would give acting a shot. And it was here I chose to delay going to a university so I could hand a beautiful little girl over to someone else.

After spending my first two years at a junior college, I was all set to spend my last two years at a university. But once my daughter was born, the guilt of having given up a child in exchange for a career set in. I had to make good on that, so I blew off the remaining two years of school, headed for Los Angeles, and took terrible jobs in order to pay the bills—all just to get what I had sacrificed her for.

While giving a child to a deserving couple is beautiful, doing it for the wrong reasons made me ugly. By extension, despite the pain he was going through, how Jason hid such a secret makes him ugly, too. What he did was also underhanded and selfish.

Then again, why didn't I take my parents up on their offer to help raise their grandchild? Because I would feel guilty? Because of the pressure? Because they were so supportive of whatever I would decide it was easy for me to make excuses? I had the opportunity to handle things differently and didn't, much like Jason. How much can I fault him?

I lie on the bed and roll to face the pillow on my left. It draws my attention as if the gentle ear I need just has to be called to mind in order for it to rest next to me.

I've definitely connected with my character. She needs something no one else can give her, so she finds a way to give it to herself. Jason says the right things, but he doesn't give me the intimate connection that makes me know I am not alone. Wanting to ease a person's burden is one thing, but feeling it so deeply it is conveyed with your soul is another.

Memories of meeting Jason on the day of my audition swarm into my mind. Something about the way he looked at me made my face warm to the point where I needed to shy away. It also caused insecurity to suck me in so badly I was blowing the audition. Then Jason asked the director to give us a moment. His earnest look turned my heart to Jell-O. "I don't bite," he said, "but the director does. You cling to me, and I'll protect you from that evil jerk." He winked and I felt secure, both by being next to him and in getting the part.

Where is that sense of security when I need it most? After what happened, I am not even sure I can love Jason. How I came here to avoid him and will return home right after he leaves for a location shoot speaks volumes.

My heart grows heavy over how the last few days have shown me I need to open myself to Jason not being the one for me—especially since talking to someone who only exists in my head has become one of my greatest comforts. That fact has also crossed me over the threshold into a world that seems based in reality yet doesn't exist.

Or maybe on some level it does. Is it possible I have a soul mate? Does he know someone is here, unexplainably loving him and longing to see him again?

The heaviness in my heart builds. What if somewhere along the line, I took a wrong turn and gave up more than I bargained for?

The pangs of my newfound loneliness are unlike any I have ever felt. I grab the pillow and wrap myself around it, feeling desperate for love—real love—the kind that enraptures you—the type that challenges you to be better, because this person makes you see how much you can give. Having something in my life that is so opposite than what I need is making all I do have seem insignificant. I want to be consumed by love again. Once more, I want someone I can trust. Right now I only find that in fantasyland. The thing that bothers me most is how comforting it is, as if I am attached to an alternate reality.

This is crazy. I need to get out of here and clear my head.

I start to head out but realize I don't have friends here any more. Shoot, I get so tied up with work that the only people I ever talk to are co-workers, and the only ones I see outside of work are Jason and Bailey. While I love her like a sister, how is it Bailey has become my only true friend? Also, I never hear her mention anyone other than her own sister who lives on the other side of the continent. Shoot, I talk to my parents so little they won't know I am here until they get home from BINGO, or wherever they may be. How can I not know where they are? Again I am starting to understand why I find comfort in speaking to someone I can only hope exists.

I grab my phone and start dialing. This is crazy.

Bailey's sigh-filled hello sounds as if she is trying to

disguise pain. I don't want to be in that boat anymore and instantly let loose. "How is it all we have in our lives are men that hurt us, careers that are shadows of the ones we want, and each other?"

I can sense her looking to heaven like I am. "Time and again I have asked myself this," she says. "Yet I can never find an answer other than I have been a fool. I guess you don't feel much different right now."

I fall back onto the bed. "I can't believe I let Jason snow me."

Bailey sniffles, and I don't find the tiniest bit of consolation in knowing I am not the only one hurting. We both deserve better. I wish I could be there to comfort her. "At least you didn't have huge, neon signs flashing in front of you. Carlos being a moocher and taking all those weekends away with the boys should have tipped me off." Again Bailey sniffles and follows it with a prolonged sigh. "Thing is, before Carlos lost his job he was so dedicated, both to me and to it. Maybe since he thought work dumped him like a rotten fish, I would turn around and do the same. That's why I feel bad for trying to get him to move out of my place, because I see myself as being as bad as he feared."

I so get where she is coming from. "It is as if Jason thought because his body was betraying him, it was easier to let me think mine was too, sort of like misery loves company. It's all so twisted. God, Bailey, how will I ever trust again?"

Bailey braves words between sniffles. "I don't know. I mean, not every man is that way. There are more good people like us, right?"

I can't help but think about the mistakes of my past and how horrible I will always feel about them. "Sometimes I'm not so sure how great of a person I am."

Bailey is quick to offer support. "Katherine, you can't let Jason get to you. We *are* good people. In fact—" Bailey pauses, and I wonder if the connection has failed until I hear her catch her breath. Suddenly, Bailey sounds enlightened. "Oh God, Katherine, we are so stupid."

"For dating those losers, yes."

Due to her tone, I can envision revelation in her eyes. "No, we are missing the entire problem. Carlos slipped into depression because he gave his all to something. When it failed him, he let what he lost swallow him up. It's less intimidating for a good-looking man to put himself out there for women than for a man with less than desirable work skills to face rejection, time and again, by faceless businesses that won't even call him in for an interview. All I did was try to support someone I love through hard times, and that says a lot about my character. However, now that I know the rest of the story, whatever problems come next are as much my fault as they are his. When it comes to Carlos, I have always been true to who I am, which meant supporting him when he was down. Unfortunately, I have not always been so wise when it comes to me."

Bailey continues while sounding as if she now understands the meaning of life on Earth. "He put himself in this position and now he thinks if he denies all of his actions, I will continue to eat out of his hand and support him. It doesn't matter why he cheated. There are better things for me—things greater than I can ever imagine—and I won't find them by sitting here and suffering with his lies. It is time for me to take risks because that is the only way I will shine. Mark my words, Katherine, I will come out on top!"

I wish Bailey's enthusiasm were contagious. Instead, I feel my heart pull back. I want to take a risk and find the great things that await me. The thing is, right now I feel what I need to explore most may be in my head. However, maybe it is a part of me that is struggling to get out. I have a lot more questions to ask myself. "You know what, Bailey? I believe you. You've given me a lot to think about. I'm gonna go for a drive and clear my head a little more."

"Hey, you okay?" she asks, sounding as if some of her fire has caved to concern.

"Yeah, you are right about this not being our fault. In fact, you are right about a lot of things. I'll see you when I get back."

Crawling From The Wreckage

Brandon

Note to self: Never, ever, hang out with Dale for an entire weekend again. Merely the memory of some of the women he attracts makes me want to dump a gallon of Raid over my head.

Yet he failed to bite—not even a nibble. I'm certain he puts up a front. I don't believe for a second he enjoys all this traveling either. The man must be miserable.

Is it possible he has a hard time approaching what could be the right woman? Does Mr. Star Salesman / Mr. Womanizer have a timid side?

For hours I have lain here while staring at this hotel room ceiling. Pondering Dale's life has taken my mind off of my own issues. Even if I could manage to get some sleep, I'll regret it when my alarm goes off in an hour.

I am sticking to my original scheme of having Dale drop me off at the airport and let him think I am heading home. I'll then rent a car and spend the day popping into the places I heard Katherine frequents. I have no idea when she is returning, but since I am here I might as well stick to my plan and hope for the best.

While driving to the theatre on Saturday, I felt the same buzz of energy I did at the airport. When I asked Dale what we were near, he pointed to the left side of the freeway. "Over there is the best damn burger you'll get anywhere in the world. Behind us is suburban hell. Even you don't want to go in that direction to save your life." He then gave me a nasty once over, which I now see through. "Come to think of it, maybe you do. Tucked behind that patch of trees on our right is Majestic Studios."

After getting his confirmation that the buzz occurred near Katherine's work, I clicked the camera button on my cell phone each time I felt it. My vacation photos show only the inside of my pocket, but each one also has its location tagged. It was so double-oh-seven of me I should have been wearing a tux. If I follow through on this buzzing thing, maybe I can find something definitive and end this madness once and for all.

The room twists a bit as my feet hit the floor. Lack of sleep must be taking its toll. When I get on the plane tonight, I have got to take something to knock me out. My butt nearly falls into the desk chair, and the glare from my laptop seems to pierce into my head and make my stomach flip. Maybe I ate something bad last night. I wonder if Dale is sick.

It is of no surprise that a map of the area from the first picture looks familiar since it is near Katherine's work and I looked up the area long ago. The location of the next shot is near Harblano's, the restaurant where I saw the photo of her having dinner with Jason. The sickness in my stomach deepens at the thought of his smarmy hands on her.

Knock it off. You don't know squat about Jason Day, so cut out the bad mouthing. Stay positive, even if it pisses you off that you have to.

The map that picture number three brings up also correlates to my existing notes. It's near where one of the tabloids said she was seen having lunch with her friend.

Oh, son of a bitch!

My head drops into my hands. Of all the stupid—

"Crap!"

The only sign that I have some level of sanity is I stop myself from flipping out for fear the cops will get called on the screaming nut in a hotel room. I'm not double-oh-seven; I'm a data mining marketing guy. I preprogramed myself into thinking I'm sensing Katherine when all I am doing is recalling places I already noted she has been. God! How sick am I?

Amber believed in residual energy, so I convinced myself I felt Katherine's. But no, that's not all. One of the reasons I convinced myself I didn't fit the profile of a schizophrenic is because I'm not displaying odd behavior. Not only did I drop everything to go to Canada to *stalk* someone, since when would I ever go to a psychic, let alone believe her?

Come to think of it, I first heard Katherine not only after seeing her on the TV at Mulligan's, but also after hearing Darla on the phone. She said, "Escaping your situation only takes listening to your inner voice." I am such an idiot! Not only did I plant a seed in my head, I let it sprout. Given that, I've probably twisted ninety percent of what Jennifer said into what I wanted to hear, *if* she and shirtless guy even exist at all. I mean, she looks like freaking Stevie Nicks. That has to be in my head. The only logical explanation for any of this is the last time I was in Warped Records, one of those stacks in Vinyl Heaven toppled over and I have spent the last few days knocked out while inhaling the fumes of musty cardboard. That place is such a disaster they may not find me for a month.

Standing puts my head in a spin that has me falling onto the bed and dropping my head between my legs. I'm sick— truly sick. I'm a mentally ill stalker who has also become physically ill through stress and lack of sleep. I've crossed over the threshold into madness.

I turn to heaven for answers. "Amber, are you behind the voice? Are you punishing me for trying to move on? Please, tell me what I need to do for this to end." I fall back, and hot tears of exasperation stream down the sides of my face. My body prickles in fear that I have lost it.

Silence. Nothing but silence.

Silence that reminds me of death.

The rays of the sun peek through the crack in the curtains and land on my hand. The image of it holding a gun comes to mind. Was that fantasy? What is my reality now?

Bile burns its way up my throat, and my hand trembles as I lift it to my temple and recall the cool steel pressing against me. This time the voice in my head is my own. *"Pull it. Pull it and be done."*

I jerk and fling my hand as if tossing the gun across the room. Without a blink, I am up and headed for my suitcase. These images of suicide must be my brain telling me I feel guilty for surviving, so I need to beat this before it defeats me. Amber and I have unfinished business to take care of.

The fluffy clouds hanging above weep tender tears as I pass through the wrought iron gates of the Detroit cemetery. I probably should have brought more than a single, pink rose, but holding them reminded me of a wedding bouquet and the vows I started writing the night after we became engaged. They are still fresh in my mind; ready to blurt out when she walks through a chapel door that will never open. When it comes to Amber's death, I've always been in a damned if I do, damned if I don't situation.

The tears burning my eyes blur the headstones below, turning the ground to a fuzz of green and grey. When I see tree roots, I'll know I'm nearly there. But if I look up, my mind will envision her funeral all over again.

I can't witness her mom doubled over the casket and screaming. I can't handle feeling Amber's little sister holding my hand and crying into my shoulder. I was so wrapped in misery I couldn't even think to console her. I don't want to envision her brother looking like he was about to lose his mind because his parents wouldn't stop freaking out about every breath he and his sister took, fearing one of them would be next.

With each step, the memories become more vivid. They grip at my lower back and yank me towards the gates, yet I keep moving forward.

Brown enters the haze of green and grey—roots from the tree I've dreaded reaching. The breath I grab to prepare myself is far too shallow. Then again, I don't think I could ever take one deep enough.

One row.

Two rows.

Three.

"Hi, honey."

In my mind, the splattering of grey clouds solidifies into a muggy mass as I set sight on Amber's headstone. The fresh sprays of yellow and pink carnations on each side, along with the bright polish of the stone, make my spine shudder with the feeling our pain happened yesterday.

I take a seat at her feet and look to where I imagine her head is. I can't do this while facing her headstone. Not only should she be alive, our last names should have been shared long ago.

I want to tell her about life in Los Angeles, and the job I suck at. I want to share how life gets crazy sometimes, so I go to the record store and give Shane a bad time regarding his taste in music which isn't all that different from mine. There's also how I'm beginning to figure out the score with Dale. Most of all, I want to be sure she knows how I love and miss her, and that my heart has a hole in it so deep I am not sure it can be repaired. But as the heat of tears burns its way down my face, I choke out calm words I never saw coming.

"Dammit, Amber, you were everything that mattered in my life. We fell in love at eighteen. The night I turned twenty-one, everybody wanted us to go out, but we chose to celebrate on our own. Being with you was so perfect I wanted to spend every night of my life that way. My heart wouldn't let me say goodnight until I proposed."

The sting of tears burns so badly I squeeze my eyes closed in hopes of flushing out the pain. We didn't just get engaged that night; we laid out our future and how we would make every dream come true. "We planned to get married when we were twenty-three, and to start a family when we were twenty-five so we could be done by thirty. Our kids would be out of college before we hit our mid-fifties, so we could retire by sixty. We knew what type of jobs we wanted, how much they needed to pay, the maximum our mortgage could be, and how much we would put in savings each month for our retirement and for the kids' futures. It was all planned out to the letter, and then—"

My skin grows cold. I will never understand how a simple moment changed so many futures.

"Then you wanted ice cream. Out of the blue, you popped up and said, 'Thin Mint.' It was so unlike you."

My throat begins to burn from the sickness building in my stomach. I hate how petty pain can make people, but I can't fight it. Or maybe I can but am tired of doing so. "I offered to come with you, but you said studying had gotten to you and you needed to clear your head. For some crazy reason, even though the store was only about a mile down the road, you got on the freeway. Some idiot decided texting about a business deal was more important than protecting your life. By typing a single word, he shattered all our dreams."

The vision of what I heard happened has never left my mind. I've tried everything to erase it, yet it won't even fade. "You were just getting on. He swerved over and knocked you into the concrete barrier. You tapped it and spun, and then another car hit you head on. Some jerk may have put his stupidity first, but you were the one who wanted ice cream, and you wouldn't let me go instead. Unlike what I would have done, you chose the freeway and didn't take the city streets." I force out the words I have wanted to scream at her for so long, because dammit, even in death I have let her hold back my self-expression. "Everything is ruined! It's Monday night, and we should be seated around the dinner table with *our family*, but I'm alone because you wanted ice cream!"

I can't take being still any longer, so I pace at her feet, tossing my arms out and then slamming them down in frustration. How could she let this happen?

"We always decided everything together, but that night it was all you. Together we had decided where to live. We set the wedding date and picked out your engagement ring together."

My finger of blame gets pointed down at her head. "But you alone decided you wanted ice cream, and you alone decided to take the freeway! It's terrible, rude, and selfish of me, but I've never found forgiveness for what happened the one time you acted alone. Now, because I am angry with somebody who is dead, I may be projecting myself into a situation that is making me lose my mind. I've been hearing voices, and now I think I killed someone—that I was the driver in a car accident. Do you have any idea how much pain you wanting ice cream has caused?"

My knees hit the ground. The bulk of my anger has been released, but pain still reigns over me. I need answers, and dammit, I will beg them out of someone.

"Every time I think I'm close to letting go, something stops me. I thought moving to Los Angeles would break the pattern. I even started dating. I couldn't find the right woman, but at least I was trying. The last time I had a chance with someone, her name turned out to be Amber. I've been hearing voices ever since, and now I'm getting visions. This has to be because of you!"

Again I point blame at her only to turn my finger around and jab it into my chest, punctuating every point of my demise. "I'm going crazy! I'm hearing things! I'm hallucinating and seeing a crackpot psychic! I flew to Canada. I convinced myself I felt buzzing because you believed in that sort of stuff. Dammit, Amber, why the hell did you have to die?"

My sobs of desperation turn to wails of agony, driving me to crawl up to caress her headstone, collapsing me onto the ground and hugging the earth. The source of my pain lies six feet beneath me, and as desperate as I am to hold her again, I know I never will.

"Make it stop!" shudders through sobs. "Make it stop!"

What do I have to do to bring this suffering to an end? I try to calm myself enough to halt the sobs, but it is all I can do to lower my voice in prayer. "God, please, the voices, the visions … Amber, I know none of this is your fault, but can't you please take the pain away?"

I lie with my heart against the ground that separates us, waiting to hear a blessing of forgiveness for a crime I didn't commit—letting my pain bleed into the dirt while hoping it will somehow wake Amber and I from this nightmare.

Then something overcomes me—something I have always known, yet have never been able to vocalize. So much guilt comes with my words I can barely get them out. "Something about being with you made it easier to keep the real me hidden in the shadows. We may have wanted the same things, but I never felt open-spirited with you. I have not been able to say it before out of respect for you, but now I need to face it out of respect for myself. I was never the person you wanted me to be, nor can I ever be. That is just the way it is."

Silence slinks in. There are no voices—no sounds at all— anywhere. I raise my head and see a car drive out the gate. Its tread on the gravel is barely discernible. Maybe I have been blessed with peace.

I brave sitting and staring at the tombstone, taking in Amber's name and accepting I will never again see the woman who should forever be my wife. The one who should be called mother by the numerous pieces of joy we thought we were destined to bring into the world. Those angels died when she did.

I finally give her a rose, much like the one I robbed her of years before. Try as I might, I can't help but remember how I had once planned to plant her a picket-fenced garden full of them to come home to every night. "Not a day will ever go by that I don't miss you. Goodbye, Amber. And God, please, goodbye voices, visions, and vibrations."

My heart sends Amber a kiss, and I leave her behind. As I head to my car, more words slip out without permission. They hurt as much as the ones that came before.

"Goodbye, Katherine. I wish you happiness. I hope I can find the same. We will meet again—someday."

I Wanna Talk To You

Katherine

Although the time I spent at my parent's house helped ground me, I never felt settled. Being in my own home is only intensifying my discomfort. I haven't even finished unpacking, yet I already want to escape. Still, it's ten at night, and I need to be up at—

Screw it. I don't want to wake Bailey, but with the way things have been going she probably can't think about sleep either. I shoot her a text, *"Just got back. Want to grab some coffee?"*

I don't seem to get more than a couple of steps away from my phone when it buzzes with a return text. *"I'm at The Kingsway, escaping Carlos by watching a documentary on bowling. Tell me where you want me, and I will be there in a heartbeat!"*

Bailey loves going to old theaters such as The Kingsway. Actually, she loves pretty much anything from the forties. But to sit through a documentary on bowling means she must be desperate to be anywhere but home. That sure sounds familiar. I'll meet her someplace slightly out of the way so she has an excuse to bail on that documentary quickly. *"Carrie's Café in 15?"*

The return text is almost instantaneous. *"I'll be there in five!"*

Inside the cozy café, I peer into my menu only to tell the waitress, "Just coffee for me, please. Decaf."

"Decaf for me, too," Bailey adds, "but with two forks and a slice of cherry pie."

"Yes!" I exclaim with the addition of a fist pump. Our twisted logic dictates whomever orders it is the one who sucks up all the bad things we are not supposed to eat. I hate having to stay so freaking skinny and constantly find ways to rebel against it. I refuse to get sucked into the ridiculous body issues Hollywood creates.

A large yawn comes out of me. I should be in bed, but right now everything seems out of sorts to the point where I know I won't sleep. The comfort I have been finding in talking to someone who doesn't exist is disturbing.

"So," Bailey says, "how was the rest of your visit home?"

"It was good," blurts out of me. Bailey's head tilts like she is not buying my forced cheer for a second, so I surrender to giving her most of the story. "Seeing my parents was great. Getting away was also good in the sense that, despite the fact my heart is on the fence, I have come to terms with needing out of my relationship with Jason. How I managed to come home after he left for a location shoot, and how I reworked my schedule so I now leave for Los Angeles late Wednesday night, before he gets back, shows where my head is." Bailey waits for me to say more, but I am not sure where to start or even if I should. Making up someone to fill the void would be a lot less weird if it didn't feel so real at times.

"But there is more to it, isn't there?" she asks.

Sometimes knowing someone who can read you well isn't the best thing to help you get your mind off of your troubles. There has to be some way for all this to make sense. "The talk we had regarding our lack of friends reminded me of being a kid and playing Monopoly against an imaginary partner. Did you ever do anything like that?" I am betting if she did, she never acted as if the person was real, let alone reached out for his hand. Why am I doing that? The worst part is, it seems so natural it is freaky.

Is it really all that weird? Aren't we supposed to find our greatest comfort within ourselves?

Yeah, it's weird.

The waitress arrives with the pie, two cups of coffee, and our check. Seriously? Why do I feel I have already been kicked out?

Bailey snickers. "With Darla around, I never had enough

privacy to create a playmate. Although …" Bailey shakes her head. "I can't believe I am admitting this. When I was about thirteen, I used to daydream that I had a boyfriend. He had black hair, a gorgeous tan, and eyes as dark as sin. We had some of the best talks." She chuckles. "Yep, I had deep, meaningful conversations with a male member of the species. That alone told me it was fake. It sounds so weird now, but then I thought of it as talking to the man I was destined to find."

Her words reinforce part of my fears. "*Was* destined to find?"

She sighs. "I told myself Saturday night that, in light of my new attitude, I wouldn't let negativity slip in, but sometimes fear seeps through the cracks. I'm determined to make better choices now."

Despite the steadfastness of her words, her voice sounds nervous. Bailey sips her coffee, and my guard rises. Something tells me bad news is on the way. I let out a hearty exhale. "Don't sugar coat it. Just spill it." My nerves drive me to grab a cherry out of the pie.

Bailey's voice continues to sound shaky. "Over the last couple of days I have made some pretty big decisions." Her demeanor changes, and the sudden *thunk* of her cup on the table snaps my attention. "I gave notice at work."

My eyes widen and lock. Oh God, please no. She can't go!

"That dose of reality on Saturday night stuck. I am moving in with Darla and taking over the job she is leaving while going back to school. It is time to stop ignoring my dreams and regain who I am."

My gaze drops along with my heart. Bailey needs to make a change but …

I want to fight her on this—to offer her a place to live, rent-free even. She could stay with me while going to school. Hell, I can afford it. She's given Carlos a free ride for so long, why shouldn't she get one?

I look back at her, ready to tell her I'm happy to help, but one solid look at the strength in her eyes that reflects the gumption she struggled so long to find tells me I have to respect her decision. "I'm so glad you are doing what is best for you. I'm gonna miss the hell out of you."

She squeezes my arm, and I place my hand over hers. "I'm gonna miss the hell out of you, too," she says through watery eyes. "But hey, it's not as if you never go to Los Angeles."

Her words breathe a bit of life back into me. They also remind me of one of the things I struggled with while at my parent's house. "True, and with what I told you about Jason's twisted logic, I may be back there as soon as this season wraps. He is totally going to tank the show."

I rattle my head while trying to clear the thoughts that keep swimming around. It doesn't work, so I pick another cherry out of the pie and hope it will somehow give me focus. I need to dump my boyfriend, and my best friend is leaving. Meanwhile, I have found comfort in a fabricated reality. Bailey is making a major decision based on what she feels can lead her to happiness. I need to do the same. For as grown up as Bailey and I are, we sure have a lot to learn about ourselves. Lately I've been learning in leaps and bounds.

I blurt out, "Do you think there is someone for everyone?" Having the courage to not only ask the question but to also face my curiosity aloud drives me to go for a big bite of pie.

"You mean, like a soul mate? Similar to how I thought this conversation was headed earlier with you being vague and asking about imaginary people?"

How she has figured out a part of what I am getting at doesn't faze me, though it probably should. "You really do know me well."

She doesn't even take a beat to think about it. "Absolutely, and I wish he would show up. I'm tired of being at a carnival."

Dear Lord, me too! Jason and I are nothing more than the same roller coaster ride over and over again. It is long past time to get off.

I put half of the last bit of pie into my mouth. Bailey digs her fork into what's left. We need to dive into a new sea to find our treasure chests. "Do you think you might know him on sight?" I ask.

"I absolutely do, but only if I don't expect him to be perfect. Don't you?"

I wish I could say that I would. Once I thought Jason might be able to fill those shoes. "Not in the least, which means I have to be a lot more open-minded." I nab the check. "It's on me. You just did me a big favor. I owe you a lot more than pie."

Bailey puts her hand on my arm and stops me. "So, you are telling me that even though you have been on the evasive side, I managed to help you with whatever was going to keep you from sleeping tonight?"

Though I smile I have to choke back the emotion that threatens to show in my eyes. "I don't know how I am going to make it without you."

"I promise to never be more than a phone call away."

During my walk home the cold air has me chilled to the bone, yet my inner being is cozy. Whatever is going on is making me change, and I dig this new version who is willing to let the world open up for her. If soul mates exists, something other than the here and now must too. Maybe opening my mind to new possibilities will help me clear out the garbage in my head and rediscover the happiness I've lost.

As soon as I crawl into bed I speak from my heart. "My name is Katherine. I live in Toronto, and I choose to believe there is someone special for me. I love walks on the beach, playing with animals, and feel people need to treasure everyday. I also believe no dream goes unheard, though lately I have lost sight of that." I snuggle deep under the covers while feeling secure for the first time in years.

"If I could somehow find a way to let you know I am thinking of you, then maybe … maybe someday our paths will cross and we will find each other."

My touch to the pillow on my left is like that to the cheek of a lover. Intense longing for someone I have never laid eyes on tears at my heart, making me miss an unseen man with the passion of a great love I have known for ages. How can this not be real?

Brandon

The warmth of a gentle caress cups my jaw and nudges me awake. With a moan of happiness, I snuggle deeper into the pillow. Hmm … I need more dreams like this.

Suddenly, I realize even though I am now awake, I still feel the touch. This isn't a dream!

My eyes pop open, yet the sensation remains, causing me to nearly choke on my gasp for air. Holy shit! The voice, the visions, they are all supposed to be gone. Yesterday I walked away and came home. I spent today struggling to stay awake at work, went to bed, and conked out while comfortable in knowing I should be at peace with everything. Instead, I feel a touch—a warm, gentle touch that under normal circumstances would put my heart on a cloud. Now my body is rigid and growing icier by the instant.

"I have big decisions to make."

"No!" I pop up in bed and rattle my head with the force of a paint shaker, risking brain damage.

"How can it be after all that has happened—"

"Go away!"

The voice fades, and the gasp of air I grab in relief adds to the pain in my chest my racing heart brought on. I drop down onto my back and try to gather my wits. My words race out. "I have a chemical imbalance. I have to. There is no other explanation. Talking to myself is proof."

Okay, I need to be rational. Do I call the ambulance now, or do I drive myself to the hospital in the morning? I'm out of excuses.

No, I am not crazy. I can't be.

Yes, you can.

No, I'm not.

Then why am I talking to myself?

If I am talking to myself, wouldn't I ask, why are *you* talking to yourself?

See, that line of thinking shows my mind is still here. This is a simple, internal conversation; therefore, I am not crazy.

Am I?

God, please help me.

Okay, rational thinking says whether or not I am nuts may be questionable, but I am definitely awake. My knuckles are also white from gripping the sheets, which I had no idea I was doing.

I force my body to go languid. Compelling myself into feeling somewhat normal further messes with my head and starts to freak me out again.

Water, I need water. Lots and lots of water.

I head off to the kitchen. Three glasses later I almost feel calm, yet there is no way I am going back to sleep—not now—maybe not ever—for fear of what may happen next.

A diversion. I need a diversion.

The box of reel-to-reels Shane gave me sits on my living room floor. I plop down, determined to let the bad music I am bound to keep finding quell my freak out. Man, was he ever right about how horrible these are.

My hands jitter so badly I drop the reel I pull off of the recorder. I will focus and overcome this. I must. Think of the music. Think of how bad it is—like mind-numbingly bad. Right now, that is exactly what the doctor ordered.

Dear God, please don't let me need a doctor.

I use care to wind the last tape properly and tuck it neatly back into its box. Even though I'm pretty sure three toddlers and a cow could produce more notable work, this could be the last surviving recording of Puke Spray, whoever they were, so respect seems due.

Lord, the next tape has to be better.

Funny, I said the same thing the last five times I threaded this machine. This may prove I've lost my mind more than anything else does.

Again I gather myself and then start the player. The familiar voice of the engineer comes across the tape, just as he has on the others. *"Okay, girls, are you ready?"*

Girls? Good, this is what I need. The seventies were a

prime time for chicks with guitars. Maybe this tape won't suck bong water like the others did.

Man, I sure get bitchy when I have freak outs.

A guitar rips in, followed by the pounding of drums. A female voice starts kicking ass and … Dear Lord, yes! A woman screaming into a mic can be damn threatening. This one certainly reminds me that my hormones love being intimidated. These girls rule! Who are they?

The only marking on the box says, *"Negative Fate, 'Pangs of Love.'"*

Oh God, yes. This alone makes me feel so much better. I can be okay. I *will* be okay. Music always saves me.

My fingers tap on the coffee table, and I hum along to the simple chord progression. When we get to the break, I jump up and start thrashing, swinging my neck round and round, spinning it into heaven. The lyrics kick back in, and I belt them out while twirling and dancing my way to the kitchen.

"I am a rock and roll machine, a product of my own revolution. The road to success is dark, but flames of my desire will light the path."

I start screaming with the impassioned singer like I'm a crazed fan. I've popped the top off of a beer and am headed in for a swig when I'm sucker punched in the face. Everything in the world seems to stop, except for the music.

I've never heard this song, so how do I know the lyrics?

Okay, I'm still freaked out over the touch I think I felt. This song has to be a cover. A lot of bands demo with covers.

Who would have done something like this? It doesn't feel as if the lyrics were altered to fit a woman singing, so that narrows it down. These tapes were recorded from nineteen seventy-eight to nineteen eighty. The engineer was out of Berkeley, so the band was probably local too, meaning the original version could have been a regional hit I've randomly heard. What seventies, San Francisco area, punk band could have done this?

UXA started in San Francisco, but I'm pretty damn familiar with anything the heavenly DeDe Troit ever belted. What about California in general? The Go-Go's were once part of the punk scene. My mind flips through their catalog, starting with all of the early stuff I've only been able to hear on YouTube and going through "Our Lips Are Sealed" which hit the charts long after this tape was made.

No, that doesn't sound right either. This is going to drive me nuts.

I grab my laptop and surf on 'negative fate pangs of love.' The top hit is for punkrockgirls.com—a fan-driven Wiki listing a bunch of bands pretty much no one has ever heard of. How have I missed this site? I'm gonna waste countless hours on here.

A picture loads and—

Holy shit … There is no possible way.

My world, my mind, it all …

My brain is melting. It must be, because I can't be seeing what I am imagining I am seeing.

Four girls in black stare down at the camera. One of them is a bleached blonde with a bar painted across her eyes. She's dead in my face and owning the shot. She also jabs at my heart as if she owns that as well. God, those blue eyes …

Sleep walking. Maybe I am sleepwalking. Either that or this pain in my chest is actually a heart attack and I'm in the hospital, high on drugs and hallucinating.

The song crashes to an end, and the engineer returns. *"Let's try it one more time. Saleena, I need to up your vocals. Do you think you can hit that chorus a little harder?"*

Saleena?

Oh God.

My hand goes to my chest, feeling my heart race and fearing the pain of an attack may soon hit.

"Sure. Are you ready to give it another go, girls?" asks a voice so sweet and delicate it is the stuff bondage freaks dream of. It in no way matches the power of the voice that belted out the song, but it's a dead ringer for the one I heard during my alleged past life flashback. Its softness reminds me of PJ Harvey, who talks like a Kewpie doll but sings like a banshee. It is a contrast similar to the ones between the images I get of

129

Katherine without makeup and her public persona.

God, that makes so much sense. Katherine is trying to sell an image the way Saleena did. They have to be the same person.

But the seventies weren't very long ago. The only way she could be Katherine is if she died right after this.

My eyes race to the Wiki article. *"The band came to an abrupt halt in nineteen seventy-eight, due to Saleena Kale's untimely death in an automobile accident."*

Oh dear God.

Prickles pop up and sting as if I have been smacked with a cactus of reality. I'm Brandon Wayne. I live in Los Angeles, and I don't want to be spoon-fed for the rest of my life.

None of this is happening. It can't be.

I head off to my room, grab my suitcase, and toss it onto the bed. What are you allowed to bring when you check yourself into a mental hospital? I am guessing my shaving kit needs to stay home.

Institutionalized

Brandon

The number of mental hospitals and clinics that reside in the Los Angeles area is a little frightening. Since there were so many to choose from, I did the most (appropriately) insane thing and picked the one with the goofiest name. Yes, I could have gone to the eloquently titled Hampton Center for Mental Rehabilitation, but no; I picked Happydale. How can I possibly refuse seeking refuge in someplace so pleasant sounding? If nothing else, this proves I have not lost my sense of humor.

Even though I am pretty sure they will provide me with a lovely jacket, I've brought enough clothes to last a week. By then, Dale should be back and he can pick up anything else I need. Work can think I have fallen off of the planet. My disappearance can be a great, unsolved mystery, as if I have been sucked into The Bermuda Triangle.

What kind of food is served at Happydale? Are they called Happymeals? Regardless, I am betting sugar isn't allowed in the place.

Now I am craving chocolate. I need to pull into a 7-Eleven for one last fix. At least I didn't decide to close some things out at work first and check myself in mid-day. Then I might have settled for grabbing something out of the plant. That definitely would have proven my insanity.

Hey, maybe I am not crazy after all.

Oh, how quickly I have forgotten I am a data-mining stalker who thinks there is a psychic who looks like Stevie Nicks. One chocolate bar and off to the funny farm I go.

I pull into the lot while pondering what to buy. Shoot, who knows how long it will be until I get another chance to eat chocolate. Ooh! Or donuts! I'll load up and cram junk food all the way there. That should burn me out on cravings for at least a few weeks.

When I step out of the car, a surprising "Hey, man!" hits my ears. I look over to see shirtless guy from Jennifer's place. I wasn't exactly unaware that her house is right behind here. How fitting is it that a psychic lives right down the street from a funny farm?

I say hello while wondering if the guy who wears a hoodie, yet is still without shoes, notices the layers of crazy on me.

"Hey, good to see you, man. I guess you know Jennifer has something for you. I'm headed back now, so fall on by. Catch you in a minute."

Jennifer *has* something for me? Why? What? And how would I know that? I swear, nothing about any aspect of my life makes sense—not a damn thing.

Sure, what the hell. I'll pop by. After all, I've no more of my sanity to lose, so I might as well humor him and his rock-star lookalike … girlfriend? Sure. Why not? She's what? Twice his age? Rock it, sister.

When I knock, shirtless guy answers the door. This time he's wearing his normal attire.

"Hi, you mentioned Stevie—" I try to slam on the brake before getting caught on the faux pas, "I mean, Jennifer has something for me?" God, did I really call her Stevie?

He laughs. "Don't sweat it, man. When I first met her I went through the same thing. I'd just gotten over it when I took some stuff down to the basement and found a box filled with gold statuettes. My brain went all crazy." He scoffs. "Turned out they were soccer trophies. I swear she put them there to see if I would lose my head. Anyway, she's at Zumba class, but she left this."

He hands me a folded note. I can only begin to imagine what is in it. Maybe she knows about my Toronto trip and is calling me an idiot for being a crappy stalker.

"Knock off the wallowing, bag the talk of being crazy, and get back to work. Seriously, Brandon, end that crap now. She's looking; so let her find you. Be Batman. Do not, I repeat, do not do anything stupid, or

you'll wind up in the pokey. Get some sleep, and eat something other than chocolate and those terrible gumdrops."

I must be getting used to madness because my only physical reaction is my jaw falls ever so slightly open. Seriously, this is comical. I can see her suspecting that I think I have lost my marbles, but how did she know I would be anywhere near this place today, let alone that I bought chocolate? I feel like I'm a little kid whose mom busted him.

The pokey? Let Katherine find me, yet be Batman? Batman doesn't want to be found. "What the hell does be Batman mean?"

Shirtless guy shrugs. I wait, hoping he'll give me more to go on. I get nothing.

Be Batman? Does that mean to get a cool car with gadgets? Maybe I should put in a hotline so Commissioner Gordon can reach me.

I go for my wallet to at least leave her a twenty or something. The guy puts his hand out, and not in the way I expect.

"She said this one's on the house. Trust me, anytime Jennifer's keeping the faith it's a good sign."

I ask him to thank her, and as I turn to leave I get jabbed. "Ouch." The roses on the bush that tried to steal my blood are the color I have come to think of as being Amber Pink. I swear there is no end to the weirdness surrounding me.

"Sorry," shirtless guy says. "The gardener missed that one this time around."

"No big deal. Have a good day."

"Yeah, solid."

Man, the amount of seventies slang in this guy's vocabulary is vast. Him and a psychic who looks like a rock star ... those things alone make me look sane, that is, *if* they are real. I'm still not sure.

I get in my car and look at the note while releasing a long sigh. Man, I don't want to be crazy. Honestly, I don't think I am. I just don't know what to believe.

I reach for my junk food—a Hershey bar and two packs

of Hostess Donettes, one of which is "chocolate" coated and the other covered in powdered sugar. Yick. With how I have been eating, no wonder why I am a mess.

After a decent breakfast, I'll head into work, clear my head, and start decoding the new mystery Jennifer laid on me.

If the article I read a few weeks ago is right, and sad is where it is at, maybe our gumdrop ad should show a middle-aged woman looking at a granny-type in a casket. The caption will read, "She may have lost her family, but she can still taste her childhood."

Man, that idea sucks. Are these gumdrops really so bad I can't come up with a decent campaign, or do I truly lack the competence to do my job?

This time I got my stash straight off of the line before coming into my office. Unless Darla messed with the formula, these are safe.

Well, as safe as anything else made here.

My teeth try to cut into the orange-colored drop, but the thing already has the tension of being stale and the sugar coating scratches the roof of my mouth. At least it tastes orangeyish.

Maybe I should start a rumor campaign about how bad these are. People will buy them to see if it is true. Thing is, once they find out it is not a gimmick, we are screwed.

I pop in a red one and dare to bite down. My teeth actually cut through it with ease. Wow, did we really make this?

Then the flavor hits my palate. It taste kind of like a tangy lollipop that's been left open in a kid's pocket. Yeah, we made this.

Hmm … a kid's pocket … kids play with their food …

I line up some of the red gumdrops and then try to build another row on top of the first one to make a pyramid. Since their tops are rounded, of course they won't stack. However, they do fall into a pile that is rather circular. With the aid of a few green ones, I add a stem. The gumdrops now look sort of cherry-like, which is also kind of how they taste. Have I hit on truth in advertising? "Endeara gumdrops: Kinda tastes like fruit."

Okay, this idea isn't total crap. Something reminiscent of refrigerator art might grab a parent's attention.

With the aid of some yellow gumdrops I attempt to make a lemon. Since the drops are too big to properly form the shape on a small surface, it looks a mess. I need a bigger workspace. I grab the bags, loosen my tie, and plop down onto the floor to start playing.

What could be Batman mean? Jennifer couldn't have meant to put on a pair of tights and a cape. Then again, it would get me attention—for being a lunatic.

I lean back and check out my art. The lemon idea sort of works. What if I use black to form a tree trunk and the other colors for leaves and fruit?

Maybe being Batman means Katherine wants a savior.

This black tree trunk implies Halloween. It might look cool with a lemon moon. A seasonal look is too limited, but there is an idea in here somewhere.

Could be Batman mean to be her superhero? Maybe it has something to do with self-confidence.

Darla's sudden laughter snaps my attention to the doorway. "Oh. My. God! That is hysterical!"

This is a good sign. Maybe my idea has some merit after all. "You actually like it?"

"You are taking your last name way too seriously. That might be the hokiest thing I have ever seen. " Darla walks off, yet her laughter continues while she heads down the hall. "Please send me a picture," she yells. "That one's a keeper!"

What the hell is she talking about?

I stand to see my gumdrop tree trunk from the same angle she did and find my art skills suck worse than my marketing ones. Man, that thing is ugly. It looks more like a bat. And with all those yellow gumdrops spattered about it looks ... Oh my God, I created a gumdrop version of The Bat Signal.

This might be the first time Darla has ever been wrong.

My art isn't hokey; it is brilliant! Batman gave the signal to Gotham as his way to be found while remaining under the radar. I need a way to get Katherine's attention despite being just another face in the crowd. How do you reach everyone while blending in?

Social media! Everyone is glued to it. You can't walk into a restaurant or a party without seeing half the people with their phones in their faces.

How can I take advantage of social media when celebrities get their fans' attention with Facebook, yet they block our ability to send private messages and don't interact with our comments? Mentions on Twitter are as easy to ignore, and if you send too many, you are labeled a stalker and blocked.

But studies show people turn to Facebook when they are bored. So after posting, Katherine probably sticks around and does what I would do next, which is see what my friends are up to.

Posting Facebook comments is considered perfectly acceptable, community participation. If I regularly comment on her post while she is still online, she'll see a notification pip pop up and may take a look. She has a ton of fans, so people start commenting immediately. That means I not only need to jump in quickly, I also have to do it with flair so mine doesn't blend in with all the others.

I need branding—eye catching, memorable branding.

How do I brand Brandon Wayne?

My eyes lock on my terrible version of a Bat Signal—my new profile picture. It is time to charge forward, and I'm going in full throttle.

I'm Batman.

Instant Replay

Katherine

After all the years I have spent flying for work, you'd think I'd be used to sleeping on planes. Yet after a long night of flying from Toronto to Los Angeles, I'm grateful for this hotel bed. Back home it may be six in the morning and long past my standard call time, but here it is only three, and I don't need to be anywhere for hours. Thank God.

At least I don't think I do …

Yeah, it's Thursday morning. I'm supposed to go to the studio this afternoon for final fittings. Traveling messes with my head and my ability to track time. However, as long as I get to sleep, there's not much I care about right now.

Moments after slipping into bed, bliss slinks over me …

Colored lights creep into a sea of black, illuminating people wearing the most God-awful fashions—orange bellbottoms, rainbow suspenders, satin jackets, and by great contrast, a couple in the corner is dressed in something cool—tattered jeans and studded, leather jackets. Looking down, I find my own clothes to be a wall of black—high boots, microskirt, a form-fitting tank top, and studded bracelets. How the whole scene reeks of nineteen seventies' fashion in its various forms makes me feel I am in a movie.

Things seem as foreign outside. Stepping stones of mosaic butterflies pave the walkway. The rectangles on the roll-up garage door are painted in a rainbow of colors that remind me of the dance floor in Saturday Night Fever.

A man with short, spiked hair, a tattered, Runaways T-shirt, and frayed jeans steals my attention. He gives me a peck on the cheek, and the smile he gives makes my heart flutter. The needle on the record player slips, ripping off Led Zeppelin. Cheers roar when "The Hustle" kicks in. Now the guy looks as if he is praying for death. "Kill me," he says with a groan.

I'm not crazy about it either. "Give it time. This song doesn't last forever, you know?" Wow. My voice is so soft it is disorienting.

"Thank God. Whomever invented disco should be drawn, quartered, and tossed into a shark tank."

He pulls me to him, and my heels get caught in the dirt, causing me to stumble. I giggle. He kisses me, and I swoon over the heavens at how cherished I feel.

"The Hustle" blends into another song that rubs me the wrong way. It takes a moment for me to recognize "Instant Replay", something I only hear when my friends watch Dance Fever *on TV.*

The man of my dreams yanks my arm. "That's it! It's bad enough Dan Hartman left Edgar Winter to play crappy music, but there is no damn way I am listening to it." He then lowers his voice to a grumble, "Damn repetitive four-on-the-floor beat with a high hat on the eight. It's like having every tooth in your head drilled."

I smile and wave goodbye to our friends. "Bye, Saleena," one of them yells. "I'm surprised Johnny lasted this long."

The instant we get into the car, Johnny pops in a cassette. The wail of a guitar fills my ears, followed by drums, and then a woman's voice that is brash and wild. "I am a rock and roll machine, a product of my own revolution," *she screams.*

Why do I think I am the one who is singing?

"I'll take this any day over that mechanical sounding, corporate rip-off crap," Johnny says with a grumble. "God only knows what the eighties are going to bring, let alone what atrocities our children will suffer."

As we drive into the night, we pass through modern suburbia with Victorian-era homes sprinkled through it. Ahead of us is a theatre marquee reading, Alameda. Where is—

Though something wakes me, the tune still plays in my head. I can't place it, even though I feel I know it as if it were etched inside me.

I try to put myself back into a lucid state while remembering what I just saw. While the memory fades, the melody lingers.

Brandon

The sound of my heart—not its beat, but the flaps of

valves opening and closing, accompanied by pops of air, nudges me out of a deep slumber. I try to shake it away, but the pressure seems to build. I try smacking the side of my head. This is dammed annoying. The only other time I have felt anything remotely similar was on the plane to Toronto, when I saw houses I suspect turned out to be Katherine's vision ...

Which happened because our flights where near each other.

I bolt up. Katherine's in Los Angeles!

I damn near jump out of bed and race for my phone. Killing the volume so I could get some sleep caused me to miss the alert of her earlier Tweet.

"Great to be back in LA, if only for a few days. Can't wait to start shooting."

Confirmation! I have true confirmation that I can sense her!

Holy crap, I'm turning into a giddy schoolgirl. She's here, and I could tell!

Now, how do I get to the woman who is either locked up on a studio lot or surrounded by bodyguards? Why do cheesy seventies sitcoms where people hide inside room service carts and sneak into hotel rooms come to mind? Hey, it may be lame, but that plan always worked on TV.

No, Jennifer warned me not to try anything crazy. Unless I can come up with a solid plan, I've no choice but to wait for the right time to put up the Bat Signal.

Surrender

Katherine

My teeth press down on my finger, biting it in hopes of releasing stress. I'm used to day-after-day of early calls, hanging out in a makeup chair, and then waiting on seemingly endless setups, but on this production I get the added bonus of a director who races actors through scenes. Between that and the pressure to give the performance of a lifetime, I barely managed to make it through yesterday—and that was the easy scene.

I take my time in releasing a deep breath. I've been so on edge I haven't even been able to make the Facebook post my publicist asked for. Being on set is stressful. Anyone who can't handle pressure at every corner should not be in this business. However, there are some directors who understand what actors need in order to give the best performance possible. This guy is not one of them. While shooting an emotion-filled funeral scene yesterday, he actually told someone to speed it up and crank it out. Unbelievable.

My co-workers also have me stressed to the gills. Harvey Davison may be a great actor, but our extreme lack of chemistry makes it hard for me to convince anyone I could ever love the guy. He is also so smug he hasn't bothered to say hello to me—the girl he is about to fake making love to. Right now, even though he is looking up at the guy he is talking to, Harvey is so condescending I'm pretty sure the guy is able to see up Harvey's nose.

All this thinking isn't helping. Hopefully posting those photos will get my head in a better space. It has to, because if I blow it and Jason sinks *Vampires Undercover*, I might as well start filling out barista applications—not that I am at all qualified.

Brandon

This waiting is driving me crazy. For God's sake, it is Saturday morning. I know she's in town, yet it's been total radio silence since Thursday—no voice, no Facebook post, not even a photo on Instagram. I'm gonna lose my ever-loving mind.

Inside my jean's pocket, my phone vibrates. It's probably another text from Dale, whom I've completely lost track of because he keeps getting shipped off to God knows where.

I look to my phone, and my heart speeds up. Finally! It's about freaking time Katherine resurfaced.

I lean against one of the bins at Warped Records to check out the post. The glimmering, emerald dress she wears in the photo displays so much cleavage that I can't help but lock my eyes on it. Damn! I wouldn't mind sticking my face ...

Focus, Brandon!

"Presenting at the Emmys last year. I never thought they would even let me in the door. :)"

How does this post already have over two hundred likes and forty-one comments? Are people sitting at their computers while waiting on her every word? Don't they have lives? How crazy.

Why yes, Brandon. Crazy indeed.

Oh, everything about this is crazy, including how I need to get noticed in a sea of fans.

Does seeing all these comments about how hot she looks ever get old? Sure, people need ego boosts, but artists also care about their craft. All that stuff she does to her body is hype, similar to how Saleena altered her appearance in order to stand out.

There lies the key. I may not know how to talk to Katherine, but I once knew how to talk to Saleena. My inner voice is the one who needs to comment. *"You should have been there winning instead of presenting. It's only a matter of time. Let passion be your guide."*

The door swings open and nearly slams shut. A wannabe

skate punk heads toward the counter. The waistband on his pants hangs nearly to the top of his thigh like he has a death wish. Loose fitting pants while skating? Sure, but you need leg swing without your belt being in the way. Oh, well. We all learned the hard way, hence the permanent bump on the right side of my skull.

I sneak a peek at Facebook. Unfortunately, my comment is raking in the likes by everyone but Katherine.

The kid huffs and clears his throat. Shane holds up a finger to tell him to wait while he finishes reading some relic. Finally, he pops his head up. "Can I help you?"

"Yeah, what's that band that sounds like Green Day?"

Shane shrugs. "Which one?"

"You know, that other punk band."

My insides clamp. I was right about him having a death wish.

"*Other* punk band?" Shane sounds indignant. Here we go.

The kid shrugs. "Yeah."

"Kid, punk is about aggression and anarchy brought on by going against the norm. Green Day is the norm. At best, they are pop punk."

"Don't be a hater of the cool. Green Day is totally punk."

Yikes! What he loves isn't the issue; not dissecting his passion is. You can only grow once you see beyond the obvious. If you dig a band, look at their idols. If you are into a genre, trace its roots. Green Day uses punk tempos and chord changes, but their melodies and subject matter are pop. Figuring out what he likes about them will open his world. Because of this kid's attitude, Shane is leading him down that road the only way he will understand the journey.

"Yeah, sure they are punk," Shane says. I don't have to look to know his eyes are rolling. I check my phone again for an alert from Katherine—nothing.

"Are you going to tell me who I am looking for?" the kid asks.

Shane pretends to scratch his brain. "Hmm ... Blink 182 is pop punk."

"Old dude, are you deaf? Not pop punk. Punk!"

On second thought, this kid should run for his life while he can. Despite the insults, Shane plays along by snapping his fingers as if he is about to be brilliant. "You want the soundtrack to Full House."

Snort!

The kid's head snaps at me. "Seriously," Shane says, " '21 Guns' snags part of the theme song. It also sounds like ELO's 'Telephone Line' and Mott the Hoople's 'All the Young Dudes'. Oh, and 'Jesus of Suburbia' totally sounds like Bryan Adams' 'Summer of 69'."

The kid crosses his arms and gets testy. "Bryan Adams isn't punk."

"Neither is Green Day!"

"Yes, they are!"

Shane thrust his index finger toward the door. I'm surprised it's not his middle one. "Kid, you are giving me an aneurism. Get out of my store."

My phone buzzes with a Facebook notification—from Katherine!

She responded?

"Thank you, Brandon. You have no idea how fantastic your timing was or what those words did for me!"

Holy …

She tagged me!

In the grand scheme of life, it means nothing, but in light of our situation, this is huge. I have to hold her attention! But how?

I'll paraphrase something she said in one of the visions. *"I've always believed no dream goes unheard."*

Shane's customer starts to head out. Oddly, Shane seems to feel sorry for him. "Okay, hold on. I've got what you want."

This is what it has all been leading to. Shane and I became the way we are because we were handed the right seed to plant. I got mine at fourteen while standing in front of my cousin Diane's record collection in awe. She asked what I listened to and why I enjoyed it. My head had always been stuck in the Top 40. When she laid the needle on *Cheap Trick at Budokan*, the opening notes to "Surrender" hit, and a call to war bounced off of the speakers. Instantly, the fire of passion was ignited. Now I may get to witness that magic with this kid.

A drumroll plays in my head as Shane hands him a copy of … *The Kinks Are The Village Green Preservation Society*. Brilliant! Always look to the idols. When it comes to numerous bands, you start with The Kinks.

"Listen to 'Picture Book'," Shane says. "The circulating intro sounds a lot like 'Warning'. Messes with me all the time."

"Dude, this thing is ancient history. They didn't have punk in the sixties."

Now Shane's not the only one who wants to kill this kid.

"Punk originated in the sixties," Shane says. He grabs a copy of The MC5's *Kick Out The Jams*. "Early punk, though they are far from the first. It's on me. Take The Kinks too, and see what I am talking about." He heads to another bin and pulls out some TSOL. "This is punk. Hone in on what you groove to, and I'll help you track down whatever you are looking for."

This is why I respect the hell out of Shane. He could have sold that kid pretty much anything—maybe even a stack of it. Instead, he opted to open his mind. This is akin to watching poetry.

My phone buzzes, snapping me out of rock and roll heaven and filling me with hope.

Katherine replied, "I agree!"

We had a conversation!

I slip the phone back into my pocket and divert my attention to a bin of records while trying to hide my canary-eating grin. Shane sends the kid on his way and then walks up to me. "Please tell me we were never that dumb."

"We both know it would be a lie. Any clue what he actually wanted?"

"Who cares? He walked out of here with The MC5, The Kinks, and TSOL. The kid owes me his life."

In the course of a few minutes I got both a response from Katherine and to watch the foundation laid for a kid to build a love of music. Life is awesome!

Katherine

Fresh in from work, I fall back onto the hotel room bed. It may be the dead of night, but I feel enlivened—as if I am diving into a pool of cool water on a sweltering day.

"I did it!" I scream. I found the part within myself that made me believe I loved that creep. I went up against one of Hollywood's best, took a tiny scene, and avalanched everyone with it! Even the curmudgeonly director applauded. My dreams are coming true, all because I was able to gain inspiration brought about by a fan who took a moment to remind me to have faith in my dreams.

I have fans! How long has it been since I thought about that? I've been so wrapped up in day-to-day life I've lost sight of the fact I am already living the dream.

A combination of excitement and exhaustion makes it difficult to type on my phone, but I'm eager to share the good news with those who want to hear it. *"Had a great day on set! Thank you all for the inspiration. I couldn't do this without you."*

But how I share my excitement is bitter sweet. I prepared for this performance with the help of a man who only exist in my mind and heart. He is the one I want to tell because without him, I never could have pulled that scene off.

I tuck a pillow into my arms while daydreaming I'm resting my head on the chest of someone special. With him I share the heaven in my soul. "I didn't realize it until now, but my dream is coming true. I've been so caught up in work I've forgotten to appreciate the little things. You know, sometimes I wonder …"

Brandon

"... sometimes I wonder how I let myself get this way. I don't want to be like this anymore. From now on, I will change that."

Katherine's voice nudges me awake. At first I feel a light ache in my chest as if I have strained a muscle. Then pressure builds. My eyes creep down while not knowing if what I feel is a heart attack, a cat I don't own, or something unimaginable—yet nothing is there. The hair on my body begins to prickle as I come to understand the sensation of a head pressing down on my chest and a warm body curling next to me.

"Do you remember to get excited about little things?"

Though I'm starting to find acceptance in hearing it, every time that beautiful voice comes into my head I can't help but flinch and gasp. Katherine may not be a ghost, yet she is haunting me nonetheless. If she can do this while alive, how is it Amber has never done it while dead? Am I sure this isn't Amber?

I try to force myself to relax and come to peace with the presence I feel. Not only does the timbre of the voice tell me this is not Amber, so does the tone of the energy.

"I miss embracing life. Has life turned out to be all you want it to be? Are you happy and healthy? Are you with someone?"

I bring myself into the beauty of the moment, curl to my right and imagine her head is tucked under my chin. *"No, Katherine, I'm alone and missing someone I've never met. Can you hear me, too? I ask it all the time, yet I never get an answer."*

"I'm always afraid to ask about you because it implies I believe you are real. If you are, you may be happily married and I am out of luck. I hate that I can't live a life of fantasy without the pain of reality being apparent. Does the pain of reality cross into the beauty of your dreams too?"

"All the time."

"My mother often says because she always thinks of me, I should know I am loved. I feel her love all the time. Do you feel mine?"

Her voice drifts off, and I sense the peace of slumber. I wish I could join her in that bliss, but this conversation has me wide-awake. There must be a way to get through to her. If

I could respond …

Maybe I can.

I turn on my phone and a Facebook notification tells me about the great day Katherine had. It's late, so there aren't many comments yet. Perfect.

I wish her good night with words that I hope resound. *"I'm so glad your day was wonderful. Mine was but only because the pain of my reality was erased by the beauty of my dreams."*

Rat Trap

Katherine

The five AM sounding of my alarm clock has me again wondering why I have chosen to work in a profession that doesn't allow me to sleep in, even on Sundays, yet insists I always look well rested.

As I contemplate the day, the song that again infiltrated my dreams slips into my head.

"The road to success is dark, but flames of my desire will light the path."

I swear I know this from somewhere. Weird.

Weirder still, why did I think the voice singing it was mine? My voice sucks.

Getting up sounds as if it is the worst idea mankind has ever had. Since my cell phone is in reach I delay the inevitable by checking Facebook. My last post is still showing, and before I can close it, my eyes lock on one of the comments. *"I'm so glad your day was wonderful. Mine was but only because the pain of my reality was erased by the beauty of my dreams."*

Hey, I've seen this profile picture before. What is it with things sounding weird to me? Like, that sounds so familiar it's creepy.

My thoughts break as a call comes through. Jason's name popping up makes my muscles twitch. I can't avoid him forever.

My hi gets cut off by his enthusiasm. "Guess who's boarding a flight bound for LA! Your assistant told me you are scheduled to wrap early today, so be prepared to be wined and dined."

Oh God, seriously? He can't be blind to how bad things are. "Wow, this is quite the surprise." I sounded surprisingly polite. My acting coach would be impressed at how well I pulled that one off.

"Fantastic! I'll swing by your hotel around six. See you then."

Brandon

Since there is no way I will ever get into whatever studio she is filming at, my only hope for running into Katherine is to put myself in places where she would go. Intuition has always told me she loves the beach. How beautiful would it be to see her in the light of the sun as it is reflected off of the water on a perfect Sunday evening?

Still, I can't escape the ghost of my past—a past that my body didn't experience but my soul did. Finding reality in my association with Katherine means accepting the full picture.

Waves crash onto a cluster of boulders before me. The sheen the water leaves behind reminds me of the steel of a gun. As much as I feel the urge to race past the rocks, I'm drawn in as if it is a spectacle of horror—a train wreck I can't turn a blind eye to. The guilt I carry may not belong to Brandon Wayne, but it belongs to his soul.

Another wave hits the rocks, bringing back the sheen that tears at my heart. Memories of the past life regression surface, and Johnny's pain slips into my soul. I'm quick to divert my eyes and start to take off with my head low, yet a pebble catches my attention. Unlike the smooth rocks around it that have taken a beating by the waves, this one is jagged. It appears to be a lava rock, yet it is surprisingly heavy for its size. It reminds me of the burden I bear—dark, jagged, and weighty. I slip it into my pants pocket and continue on my way.

The sun begins its journey behind the waves, and the air turns chilly. I tighten my jacket around me, blocking the wind that nudges me back. Like a rainbow chaser, I look at my screen shot of the online conversation Katherine and I had yesterday. Even if all this was to end now, and I never heard from her again, this experience would still be nothing short of astounding.

Waves roll in, barely missing my boots. Suddenly, my chest is shocked into quivering, and my body freezes at the warning. There is no mistaking that was a chill of impending danger—not to me, but to someone I love.

The sensation hits again. This time it comes from behind, nudging me. Enough holding back. I've been given the gift of sensing her for a reason, and intuition is screaming something is wrong.

I'm headed down Highway One in a flash. The chill pays me another visit, and I jump off the highway, dropping me in Santa Monica and sending me winding through streets. Pressure forms in my head and is accompanied by the emotional crumbling of my chest. What could possibly be happening to Katherine?

The pressure continues to build, making me nearly dizzy. When it begins to ease, I know I have driven too far.

I pop an illegal U-Turn and speed back to where I felt the sickest, get out of my car, and start running. My ears fill with the sound of my heart valves popping open and then closing. The intensity grows until I find myself in front of a restaurant so exclusive that drivers wait in parked cars and reservations are checked before you can get in the door. Shoot, even the paparazzi have taken up residence in front of this place.

Is she here? Is what I am feeling simply a signal to bring me here for an appointment with destiny? My heart races with the hope of seeing her, yet it feels so broken that I fear for her. What could happen that would be so bad, especially in such an elegant place?

Cheers come from inside—loud cheers reminding me of a sports bar when the home team has scored. I step to the window in hopes of seeing what the commotion is about, but standing people and flashing lights block the spectacle. An older couple dashes out, laughing. "I can't believe we saw that," the woman says.

The man wraps his arm around her and smiles. "You and your star lust."

"You have to admit the look on her face was priceless. And the size of that rock! I didn't realize he made *that* much money."

"It's obscene how many so-called stars rake in the cash— even bottom feeders like Jason Day."

Oh, no.

No way! There is no possible way this is as it seems. She's mine. I'm hers. It's always been that way. At some point we made a vow for eternity. I know we did. God brought us together, and Jason Day is not allowed to mess with that!

I try to keep my cool while tailing the couple close enough to eavesdrop but not for them to fear I am about to mug them. They need to tell me I've got the story wrong.

"The tabloids should be buzzing tomorrow," the woman adds.

"Yeah, we are going to be more inundated with Kason jokes than ever. I already want the divorce over with."

The sucker punch to the gut causes the world around me to slow; yet the flashes from behind make my head spin. In the cracks between the paparazzi I catch a glimpse of Katherine's fluttering hair as she and Jason duck into a waiting car. The boldness of his grin eats at my soul.

I've lost her, and I never even got the chance to show her the light she puts into my eyes.

Come back, Katherine. Step out of that car and look at me. See the love I have for you. How can it ache so much if my love for you isn't true?

For the second time in my life, my heart slips out of my body and splatters on the pavement for passersby to walk on. My hands scrape across my face—my fingers digging into my hair and squeezing. I surrender to the pain and slip my hands into my pockets, needing to turn and walk away. The rock I found on the beach scrapes across my skin, reminding me no matter how bizarre the craziness is, the pain in my heart is very real. We were just finding each other again. What about all those dreams we once had?

God, Katherine, how do I get through the rest of my life knowing what I do? How do I face a lifetime of understanding it may take us both dying to be together again? Even if I find someone, how can I give her the unbridled love she deserves while you are still out there?

Bitter reality has invaded my dreams. Yet again, my hopes, my fantasies—everything my heart holds dear—have all been shattered by the hand of another.

Ten minutes ago …

Katherine

Soft music seeps through the air, serenading me while I wait for Jason to arrive. Instead of him picking me up as planned, he sent a driver who politely suggested I wear something a little more suited for this place. Foolish me, who has learned to never travel to this town unprepared, played along. Sometimes I am far too accommodating.

Given these surroundings, Jason probably has romantic intentions. I have contradictory plans. He'll sit, I'll say it is over, drama will unfold, I'll catch a cab back to the hotel, and then I'll order food from room service. Perfect.

A waiter stops at my table with his tray high in the air. "Compliments of Mr. Day," he says. My heart damn near stops before the champagne glass can even hit the table. Holy crap, the rock in that glass is huge! Jason could have ended world hunger with the money he forked over for that.

Suddenly, he is right next to me, down on one knee and—

Why are those photographers kneeling behind him? Jason's lips move, and the words I don't want to hear go unnoticed.

The world starts spinning faster as a flash blinds me, and the patrons go crazy. In a flash, Jason has his hand behind my neck and is kissing me. I'm even more flabbergasted when he downs my champagne so he can slip the ring on my finger.

Flashes continue to attack from all angles, and the music turns louder. My champagne glass gets refilled, and a platter of oysters arrives. Is this even happening?

Jason settles into his seat, and answers a question thrown at him from a man with a camera. Has he already forgotten I am here?

I am here, right? This is surreal.

I used to dream of all the sweet ways Jason could ask me to marry him—soft music, candle light, and champagne were all on the list—but never once were photographers. I know they are everywhere around here—in people's driveways, outside of studios—hell, you can even find them at bus stops. Regardless, he had to have planned this to the letter for so many of them to magically be here at this very moment.

I can't even pretend to be a part of this. I don't want it, not to mention I haven't given an answer.

I pop up to leave. Before I can get a single step in, Jason has his lips on mine—forcefully. He's not giving me a prayer of pushing him away without making a scene, which he knows I won't do. I was raised better than that. I thought he was raised better than all this, too.

I smile sweetly and say just loudly enough for the people around us to hear, "I think we need to do some private celebrating."

My words seem to remind Jason I am standing next to him and pull him into the moment. A smile breaks across his face—a genuine one that is far warmer than he could ever stage. Jason takes my hand, and we try to break through the crowd of photographers. Another camera gets in my face. "Miss Miller, when is the wedding?" the guy yells toward me.

I should tell him I haven't given an answer, and when I do, it will be no. I should get in Jason's face here and now, but I don't want a bigger scene than there already is.

Once we get outside, another paparazzo asks about the wedding. Jason puts on a canary-eating grin. "Sooner than anyone realizes, but we can't give you details because we've got to do these things under the radar." He winks. "You know how it is with celebrities."

Celebrities? At best we are on the B-list. I can't believe anybody gives a crap about us, let alone cares when the wedding is, let alone would crash it. This guy is ridiculous! Why didn't I dump him sooner?

The second we're shut inside the car, I yell, "No!"

"No what?"

"No way in hell are we getting married! I love how you are acting as if I've said yes, yet I haven't been able to get a word in edgewise!" His brows knot, and his mouth slips open just enough to show me his I-don't-get-it look may have some truth behind it.

Jason tries to slip his arm around me and gets all touchy-feely. Those arms remind me of worms. "Katherine, honey, I am certain—"

"Don't touch me!" I cross my arms to send the message that even the air around me is off-limits. Great! This is all going to hit the papers tomorrow. When I make them retract it, *if* they retract it, everyone will say it was staged for publicity. With the way he played this, it must have been.

These are Jason's true colors. He manipulated me into thinking we would have kids together. Now he knows I am about to dump him, so he proposes with cameras everywhere, all to get me where he wants me. No deal!

At the last stoplight before we hit the freeway, I slip out of the car, storm into the nearest bar, and down a shot of tequila while waiting for a cab. I then head to the closest beach and make the poor driver wait for over an hour while I walk. There must be some kind of magic here, because for as angry as I am, the sensation of love in the air brings me inner peace.

Second Hand News

Brandon

Cars.

Miles and miles of cars are parked on the freeway, and I'm stuck—both here and in life.

Driving is supposed to bring a sense of freedom. I'll never forget the feeling of jumping behind the wheel and taking off by myself for the first time—windows down, music blaring, wind whipping through my hair, gunning the gas as I hit the freeway, and letting out a rebel yell that declared I had spread my wings.

If cars mean freedom, why am I parked in one while struggling to get to work? I should be flying down the road while scream-singing out the pain of losing a battle I never should have been fighting. I've been dumped, and I never got the pleasure of meeting the woman who yanked out my heart and used my blood as paint in what should be my padded cell. Only a special kind of loser can feel an imaginary lover has given him the slip.

I manage to pull a few feet forward before stopping again. Visions of Katherine and Jason standing in front of a preacher while surrounded by wedding guests have been an unshakable image since I saw her get into that car last night.

Katherine, you can't do this. I'm out here waiting, hoping, and praying for a way to find you. I've heard your prayers, and I know this isn't what you want. How could you do this to yourself? How could you do this to me? To us? To all we have been?

My eyes burn, and I swallow back the pain of losing the woman I love. As irrational as it is, I can't escape the sorrow ripping through me.

I move the car up a little more, only to get stuck again. I hate LA traffic. I came here to take an average job at a sub-par candy company because someone promised to help me fulfill my dreams of spending time with my family—if and when I have one. Because of that, the job I seem to be so dysfunctional at gave me hope. Now I am not so sure hope is worth the stress of people honking at me to move when I am as stuck as they are.

The chugging sound of Lindsey Buckingham's guitar introduces Fleetwood Mac's "Second Hand News". Great, now the real Stevie Nicks is reminding me how I feel abandoned by Katherine for some hot stud with bigger muscles and better bone structure. Hearing this is akin to getting a double-fisted punch in the gut.

I can't think about this anymore!

Frank Sinatra's version of "Anything Goes" overlays Lindsey's guitar, and I'm grateful for the call from Dale. "Hey, how's Chicago?" I ask. "Wait, you are in Chicago now, right?" I don't get how he can live this way.

"My hair looks like I've been through a wind tunnel."

I snicker. "Something tells me that with all the success you have been having, you can afford better styling gel. Are you still living the life of a king?"

"More like a god. I swear, if I break the lead on my pencil, someone yoinks it out of my hands and replaces it with a fresh one before I can process what happened. How's California life?"

"Stalled out."

"Get anywhere on that gumdrop campaign yet?"

"Oh man," comes out of me with a groan. I am so behind on that damn thing. "Why did you have to ask about it?"

Prolonged silence follows. I'm about to ask Dale if I have lost him when he says, "So, um, is it as warm and perfect there as it always is?"

This conversation is weird, especially considering I am having it with Dale. "Hey, you okay?"

He's quick to answer—as if he was caught red handed.

"Yeah, why do you ask?"

"Since when do you call me for small talk?"

Again I get a moment of silence. "You got me. A few days ago, you didn't seem to be doing so well. You okay?"

It's nice of him yet out of character. Doesn't this break the guy code of not talking about our feelings? This whole situation must have me further gone than I ever realized. I hate to lie, but I manage to sigh out a "Yeah, I'm good. You?"

"Yeah. Hey, hold on a second." Mumbling comes through on Dale's end—normal mumbling. I swallow back the sick feeling at the reminder of being on the phone with him and seeing Katherine for the first time. However, all I hear now is my radio where Rainbow screams "Since You've Been Gone" in my ears. The universe seems to have pulled out the classic rock hit parade for assistance in ripping my chest open and rubbing salt in my wounds. I'm quick to flip the station to something with random babbling. Finally, I am able to speed up and catch my exit only to slam on the brakes. Dale comes back on the phone. "Hey, sorry. Duty calls."

"Yeah, no problem. I'll catch you later."

I'm ready to hang up when Dale chimes in again. "You know how to find me, okay?"

A wave of emotion flows over me, and I start to tear. It is twisted and wrong that I'm in such a state my friends are worried about me. How can losing someone you have never met be so gut wrenching? "Thanks, man," I tell him. I hang up and stare at the red light—waiting and feeling useless. Habitually, I swipe up my phone again to check Facebook.

Dammit! I'm a freaking addict who needs rehab.

The guy behind me honks. I jump to move forward, and then slam on the brake when I see the guy in front isn't moving. LA sucks!

The deejay continues to babble about God knows what. In hopes of salvation, I flip back to the classic rock station and get washed over by The Moody Blues. Seriously? Of the hundreds of songs in their catalog, why does this deejay have to play "Voices In the Sky"?

Again the guy behind me honks while I can't do squat.

That's it. I'm done! I don't care that it's Monday. I'm turning around, calling out sick, heading off to Chicago for a few days, and forgetting about all the crap here. I'm also taking my passport in case I decide to run away for good. Before I go, I'm destroying all reminders of Katherine; website bookmarks, Jennifer's cheese (both the moldy one and the one that is starting to look a little weathered), along with the peanut butter I have only because I heard it is her favorite. When I return, *if* I return, voices or not, I'll be a fresh man—as if this whole episode never happened.

Katherine

"Yes," I say over the phone to one of our producers, "of course I understand where Jason is coming from, but that doesn't mean I have to appreciate it."

"I'm not telling you to say yes," the guy says, "I'm only asking you to think about it a little more before everything blows up."

Before everything blows up? I can't imagine things getting much worse. I also can't understand why the producers would care. Jason is leaving, so an engagement followed by an epic breakup would whip the media into a frenzy. Why would he complain unless …

I know I should be angry, yet my heart dips in disappointment. "Let me guess, Jason has not stated, but has implied, that if things magically work out between the two of us, he might hang on in a guest star capacity. Am I right?"

His pause is prolonged. Eventually he says, "Look, all we are saying is it already looks bad enough that Jason is leaving. The engagement is fine, but now there are rumors circulating around here, and the whole thing looks like a bad publicity stunt. The producers want you to be happy. Before you make any decisions public, please let us know what to expect."

I guess Mom and Dad raised me right, because despite how angry I am regarding the situation, my words come out respectfully. "You can expect Jason and I are not getting married, not now, not ever. Thank you, and have a nice day."

I set down the phone, and tears begin to well. As much as I am sick of this mess, I am sicker over what has happened to Jason and I.

Only a moment passes before it rings again. I'm so beside myself it takes a second to realize it is Bailey's ringtone and answer. "Please tell me you have not heard the news already. I'm sure you have figured out it is not true." My God, my voice makes me sound broken. I may be pissed at the fallout, but what happened with Jason has left me lost.

Bailey's words come out with hesitation. "I don't know how to say this, but I was just watching TMZ and—"

"Shit!"

"I'm sorry to be the bearer of bad news." Her pause makes me feel I need to brace myself for what is about to follow. "The buzz is all over work, too. No one can set foot outside of the studio without getting badgered with questions."

I sigh. "Well, you have Carlouse, and I have Jerkson. I've spent the entire night trying to fix this insanity, but no, they're running the story as if I said yes. The photo was perfectly timed to catch my shock. It's easy to think my next expression would be one of happiness."

"I kind of figured something was wrong. I hate to tell you it looks pretty convincing."

"The further I step back, the more I see how expertly planned this was. I can't help but wonder if this is partially my fault. I should have accepted our needing to split sooner. Even telling him over the phone would have been more humane than making him wait."

Bailey's voice turns exasperated, and I feel she is not only defending me but also herself. "No, you were trying to do the right thing. Unfortunately, that often bites us in the ass. I swear, these guys think all they need to do is show us a little attention and we will bend over backwards to lick their scrotums."

I chuckle. Good, if we can't find at least a speck of humor in all of this, we are doomed. "Do you know Jason has already gone so far as to have one of the *Vampires Undercover* producers call me? You should have heard him hem and haw his way through telling me what a great idea it was to marry Jason. Can you even believe Jason would ask him to stoop that low?"

"Not in the least. The guy probably only made the call in hopes Jason would renew his contract. Seriously, what the hell is Jason thinking?"

"I've been asking myself that all damn night." Man, what did I ever see in him in the first place? Bailey is probably asking herself the same question about Carlos. "Are things going as planned with your great escape?"

"Yep. I'm the hell out of here. I've had it with this madness."

"I can relate." I catch a glimpse of the TV and wish I didn't. I can't believe they are running this damn story again. Who could possibly care?

"Yeah, we all know Katherine Miller is a force to be reckoned with as well."

If I were that powerful, I'd be able to stop all the madness around me. "Nah. It's a facade brought on by all of the thrash and," I fake a sneeze while saying, "poser metal you catch me blasting in my trailer."

"Poser metal? You mean, the stuff you always leave out mentioning when asked what kind of music you listen to? Why do they call it that? It sounds so derogatory."

I shrug while wishing the image of Jason's proposal that is forever etched in my mind would go away. "People are weird about what they label and how they do it. It's just the pop side of metal. The only reason I don't mention it is because most people would label me as a throwback. In my line of work, you can't afford labels."

"Yeah, you keep telling yourself that."

I toss my hands up and laugh, grateful that Bailey is putting my mind elsewhere. "Okay, people make fun of it and it pisses me off. It's easier to stay quiet than get defensive."

"You need to own it. I've got to get going. Are you sure you are okay?"

"Yes, but when Jason returns, if he says even the tiniest thing to imply he and I are together, kick him in the nads!" It's more of a request than the passive suggestion I make it sound like. "And for the love of God, if he tries to talk you into siding with him and talking to me—"

"Again, I hate to tell you he has already tried. When I see him, I'm going for his nads just on principle. I'll also tell him if he is even half a man, he will let you keep the ring for all of the trouble he has put you through. That rock looks as if it is about the size of your head."

"Oh dear God, Bailey, it's fricken' mammoth! He played every card he could to get me to say yes."

"Which goes to prove we are the strong ones. Go finish knocking 'em dead and hurry home for my last day. I want to hear it went so well that you are planning your Oscar acceptance speech."

"You're on!"

Watching Bailey's name fade as the call ends puts a different kind of hurt in my heart. I won't let her become a lost friend. I need more people like her in my life—people who try to do the right thing, yet are determined not to be doormats.

I want to believe Jason's proposal was genuine, but how can I when a circus is erupting around me? Even if it was, between his deceit with not telling me about his infertility, and now not helping me correct the lies the media is reporting, let alone having people call to sway me, Jason has left me no choice but to take action as well.

The words, *"I am NOT engaged!"* begin my long-winded Facebook rant. He's got every bit of every nasty word I type coming. Getting out my annoyance is cathartic. There is no doubt in my mind that telling him he is a useless wad is the therapy I need. However, when it comes time to hit the send button, I freeze.

This isn't how I believe in acting towards anyone. Calling out Jason only further blackens our situation. This post doesn't set the record straight; it's grandstanding. It's deepening the whole we are in while tossing the dirt I am shoveling back on top of us. Besides, I've never been fond of airing dirty laundry, and I see no reason to lower myself now.

I change my post to reflect a much simpler version of the truth. *"Thank you all for your well wishes. However, the press has it wrong. Jason and I are moving forward in different directions. I wish him the absolute best."*

I should have dumped him sooner, but I was only protecting his heart. It is possible he was trying to hold on to what we had, but how he handled it erased all of my fond memories of us and replaced them with pain. We shared so much that my heart is broken over the fact I'll never be in love with him again. I can't help but feel somehow, if we stay together, we will only destroy each other's dreams.

Brandon

The wheels of my flight hit the ground in Chicago, and I'm quick to turn on my phone to call Dale. I will force myself to choke down dinner and relax with a couple of drinks. I'm also eager for serious guy talk—which means shooting the shit about nothing of emotional importance.

Texts and voicemail notifications flood in, causing my phone to flicker like a disco ball. Is everything at work going to hell so badly that Darla is trying to track me down? Screw it. My boss was more than cool with me needing time off, so work can wait.

With my carry-on in hand I head out to hail a cab. Again my phone chimes.

Fine, Darla! I'll look at your freaking text.

"Seriously, Brandon. All of this weirdness with you has me worried.

Call me, or I am calling the cops!"

Geez, I can't deal with this now.

I slip the phone into my pocket only for it to chime again. *"Thanks for the roses! How did you know pink ones are my favorite?"*

What the hell? I didn't send her flowers.

My heart jumps when the obvious hits. No, she didn't say flowers; she said *pink roses*.

The second Darla answers the phone, "What pink roses? I didn't send those," blurts out of me.

"Well, duh."

"Why did you say that?"

"Because I was running out of ways to get your attention."

"So you randomly thanked me for flowers I didn't send?"

"Pretty much."

My life is a freak show.

Suddenly, Darla accosts me. "Brandon Wayne," God, she reminds me of my mother, "I know you are a rational person, but lately you have been hearing voices. I've caught you zoning out at work and at the bar in front of the TV *numerous* times. I haven't seen you eat anything other than toxic gumdrops in weeks. You look like you don't sleep for more than an hour a night, and now you are flying out of town again. If I acted that way, I hope you would also turn into a giant pain in the ass and make sure I was okay."

My heart feels a little lighter. It's nice to have someone concerned for me, especially when I am already pretty concerned about myself. Darla is right. I am not coming off as sane lately. "Thank you. I *am* okay but just barely. I called out because I need to put me first. I promise that, if I am not doing better in a few days, I will get professional help—and not a psychic. Now, I could use some good news. Tell me about your sister. Did she make it in yet?"

"No. She was supposed to start today, but work made her an offer she could not refuse. They need her on set tomorrow to match some complicated makeup from last season. After that, she's on the next flight out."

"Makeup? Bailey's a makeup artist?"

"Yeah," Darla sounds as if I am dragging something out of her, "for that God-awful TV show you love."

"Me?" I don't watch much TV. The only thing I have seen recently is—

She has got to be kidding! I try to hide my excitement. "Bailey works on *Vampires Undercover?*" Crap, my voice cracked.

"Yes," she says with a groan.

In one of my early visions, Katherine was in front of a makeup table. Now I get why the woman with her looked so familiar. Change Darla's green eyes to brown, give her normal hair, and you have Bailey.

"I am sure you can understand why I don't tell anyone my sister gets to spend her days running her fingers all over Jason Day and that other smoking hot guy whose name I can never remember. They are waiting for Katherine Miller to get back from LA stupid-late tonight so Bailey can finish up tomorrow. Thank God. I can't wait for this drama with Carlos to be over. Bailey also can't wait to escape the drama of Katherine and Jason's bogus engagement."

The tingle of adrenaline races through my body. "Bogus?" I ask, with my voice cracking in hope. "Did you say bogus?"

Darla moans. "Yes, I swear, these actors and their drama. I tuned out half of the story, but apparently Jason set up the proposal so Katherine could not say no even though he knew she was about to dump him. Pretty damn ballsy, especially since he is now saying, 'we need a chance to think things over' as an excuse not to talk to her about the mess he has made."

That explains why I felt so bad before I even got the news. Katherine didn't want that proposal. I can't race Darla off of the phone fast enough. Right when I thought the game had ended the universe tosses me a message like this? There is no way this is a coincidence.

I search for all Toronto-bound flights out of Los Angeles leaving late today. If she flies direct, there are only two options—one of which is with United. When I sensed her in the airport, it was in the United terminal. That has to be the right one.

If I can catch a flight within the next six hours, I'll be there when she lands. Our paths will cross, and this time it won't be in mid-air.

I pull the rock out of my pocket—the one I found at the beach that I have come to think of as an extension of both Johnny and myself. "Come on, buddy. We've got a girl to get back."

Our Love Will Last Forever

Brandon

With each tick of my watch, my heart seems to race faster. Even if I have all of the details right, this is going to be a close call. In the event Katherine's flight got in early, I'm screwed.

The second my flight is down, I am up, grabbing my carry-on bag, and shoving my way through the passengers as they flood the isle. "Sorry," I holler, "my wife's having a baby, and I'm about to miss it." Most people step aside and offer congratulations while others give me death glares. Why didn't I think to fly first class so I could be ahead of everybody else and not have to be an asshole?

My feet sprint across the tile as I head towards the baggage claim, all the while keeping my eyes peeled in case she is still in the terminal. At least arriving at an ungodly hour gives me the advantage of running through a near-vacant airport. When I reach the escalator, my body starts going haywire, much like it did the last time I was at this airport right after she was here. Although I only have one guy to pass, I again play the wife-in-labor card, lift my bag over my head, and race down. Someday karma is going to bite me in the ass for this.

Finally, I reach the baggage claim for her flight.

Empty. Not a single bag awaits anyone. Son of a—

A cab! She needs a cab! If that fails, I'll head toward long-term parking. It's a hell of a long shot, but at this point I have to keep running. Worst-case scenario, I will call Darla, tell her I wound up in Toronto, and offer to help Bailey move.

Yeah, how the hell am I going to explain that I happen to be on the other side of the continent? Darla will have me locked up, which is all the more reason why I have to find Katherine now.

The line of cabs is a mile long. Why are there so many this late at night? If she needed a ride, she's gone. Long-term parking is my only hope.

Pressure begins to build in my head. At first I think it is the stress of the moment and start to sprint off. Then the sound of my heart valves *pops* in my ears, and I halt. She's here! Katherine has to be near.

I spin, slowly panning the area to catch sight of the woman who is affecting my senses. A few feet away stands a lady with her head hung low while reading something on her phone. Her hair is up in a scarf, and despite the fact it is night, she's wearing sunglasses. That has to be her.

She steps up to the curb, and the cabbie gets out.

Katherine

I brave turning on my phone for the first time since I left the hotel in LA. My Facebook post about Jason and I going our separate ways has gone viral. While the rumor mill continues to churn, now that I have stated my side I feel peace is deserved.

As soon as it finishes booting, my phone enlivens with notifications of missed calls and texts, including one from Jason. The last I heard from him was yesterday—the day after his proposal—when he finally sent me a text in response to my messages asking him to call off the reporters. All he said was, *"I think we need a chance to think things over."*

Thinking things over should have meant giving me time, not making me battle reporters, let alone have to deal with the people he tried to get to speak on his behalf. Did he have to bug poor Bailey? She has enough problems of her own with moving this week.

I take a look at the phone and absorb the words he sent before my flight took off, *"I know seeing each other tomorrow will be rough, but I am certain you and I will make the best of this. We always do."*

Yes, Jason, we have always made the best of everything, and in some ways that is the problem. Sometimes making the best of something is more making do than it is growing together. I can't see making do by saying yes even though that is clearly what you think is best.

Another text chimes in. The timestamp on this one shows it was sent about an hour after my flight took off. *"Don't worry. What I have waiting for you will make you feel much better. See you soon."* Does the guy not let up? Times such as this make me wonder how I ever loved him. Thing is, I did, and in many ways always will.

"Where to, lady?" the driver asks. I give him the address of the studio and start to slip into the back.

Footsteps race up, and I freeze. Jason did say he has something to make me feel better, so I've sort of been expecting him to ambush me. Then again, he probably wouldn't risk making another scene. Or would he? I just don't know anymore.

"Hi," a man's voice says. "That's near the Excelsior, right? Would you mind splitting the fare?"

I'm so relieved it isn't Jason, or someone we know, again trying to talk me out of saying no, that, "Sure," slips out. As long as the ride is peaceful, maybe company will keep my stress at bay. Heaven only knows what questions I will face at work.

The man gets in yet minds his distance. There is a touch of nervousness in his eyes. It is contradictory to what I would expect based on his studded, leather jacket. While it and his combat boots show he has the fashion sense of a modern-day punk, his pressed, white dress shirt and jeans that look well-loved yet neat and perfectly clean, pique my fascination. I remove my sunglasses for a better look.

"Where did you say you were going?" the driver asks him.

"The Excelsior, but please take care of the lady first." He looks to me with a gentlemanly smile. Given the recent circus my life has been his politeness is deeply appreciated.

The driver pulls out, and the man looks to the road as if trying not to stare at me. Could it be he recognizes me even though I am without my signature makeup and colored contacts? If so, this will only be the second time that has happened.

The way the streetlights hit him showoff the gentleness of his features, yet there is a slight ruggedness about him. Actually, it's more of an edge. His kind demeanor seems genuine, yet it doesn't scream pushover. I'm intrigued.

He turns and offers his hand. "Hi, I'm Brandon."

There is a sweetness about him that nearly forces me to smile. "Katherine," I say, reaching for his hand. At the touch, a zap races through my fingers and up into my heart, softening the stress of the last few days. I've had guys sweep me off my feet with their looks and woo me with their charm, but never has one brought me such instant comfort.

He seems to search for words. "Are you here on business?"

"Sort of. I live here because I work here." Something about him seems familiar. Do I know him?

"Oh, where are you from?"

After two days of choosing my words carefully to anyone who will listen, basic small talk with a nice stranger is comforting. "Seattle, originally. You?"

"Detroit, but I live in Los Angeles now."

I nod. "I lived in LA for a while. Part of me really misses it, another part is thankful I'm not there anymore. There's a lot of pressure in that town." Shoot, in this business there is always a lot of pressure, even when life is going well. Hardly a day goes by I am not stressed to the gills.

He blows out some air as if he feels my pain. "Yeah, no kidding." Maybe he is an industry person. He seems so darn familiar. I'm pretty sure that if I had seen him before, I would remember him, but his features are not what is grabbing me, it's … him. Gosh, this is weird.

My cell phone chimes, and the fear of who it could be brings pressure to my head. Please, don't let it be more Jason drama. Let it be news that the shoot is pushed back a few hours. I would not exactly mind a nap.

On second thought, a cup of coffee with a nice stranger

sounds even better.

My stress races back the second I get a look at the screen.

"By now you should have been greeted by my messenger. What do you say? Can we talk about this?"

His *messenger*? My shoulders drop in exasperation. I'm such a fool. This Brandon guy must be some hack Jason hired to butter me up for the big sell. No wonder why he came dashing up as I was getting in the cab, even though there were other cabs around and thus no need to share mine. And no wonder why he is nervous; he has a job to pull off. Hell, his nerves could have gotten rattled because he didn't recognize me right away and thought he screwed up. Before I gave him my name, he was probably worried that he got into the wrong car.

I have to hand it to Jason. He managed to make me a captive audience. He blew it by exposing his hand though. If I wasn't so damn tired of this crap, I'd ignore the text and see where he intends this to go. Instead, I have zero interest in whatever message this guy has. In fact, the more I look at him, the more the pressure in my head builds and my blood starts to boil.

"Really?" I ask indignantly while staring straight at Brandon. "*You're* the messenger? Why did Jason think you were the one to send?" He looks like his brain is sputtering. I thrust the phone into his face and show him the text. "I've seen Jason manipulate people before, but who are you?"

The driver jumps in, "Lady, are you okay?"

I almost say I am fine so I can hear Brandon's excuse and find out what Jason's game is. However, after forcing myself to remain calm for the last two days despite all of the drama around me, I have reached my limit. "No! I am anything but okay!"

The driver pulls the car over and jumps out. A look of panic hits Brandon's face. It is pretty convincing. "You've got it all wrong," he says with his words racing out. "I'm a marketing guy for a candy company that makes terrible gumdrops. I don't even know Jason Day." The driver yanks the door open and starts pulling Brandon out, but he resists.

"Please, let me explain. No dream ever goes unheard."

What the hell is he talking about?

The driver pulls harder and finally gets the guy out. Still, he keeps sputtering gibberish. "Sometimes you have to remind yourself the pain of your reality can be erased by the beauty of your dreams."

Of all the crap Jason would have him pitch, what is this supposed to mean? "Even if Jason didn't send you, you are clearly crazy."

"We talked on Facebook!"

My eyes roll. How many times have I heard that song and dance? This guy is quite the piece of work. Either he is nuts or Jason had a contingency plan that if all went haywire, the guy was to act like a stalker and make me think Jason has nothing to do with this. Regardless, I'm done. "Go away!"

The driver slams the door and gives Brandon a death glare, yet Brandon leans down to the window and yells to me, "Wait! Bailey! We have a mutual friend! No, but sort of. I can explain!"

Oh, man! Not the Bailey card again. Wasn't Jason trying it once enough? This guy isn't even playing it well. He *sort of* knows her? Yeah, that's a great excuse for when she has no clue who I am talking about. I'm not even gonna tell her about this one. If I did, Jason would lose his balls, not that I would mind. Bailey has bigger problems than facing jail time.

The driver tosses Brandon his bag and screams something about repositioning his head to another part of his body, yet the guy won't give up. "Dammit, Saleena!"

The driver hits the gas so hard the tires squeal. "Don't worry, lady. I'll have you at the studio in a flash."

We speed down the road, and just being away from the guy causes my anger to quell. Regardless, I'm so stunned by the event I can barely think to text Jason back. *"How dare you play games with me! Who was that guy? You have finally managed to get me to flip from being distraught to pissed!"*

Jason has me totally blindsided and feeling I am missing the obvious. What is this game about?

My phone chimes. *"What guy?"*

Is he real? He is the one who started this by mentioning Brandon in the first place. *"Your little messenger!"*

The cab pulls up to the studio gates, and I tip the driver triple the fare for his trouble. The second I am out the door I begin stomping my way across the lot. My phone buzzes again.

"Umm … I think something may have gone wrong."

Oh, you bet it has.

A guy in a golf cart pulls up and offers me a ride to my trailer. I'm so agitated I want to lash out and bark no at him, but that is not me. Anger is counter productive to anything even remotely constructive. Right now, all it would do is hurt a nice man's feelings.

I thank him and hop in. As we ride, the cool air whips up my nostrils and helps me clear my head enough to further see I am not being myself. Something is bringing out the worst in me, and I won't allow it to hurt others.

I also have to question what has me so riled when I have held it together for so long. Two weeks ago I thought I was pregnant. I've since struggled with telling Jason, lost a baby, and got devastating news of Jason's deceit—all of which brought me to see what a disaster he and I were and got me longing for something better. Regardless, I held on even though I knew I shouldn't. Then he proposed and …

Tears well in my eyes, changing the reason for the burning in my cheeks from anger to hurt. Jason and I were once so in love. Everyone said we were a dream couple, and it seemed they were right. I miss the smiles we shared. When I really think about it, we were never perfect, but that doesn't mean I wasn't happy. I miss being happy.

Dammit, I want to believe his proposal was genuine. Any other time and any other way, I would have said yes in a heartbeat. Instead, the moment I dreamt of for so long was a circus. I haven't let myself think about anything other than the drama because the reality of facing Jason and I ended long ago will shatter me.

The nice man drops me off, and I hide my eyes while wishing him a good day. My tears blur the ground and obscure the stairs leading into my trailer. Opening the door makes me feel I am entering a void. I used to be so grateful for this job. Now I don't know that I want to be here anymore.

Flipping on the light brings another jab to my heart as I find a bouquet of flowers on my coffee table. For days I felt Jason has been trying to wear me down. As much as I need to be true to my resolve, a part of me is not so sure that caving is very far off. The pain of this situation is exasperating. Everything about it hurts. It also causes me to get drawn to the folded sheet of paper tucked into the bouquet that begs, *"Please read me."*

Footsteps race up my stairs. I look to the door and see Jason stop in the threshold. When our eyes meet, the redness in his tosses on another layer of heartache. Being disappointed in someone is one thing, but facing him is another, especially when all you see is pain in his eyes.

He looks to the flowers. Solemnly his words come out, "I guess they made it after all." I feel him fight the urge to talk about all the things we don't have time to now. "Please, read the note." He turns to leave. "I hope we can finish this at home after work."

Hearing his shoes as they slowly *thunk* down the steps reminds me that all we have been through in the last few days is nothing compared to the rest of our story. With trepidation, I begin reading.

"I've always been a dreamer. Somewhere along the line I forgot the dream I had in you was as important as all the other ones I hold so dear, and I lost sight of how much I love you."

Foolish as I feel for it, his words deepen the cracks in my breaking heart. It wasn't all that long ago Jason and I had something worth cherishing.

"I hear you, loud and clear. When we get home, let's settle this on the best terms possible. I love you, and I am so, so sorry things went the way they did. My heart may be broken, but neither of us can hurt any longer."

The truth hits—just because we are done doesn't mean it isn't going to hurt. I thought the drama Jason put me through erased my pain, but remembering how much we have loved each other and the experiences we have shared tells me I am wrong.

It's All Over Now, Baby Blue

Katherine

The distress brought on by a few days of problems hardly overshadows the pain of breaking up with someone with whom I have shared so much. It's not a question of if I love Jason, but more a matter of accepting how we fell from grace.

Jason's key slips into the lock on our front door. When he enters, "Hey," said with downcast eyes tells me he is resigned to whatever salt I am about to pour in his wounds. The Jason I know would be hopeful of reconciliation. But this guy here … He's hurting and is as done with this relationship as I am. Where did we go wrong?

My heart sours as it comes to accept more of the truth. "You were actually serious about the proposal, weren't you?"

Finally, I get eye contact—his red and burning ones to my sad ones—and I wish his eyes had stayed hidden. "Yes."

My hands flick out—a muted tossing them up in bewilderment. "How could you possibly think the way you did it was acceptable?"

How he looks lost over what to say has my body feeling weighted. Giving up isn't something Jason Day does lightly. "I did it for us," he utters. His sincerity stabs my heart. "For so long, you wanted to get married and start a family. I kept promising it would happen, yet every time we talked about it I found myself pushing the date back. When I leveled with you, I was forced to accept what I did wasn't some career-minded game like everything else I do. I hurt a person I love because I was selfish. I should have known better."

"And yet you expected me to say yes?"

He sighs and tosses his keys onto the stand by the door. "Yeah, power of positive thinking and all."

I don't get him. "Why were you suddenly so eager to get a

ring on my finger if it wasn't a stunt?"

Jason scrapes his hand across his face as if slipping from wallowing in sorrow into fighting back frustration. "Because I had to jump in or risk losing you. We both said so many times us getting married was a sure deal that I never expected a proposal to backfire. Besides, after all those years of me pushing back, taking advantage of the opportunity for some publicity seemed the only way to make it up to you."

"Me?" Is he kidding?

"Yes," he says with his tone growing firm, "it was the best of both worlds—move forward with the life we dreamed of while getting some attention. Remember, the plan to put our careers first was your idea."

"Oh, please! I never said that." This man needs to look in a mirror.

Jason's eyes go aflutter with disbelief. "Are you kidding? When we first got serious about our relationship, we set up a plan. You said you— Never mind."

"Never mind what?"

"You know," he states strongly, "and I don't think you want me to say it."

My hands fly out as I hope to grab understanding of what the hell he is talking about. "Know what?"

"Really, Katherine, who are you? You said you owed it to someone to have a successful career. Only then could you move on with your life. So yeah, when that wasn't happening, I pushed the date back, but you were the one who came up with the plan."

Whose idea it was isn't the issue. "Yes, but I had a time frame."

Jason steps toward me, and although his approach is physically non-threatening, emotionally I feel he is about to put me in my place. "No, *I* gave it a timeframe. When the goal didn't get met I extended it so you wouldn't freak out. There are three reasons behind everything I do. One, we have to strike while we are hot. Two, we don't want to be stuck in the shadow of this show for the rest of our lives. Three, you, as you often remind me, don't exactly have forever. When everything came to the surface about me, not only was I afraid you would bail, I was also afraid you would lose it over how far you still were from your goals. Since we planned to marry anyway, I tried to get some publicity in hopes of boosting your career. Face reality, Katherine. All that stuff I said a moment ago, when it sounded as if I were blaming myself, was me, again, sheltering you from who you are and the decision you made."

I stare straight at him yet miss all in my sight. In some distorted way, Jason thinks he has been protecting me and uses that as a reason to justify his deceit. What kind of depraved relationship do we have? Have I been dodging reality and don't see it, or is he cowering from his actions? "If you are looking out for me so much, not to mention the fear of my having a meltdown, why are you bailing on the show?"

He shakes his head at me and then sucks in his bottom lip and eyes the room. Whatever comes out next is going to be a doozy. "You've just proved my point by not stepping back and seeing the full picture again. Stop to think how my leaving puts you in the spotlight. The show's focus is on a love triangle in which my character provides the tension. Take away me and you have a boring love story. The logical thing is to kill that whole love element while strengthening the pivotal character—meaning you. Bam! I'm on the A-list, and you are now the true star of the show."

Why won't he admit quitting is what is best for him? "This isn't the same story you tried to sell me the other day."

"Do you really want to hear I am setting you up so the career boost you get is not the one you want?"

No, not at all, but much like how I know he was hedging his bets when he tried to work an angle with the producers, I also know in this business one person's loss is another's gain. That's just the way it works. Besides, I am convinced the show will tank when he leaves. His being a guest star could give us a saving boost.

"Right or wrong," he continues, "I did it for us." He hangs

his head and shakes it. "I really thought I was doing the right thing, which is why I tried to get Bailey to side with me. When I couldn't, I knew all hope was lost. I should have called the press then and there, but I couldn't bring myself to do it." He quickly adds in, "I swear Katherine, I absolutely swear I did not contact the producers. They called me when the story broke."

I want to believe him, and I would if it were not for one thing. "What about your messenger?"

He snickers, but there is no sign of amusement anywhere near him. "The flowers? I needed something to act on my behalf. I couldn't admit we were done to your face, so I had to find another way to let you know I backed off."

Backed off? The bouquet was the messenger? Oh no. "You didn't send someone?" Oh, that poor man in the cab. I don't think I'll ever get his expression of shock out of my mind. In my defense, kicking him out was probably for the best. Towards the end, he really was sounding a little off.

Jason looks oddly at me. "No, I put them in your trailer when I got in. From the sound of your text, I thought you were upset about it, so I came running as soon as I could get away." He now looks as if he fears he has offended me and races to plead his case. "I'm sorry if I did the wrong thing by going into your trailer, but it was bad enough I had to say those things in a note. I couldn't let someone else deliver it." Jason gives himself just enough of a moment to beef up his resolve. "Anyway, your messages made it clear you are done. After seeing the big picture, I am more than ready for that myself. I'm going to grab a few things and get out of here."

Maybe I am a fool, but now I truly believe Jason thought his reasons were legitimate. How could I ever think he would send someone into the cab like that? Jason knows when to play cards, and he may stack the deck, but he would never show his hand or intentionally do anything to hurt someone. The fact I would think he would stoop so low shows we have no business being together.

After clearing all the drama and sifting through mind

games, the truth of our situation sinks in. What hurts most about saying goodbye to the man I once thought I would spend my life with is that, in light of my revelations over what a mess we are, breaking up doesn't hurt much at all. "Take your time," I tell him while I head for the door.

I always knew I was driven, but I thought that between the two of us, Jason was the bulldozer. While I question the validity of much of what he has said, he is right; I'm just as bad.

I reach for the knob, and Jason's gentle touch to my arm finally conveys the deep understanding I have always longed for. "Hey, we are not bad people. We just have our priorities wrong."

Jason has made a lot of decisions involving me based on personal assumptions—so many that I can no longer venture to guess who is right. All I know is I don't like how Jason sees me, and if that is how I really am, I need to make changes. Our problems are a two way street. When you blend toxins, the effects of the fumes can sneak up on you. I don't want to be toxic any more.

We show solidarity in knowing it is time to move on—me by stepping out the door, him by closing it behind me, and both of us by quoting the words I posted on Facebook about our situation. "I wish you the very best."

Strength To Endure

Brandon

I don't get it. I still just don't get it.

Yesterday, everything came together, and I shared everyday small talk with Katherine while my heart fluttered all over the place. I watched my every move to make sure I didn't say anything stupid. Hell, I was even upset at myself for not having the foresight to polish my boots. Then, completely out of the blue, she thrust her phone in my face and got indignant, all while babbling about Jason.

I park my car in Endeara's lot, shut it off, and fall back into the seat. She had to have me confused with someone else. Regardless, I didn't help matters any. All I could think to do was spew out clues I hoped would resonate. Given her tone when she told me to go away, I'm surprised she didn't call me a freak. I can only begin to imagine what she would have called me if I told her I had been hearing her. Besides, that cabbie probably would have beaten the crap out of me.

Dammit, I just want to be happy again. I'm a nice guy with at least half a brain. I have a well-paying job, and I don't think I am the ugliest guy who ever existed. Even if I were, I only want to be the person who makes someone smile when life goes haywire. Tell me, God, how is that too much to ask?

I look up for answers and get the same silence I always do. Yet again, the insanity I have found myself in leaves me to fend alone. However, I am damn grateful that I haven't heard a peep out of Katherine. If I thought I was being driven crazy before …

But there was so much more to it. Every bit of madness, every visit to Jennifer, every time I looked at that damn cheese, brought me hope. Reality sucked, and if a fantasy was all I could have, I subconsciously embraced it. Although there was at least some truth behind my experience, I have no choice but to think of it as a dream, else I will forever know what I have lost. I'm not only saying goodbye to another person my heart longs for, I am burying the part of myself that created my perfect love.

I pull the rock I found at the beach out of my pocket and rub its jagged edges. My throat squeezes as I force myself to face it is time to reinvent part of me again. It is also time to walk through Endeara's doors and brave my inescapable reality as it slaps me in the face.

I don't let myself form another thought before bolting into work. Knowing what to expect only grants a small amount of comfort. Behind the reception desk sits a woman I have never met yet I once saw in a vision. If Darla hadn't told me that Bailey worked with Katherine, my mind would melt from the madness of her appearing before me.

Whatever. Katherine rolled her eyes at the mention of Bailey, telling me that I probably value Bailey more than she does based on her association to Darla.

I'm two steps into the lobby when Darla slips up from behind and links arms with me. "Welcome back!" she blurts out. She then whispers, "You okay?"

I lean in and whisper a lie, "Yes, I'm much better," and then look her dead in the eyes to tell her the truth. "Thank you for being concerned. I appreciate it."

Without letting myself think about it, I spin around and extend my jittery hand to Bailey. Even though all has crashed and burned, she knows the woman who invaded my dreams and made my heart sing. That makes her similar to royalty. "Hi, Bailey. I'm Brandon."

I have a zillion things I want to ask her. There are even a few I should, such as if she is exhausted from flying in last night after working yesterday, and is there anything I can do to help her get settled. Instead, I stand like a fool—a smart fool who can't get in trouble if he doesn't open his mouth.

Bailey returns the greeting. My eyes lock on our hands as

they shake. If Bailey saw Katherine after the run-in we had, does it mean she knows about the freak in the cab? Man, I wish I could comprehend how one tiny misunderstanding could appear from nowhere and shatter so much.

A chill creeps up my spine. That reminds me of how Amber's life was taken in an instant no one saw coming. Life is a delicate chain of events leading to fate. One broken link and all of the pretty trinkets fall off.

But what happens if two chains break and different halves are seared together? Would they transform into a new path? Maybe I should ask Bailey about her old job, and that will somehow lead to fixing things with Katherine.

No, because Darla already knows about my *Vampires Undercover* marathon. If she starts putting all this together and the freak in the cab, who also happens to be named Brandon, comes up in conversation, I'm screwed. There are far better things it would be wiser to do, such as try to scale Mount Everest while relying on the strength of a spool of thread. Regardless, I can't stand here like an idiot.

A crust and dust covered binder bearing the Endeara Candies logo sits on the sign-in counter and catches my eyes. The thing looks as if it is about fifty years old, if it's a day. "What's this?"

"Our formula book," Darla says as if it is as common as the Yellow Pages.

"*Formula* book?" I ask. "That sounds valuable. Why is it sitting on the sign-in counter?"

Darla bows to Bailey in a signal for her to take over. How Bailey rolls her eyes tells me she is already in disbelief over this place. "The plant manager left it there yesterday afternoon and told Darla not to move it. Apparently, he needs to do some research and things on his desk get ignored. Thus, he asked her to 'tell the new girl' to give it to him first thing this morning."

I don't want Bailey to think I don't have faith in her abilities but ... How do I word this without insulting her? "The plant started up two hours ago. Why didn't you give it

… " Oh, God, I'm gonna sound like an ass if I finish that sentence.

Darla looks at me as if I am the most clueless creature in the world. I probably am. "Really, Wayne? You have to ask? Tell him, Bailey."

"I tried to give it to him, but he told me to leave it there because he didn't have time. If it is still there at the end of the month, I'm to remind him about it again. At first I thought it was an initiation, but Darla assures me this is the way things work around here."

I flip through it. This is our entire playbook—our bible. "Should this thing be left out? What if it gets stolen?"

Bailey chimes right in. "To answer your first question, no, that's almost as risky as walking down the street while shouting your social security number. However, you've tasted the stuff we make here. If that thing goes, we would have to reformulate everything. Theft would be a blessing."

"Damn!" I jerk back. "You really are Darla's sister!" I also can't dispute her. I have half a mind to slip it into the incinerator myself. "Welcome to your new life, Bailey. Something tells me the transition will be seamless."

Now I remember the thing I love about this place. As long as I work here my reality will be as bizarre as my fantasies.

With a chuckle, I head to the elevator and return to the life I once led.

Gumdrops.

Piles and piles of gumdrops.

Mocking me.

For the two hours I've been here, these stiff gobs of goo have had me in a staring match.

I press a green one between my fingers, slowly kneading it. Its texture reminds me of the thickness that has been in my throat ever since I saw Katherine's beautiful face contort in discomfort. The beads of sugar dropping onto my desk form a portrait of my loss. Like anytime a special relationship ends, I am finding that moving on is not so easy.

I roll the gumdrop over the sugar in an attempt to make it whole again.

I can't take this.

I can't take the sorrow. I can't take the loss of hope. More so, I can't take the tug of war between prayers that I never hear her again and concern for her because all has been silent. As much as I miss it, I need her voice to be gone forever. Wondering if and when it will pop into my head is driving me insane.

Enough!

I swipe the sugar off of my desk with my sleeve. Dammit, I made a decision to walk away, and I will stand by it. I'm going to be certain I never hear the voice of Katherine Miller again. There has to be a way, and I know how to find it.

Shirtless guy answers my call to Jennifer on the second ring. I hate how I got so wrapped up in a mess that I lost all manners and have never asked his name. Before I can open my mouth, he says, "Hey, man. It's Rob. Jennifer is at her fencing class, but she left you a note. You wanna fall by or should I lay it on you?"

Did he say his name because he was stating who was answering, or because he knew I was going to ask what it is? And how is it that she again knew I would be in touch? I know this should faze me, but frankly, I don't think a cow tap-dancing could faze me now. "Yeah, sure, lay it on me."

Rustling comes through the line, followed by the sound of paper being unfolded. "She said, 'You and Katherine have been led to water. Partners work together, but a loved horse is one that is not forced to drink. Now that the universe has been given a nudge, you won't hear her any more, but it doesn't mean you are not loved. Meanwhile, get to work. You can't afford to get fired. Retro is always in.' "

I can only begin to imagine how my face is contorting in response. I don't know where to begin with questions, or even if I should. I think I am relieved about the voice but—

"Hey, sorry," shirtless guy says. "Gotta mosey. Someone's at the door. Later man."

I return the goodbye in a way he can groove to. "Yeah, solid."

Why can't Jennifer leave me a message that isn't cryptic? Seeing the mounds of gumdrops on my desk makes me feel even more overwhelmed. I need a break. Times like these I wish I smoked. Instead, I go for a gumdrop. Hey, both will kill you, so it is sort of the same thing. Hell, they practically taste the same.

Endeara Candy: Almost as bad for you as cigarettes.

Man, she is right about needing to get my ass in gear with work. I said I was moving on while creating a new version of myself, and that is exactly what I am doing. As of now, if I can't get over my situation, I will work with it.

And yes, Jennifer, retro is always in. People are suckers for nostalgia because the past seems like it was more fun than the present.

What was up with the horse analogy? I get the general sense of what it means but …

How can I move forward with this new mystery over my head? This is gonna drive me crazy.

As I bite into another gumdrop, I'm reminded how people view crazy is relative to many factors.

Okay, my situation is making me think of horses. That plus the retro comment remind me of Fruit Stripe Gum. Those guys had it all—colors, stripes, animals. Did they ever make stuffed toys? That would have been perfect.

That is what we need! A cute mascot, such as … The Endeara Deer! How has no one thought of this before? Montgomery Ward gave us Rudolph The Red-Nosed Reindeer, so why can't Endeara have a mascot? Oh man, even if our candy sales continue to suck, my inner voice is telling me we can make a killing in the toy market!

No more voice. God, what a relief.

Is knowing I am not going to hear Katherine again really a relief? How can I move forward when I miss the hope she brought me?

I need to find a new kind of escape, such as I did when I lost Amber and became engrossed in music. I also need something that gives me a prayer of keeping my job. At least this retro thing seems to be clicking. Maybe I should watch some old commercials.

No, look at what happened the last time I paid attention to a commercial. Dammit, I'm supposed to be making my situation work for me, not returning to a path that will have me back in my car and aimed at Happydale.

I start to go for another gumdrop but gather the smarts to stop stress eating. After all, there will be no new version of me if I poison myself.

I Google "famous candy marketing campaigns" and quickly get annoyed. Seriously, Sugar Daddy's used to have prizes? Those bastards! They didn't when I was a kid. There goes my memory of the sweet taste of childhood dreams.

I gasp at my brilliance in accidentally creating a tagline any adult can relate to. Yes! Endeara Candies, the sweet taste of childhood dreams! Could it be that just knowing the voice is gone is bringing my mojo back, or am I really determined to move forward this time? Maybe I am pissed at the madness around me and am learning to deal with it.

My desk phone rings. When I answer, my boss sounds stressed to the gills. "Drop everything and get into my office. The CEO is on his way over, and if we don't have something—anything to help us move this crappy candy—we are both fired!"

My words are quick to come out when Dale answers my call. "I'm brilliant, and it is celebration time! I'm getting into my car now. Get out of that office at a decent hour for once, and meet me for drinks."

"This is a welcome change," Dale says. He sounds relieved by my attitude. "What's got you so happy?"

A lot of my cheer is forced, but I am allowing myself to

get excited about life. With how self-absorbed I have been over the last few weeks, putting a new head on and pulling off what I did is huge. "I've come up with a slogan to market Endeara's candy in a way that doesn't make me feel like a lying sleaze ball."

Dale's laugh sounds both humored and ironic. "You mean, you have found a way to market candy that taste like boogers without feeling as if you have succumbed to being a wretched salesman."

"Pretty much. I also created a long-term plan that, when we work the right deal with a toy manufacturer, will put my stuffed animal design on the beds of millions of little kids for years to come. It also has the power to launch a major Christmas special. Endeara the Deer will become such a cherished part of their childhood that when they are our age, they will fork over a hundred bucks just to get their hands on another one. Let's grab cocktails and dinner at someplace awesome."

"Wow. That sounds pretty amazing." Dale's enthusiastic voice turns cautious. "Actually, can you meet me at Mulligan's? I've got something big I need to talk to you about, and I think I need to be here when I do it."

Talk? Dale? "Hey, you okay?"

"Yeah. How soon can you get here?"

It's not even five, and Dale is already out of the office and at a bar? Something is up. "I'm out of the parking lot now. I'll be there as fast as LA traffic allows. Meaning even though you are only a few miles away, I'll see you in about two hours."

When I arrive at Mulligan's, Dale signals the bartender and orders us a couple of glasses of their best Scotch. My raised eyebrow asks why. "Celebrations call for something special," he says. "Besides, I'm trying to figure out how much change I am up for."

Yeah, something is up. "So, what's the big thing you need to talk about? Are two new strip clubs opening and you can't decide which one to waste your money at first?"

"Ha! I swore off of strip clubs after your visit. In fact, I've sworn off of a lot of things. Strange as it is, I have to admit I feel a lot more secure in my manhood."

What? Who is this guy?

When the waitress arrives with our drinks, Dale gives her a polite thank you and a kind smile. She's pretty, but also a little trampy. Dale may always be polite, but she's not at all the type he shows gentlemanly respect to. This sounds like the guy I always thought Dale could be as opposed to the guy I've known.

Dale continues. "Our little chat in Toronto is the reason I want to talk to you now. Something big happened—something I have busted my ass for. But first," he raises his glass, "congratulations on today." We *clink* glasses, and as I take a sip, he whammies me. "I got an offer for a promotion. A huge one—like astronomical. We are talking double what I make now, and I would no longer be a slave to commission."

"Wow. That sounds amazing." I'm still trying to figure out what is going on. Dale has spent years busting his ass for this. He shouldn't sound as if he has been doomed. "What's the catch?"

Dale's phone rings. When he gets a look at the number coming through, he groans like the world is ending. "Sorry, I'll be right back."

Out of habit, I pull out my own phone to check Facebook while cursing myself for being an addict. This constant stalking has to stop. I delete the app and slip the phone back into my pocket. It is time to think about something else. That is pretty difficult considering the TV I first saw Katherine on is right across the room.

I stare at the screen, hoping to see her almost as much as I dread it. My leg starts jittering at the thought. Another sip of Scotch is a short-lived diversion. Dale needs to speed it up before I drink his too.

My eyes continue to feel drawn toward the TV, seeking the woman who puts longing in my soul.

Gah! I need a new obsession.

Games. I've got to have Solitaire or something on my phone.

Darla grabs my attention when she slips into Dale's seat. Thank God. Looking for a diversion was driving me nuts.

She steals a sip of my Scotch before shaking her head in disbelief of what she is about to say. "I swear, Wayne, you are going to drive me crazy. I've met some nut jobs before, but you are a mental case all your own."

Is she serious? She can't be serious, can she? Sometimes with Darla, it's hard to tell. This could be about anything.

Her narrowed eyes enhance the sarcastic tone in her voice. "I overheard the most interesting call a moment ago."

Oh no.

I grab back my Scotch and attempt to casually take a sip while fighting the urge to down it.

"Bailey was talking to a friend of hers—someone you met early yesterday morning."

I close my eyes and brace myself for the berating that is sure to come.

"Given how you have been acting, your back-peddling about hearing things, and with power watching a show that happens to have an actress you met when you bailed on work and wound up in a cab on the other side of the continent, things are sounding a little, shall we say, stalkerish."

My cringe deepens. I can't even begin to think of a way out of this one.

Darla touches her finger to her chin, tapping it as if she finds something to be curious. "Then the story took a strange turn, so much so that Bailey searched for a pen and paper to take notes."

Oh, God! I shudder to think where this is going. Can't she bust out with it like a normal person?

Darla slips me a piece of paper, and the joking demeanor drops and caves to ... trepidation? My widened eyes scan downward, fearing what Bailey may have written. I let out a huff of surprise when I see Katherine's name and phone number.

"Apparently Katherine thinks she owes the freak who got into her cab an apology for her being a total bitch."

This is unreal! As much as I hoped for it and knew in my heart it was possible, I didn't dare believe this would happen. Thank God! Maybe now I'll be able to make sense out of everything.

Darla squeezes my arm, and the depth of her concern becomes clear. "Brandon, I can't even begin to imagine what is going on, but I've been awfully worried about you, and Bailey said Katherine sounded a little weird."

My words race out. "I didn't mean to scare her. She thought Jason sent me, and things went crazy from there. I didn't know what to say."

Darla sucks in her lip. "It seems she's a little freaked out in a different way. She didn't give any details, but whatever you said left quite an impression." Darla pauses, and I sense she is choosing her words wisely. "Saying she was trying to find a marketing guy from a place in Los Angeles that sold bad gumdrops got my attention. However, with the way you have been acting, hearing the guy spoke in puzzle pieces is what convinced me she was talking about you. Are you absolutely sure you are okay?"

I stare down at the note, and my thoughts jumble. Did I leave an impression on Katherine because what I said was so strange, or did she figure out what I was getting at? At least now I can have a real conversation with her. As much as I know what I experienced was real, a part of me could use some confirmation. "I'm fine. In a way, I always have been. In others ... Man, there is a lot about the world I don't get." Darla keeps staring like she wants to believe me but is still concerned. "Really, I'm fine. When I get into the office tomorrow, I promise to tell you a story that will blow your mind."

Darla pats my arm and chuckles. "Yeah, good luck with that. Remember, I'm the one who led you to a psychic in the first place." She slips out of the booth. "I have to get back to the car. Poor Bailey, I swear she is so tired that when she and Katherine started deducing what happened she sounded as if she had seen a pink elephant. You truly are fine now, and I will see you at work tomorrow, right?"

"Yes, I promise."

With a squeeze to my shoulder, Darla heads off.

A tingle of happiness enlivens my soul. I did it! I'm in touch with Katherine! A real conversation is only a phone call away.

Does she know what has been happening? Did the puzzle pieces I dropped pique her curiosity, or has she come to realize I was an innocent victim and she wants to apologize? If that is the case, should I let the situation lie and hope we become friends so someday I can tell her, or is she not supposed to know what brought us to the point that makes this call happen?

Dale slips into his seat, and although I force myself back into the moment with him, I refuse to let the wonder of what I just experienced escape me. Things happen every day that are beyond our comprehension. If people were not so closed-minded, maybe those who experienced amazing things would speak freely, and more often we would see that wonders can unfold before us.

Dale starts his words with a heavy sigh. "That call drives home my point—other than the fact I would have to move to Chicago next week."

"Next week? What do they think you are? Cattle to be herded?"

"It's not that big of a deal." From the tone of his grumble, I don't believe he feels that way at all.

"It *is* a big deal. That is a lot to ask of someone."

"They would make it worth the effort."

"Yeah, but what about the stress?" I ask.

"Great point. That is one of the places I am going with this. I'd wind up spending even more time married to my job, which leaves me zero time to find, let alone pursue, anything else. As much as I am pretty sure I know the answer, what would you do?"

This is a no-brainer. I've always felt how Dale lives his life is foolhardy, yet I'm wondering what I have to do with this. "Why are you asking me? And why did we have to meet here?"

Either there are a hundred things far more interesting than me or he is avoiding eye contact. "Because, Mulligan's has come to be a second home, and as much as it pains me to admit this, you and I have the same goals. I actually believe you are going to meet them. Me … not so much. How do you do it?"

"Do what?" Wow, did he really say *we* have the same goals?

"How do you keep hope for all those dreams you had with Amber when you can't even bring yourself to go out on a date? Right now, you've got zip. You took a job you are not too keen on because you were promised that when your life worked out, your boss would be there for you. You don't have a single, female prospect on the horizon. Yet here you always are, looking as if the whole world is about to burst open and pull you into bliss. How do you do it?"

When I woke this morning, I never would have seen Dale as being right. Even now that I am about to burst over my news, it is still hard to see. But the funny thing is that Dale called me about having this conversation regarding hope for a better life before I heard that Katherine wants to talk to me. Meaning, even though I have been a disaster lately, he has still been able to see who I am. Maybe that cheese from Jennifer wasn't telling me what to do. Maybe it was passing on wisdom by showing me who I am. If Dale wants to be like me, he needs those words, too.

"Follow your heart," I tell him.

Dale stares, waiting for more, and I just smile like a fool who has struck gold. "My heart?" he asks. "But I am talking about whether to take a job. A job is a paycheck. What does that have to do with my heart?"

For what may be the first time in my life, I feel profound. "Your heart accepts things logic ignores. Did you ever stop to think my not being tied up with thoughts of the almighty dollar is what keeps me feeling free? Sure, we all need money, but once the bills are paid and the food is on the table, everything else is a luxury. Money buys the ability to travel to foreign lands, yet without it we are more likely to walk to the park and hear children laugh. Follow the sounds of your heart, the sounds no one else hears, and you will be like me."

I don't even bother to finish my drink. I'm surprised I've been able to contain myself this long, yet I won't leave before telling Dale the rest of what I feel. "Thank you for seeing what I am about and for reminding me of that fact as well. I always knew there was a reason why you and I were friends. For what it's worth, I hope you stick around. I'd love to be there when you find the girl who tames the beast. He doesn't need as much coaxing as everyone thinks."

Dale grabs my arm as I start to head off. "Hold up, buddy." His eyes lock into mine and narrow. After an audible exhale, he sets his elbow on the table, cupping his chin in his hand. I've never seen him look perplexed before. Finally, he nods. "Yeah, I'm staying."

"Just like that? You're going to let everything you worked for go?"

"Yep, just like that. Something tells me if I keep chasing rainbows, I am going to lose. Instead, for some crazy reason, I'm staying here with a wack job friend." He looks to his drink and shakes his head while waving me off. "It pains me to admit I need you to keep me in check. God help me."

Imagine, Dale following his heart. Something tells me it is going to pay off. It must have for me because when I step out of the booth, my feet feel as if they are floating on air.

Crazy World

Katherine

It has been less than an hour since I got off of the phone with Bailey, yet I can't stop pacing a hole in my bedroom carpet. My head won't stop racing, which is probably why it seems like the clock can't catch up to where I think its hands should be. Why hasn't he called? This is unreal. It can't be the same guy.

Maybe he doesn't think this is important. Maybe he is angry with me. Hell, I would be. I was such an ass.

I need to get a grip.

My phone rings, and I dive onto the bed to grab it. I try to force out the most normal-sounding hello I can muster for fear I will come off as more of a loon than I already have.

"Hi, Katherine?" The guy sounds like he is freaked and trying not to show it. "This is Brandon. Bailey's sister asked me to call and—"

I don't mean to cut him off, but not only am I eager to get this conversation underway, it's not fair to make him wait for an apology any longer than he has. "Thank you for calling. I feel horrible about what happened. I'm not even sure how to explain, except I was under a lot of stress and wasn't thinking clearly. I am also embarrassed that you are not the only one I misjudged at that moment. I hope you will accept my apology."

His words jump in, and I finally feel like I am able to unclench from the stupidity of what I did. "It is fine. Really. We all have moments when we get blindsided. It is kind of amazing that you were able to find me."

Good, he is willing to talk. Coincidences won't stop nagging at me, and I've no idea how to approach them. "I have you to thank for that. When I called to see how Bailey's first day at work went, and she mentioned thinking she needed to get her stomach pumped because the candy there is so bad, things started coming together."

He snickers. "Man, it's about time that garbage was good for something."

I chuckle both out of amusement and relief he has given me another chance to take this conversation further. "If it's that bad, how do you stay in business?"

"I'd like to think it has something to do with," he clears his throat, "brilliant marketing."

I roll onto my back and stare at the ceiling while trying to relax. He does seem like the nice guy I thought he was. "Ah, yes. You did comment that you were a marketing guy. Does that mean you sit at a drawing board all day? I'm envisioning you scratching your head, crumbling your latest masterpiece, and then tossing it on top of piles of other discarded ideas."

"I wish I were that prolific. What it means is I push gumdrops into lame pictures while hoping to get an idea that doesn't suck."

"It kind of sounds like you are a toddler making macaroni art." Suddenly, I clue in to the new puzzle piece he has given me. "That's why you mentioned Facebook! You're the guy on my fan page with the Bat Signal made of gumdrops! Once I saw your last name is Wayne, I thought it was pretty funny." Brandon tries to mute a gasp. I've probably embarrassed him. My brain starts putting the pieces together. He's the one whose words got me to push aside my fears and give a strong performance. He also commented again later that day. All that talk about dreams was a reminder of what he said. Thank God! I was starting to get some crazy thoughts about why those things sounded familiar.

Yeah, but they sounded familiar then too. That is only the tip of what has me weirded out. Why do I think I know this guy? The stuff he said reminded me of the film script, yet he wasn't on set, nor is he listed anywhere in the crew notes. Maybe he knows the writer. "Hey, I need to thank you. You said some stuff on Facebook that gave me a boost right when

I needed it. It was almost like you could read my mind."

"Really?" He sounds excited, and I am not sure if he is having a moment of fandom, or if he is catching what I am getting at. I have to stand and pace because all this is making my nerves jitter.

"Yeah, in fact, you seem familiar. Have we met before?"

"Umm … Not that I know of."

I swear there is something going on here. I feel stupid for not cluing in. "It's just all that dream stuff sounded familiar. Did you get it from somewhere?"

His chuckle is a nervous one. It also sounds hopeful. I thought I was leading the cat and mouse game. Now I am not so sure. "Maybe, you know how sometimes a little voice in your head says something? Sorry, that sounded weird."

Is he saying what I think he is? This conversation is making my skin break out in bumps, but I can't let him know that. "No … not so weird at all." I sound like I am a mess. I pretty much am.

"It's just— You don't always need words to catch on to what a person is thinking. I once knew someone who was a firm believer that a person's energy leaves a fingerprint for others to pick up on. Maybe that is all it is. I've heard stranger things."

Again, he is talking in puzzle pieces. However, I do get how someone's energy can convey his emotions, even if he is trying to hide them. Actors use that trick all the time in order to sell a scene, but it doesn't change how what I am about to say scares the living hell out of me. "So, it is sort of like you could hear my thoughts as if I were talking to you?"

I bite down on my nail and wait. Since I stepped back to see all the places I have been screwing up, that cab ride has haunted me in many ways. "Yeah," Brandon says, sounding as nervous as I do. "You can *definitely* say that."

His emphasis makes my skin feel raw. Some of my findings have been simple explanations while others have been a bit of a stretch to accept. That emphasis is telling me something though, and I need to either face my fears or run.

Why do I fear what I hoped would happen? I may be on the verge of uncovering a miracle.

There are many ways to phrase my next question, but I won't allow myself to word it so it is easy to dodge. Logic yells at me to keep silent, but I brave words that seem innocent yet carry worlds of weight. "Brandon, how did you know about Saleena?"

A pause of discomfort creeps through the line, putting my nerves further on edge. He probably fears that if he tells me the truth, I will think he is crazy. He deserves help with this because if my suspicions are correct, this poor man has already been through enough. My words come out slowly and well calculated. "When I was in LA and you were making those posts, I had a dream where someone called me Saleena. Since then, I've had a song stuck in my head that I can't place."

He doesn't have to get much out before my nerves turn to ice. "The road to success is dark, but flames of my desire will light the path. Are you the one who dares to stand in my way? You may get destroyed, or I just might be saved."

My breath hitches, and every part of me quakes. Brandon waits for my reaction, but he has freaked the crap out of me so much I have to place the phone down, close my eyes, and remind myself that I am safe. I put the puzzle together last night, and as much as logic told me I had to be wrong, I couldn't hide from knowing there was truth hidden somewhere. I lie down to prepare myself. My words barely make it out as I brave the question I am pretty sure I know the answer to. "Ha-Ha-How … How did you know what to say about dreams in a way that would stick with me?"

Tension comes through the line as Brandon forces out the words, "Because I heard your thoughts." My body jerks, sending me upright and frozen. He sounds as freaked as I feel when he says, "One time you said, 'If I could somehow find a way to let you know I am thinking of you, maybe … maybe someday our paths will cross and we will find each other.' It seems to have worked."

I want to run; yet I need to know more.

"Katherine? Are you okay?"

It takes a few swallows to get the dryness out of my mouth before I can speak. "Yes, please keep going."

His words sound methodic, as if he has experienced the panic I feel and wants to help me hold it together. "I kept hearing a voice as if it were addressing me but didn't know my name. Eventually I matched the voice to you. I swear to God I thought I was losing it." He pauses, and I am grateful he has given my mind a chance to catch up to my sprinting heart. However, it also feels like a warning for the shock to come. "Then I started getting visions. You walked into the bathroom and looked in a mirror. Since you didn't have make-up on, things made less sense than before. I was so freaked out. I couldn't sleep. I couldn't eat. I almost checked myself into a mental hospital. I was actually on my way to do it, and I ran into someone who— Man, that part of the story is a tale all its own. Katherine, just ... Please tell me you are okay."

I look down at my white knuckles and feel the tension deep in my gut. I swear every muscle in my body is cramping. "Oh, I am pretty freaked out," shudders out of me. "Thing is ... What I can't believe right now is that I believe you."

"Oh, thank God." The relief in his voice is so heavy I almost feel touched by it. "Katherine, who were you talking to? Do you have any idea why I was able to hear you?"

I sit back and brace myself for what I consider to be the strangest part of all of this. My words were aimed at one person—one very specific person. "I was talking to my soul mate. As crazy as it sounds, I think fantasy crossed over into reality."

"Katherine, nothing sounds crazy to me anymore."

Brandon

The relief that fills me is a true gift from heaven. For weeks my mind has bounced back and forth between accepting what I felt was real and fearing for my future. Now I know every moment of the last few weeks was based in reality, and I could not be more grateful.

Katherine and I stay on the phone for hours, each sharing our sides of the story. Every time I think I have told her everything more details come to mind. The conversation has a magic all its own, but then another wonderful thing happens—we start talking about other subjects. It starts with music and moves on to morals, thoughts on the meaning of life, and the dreams we have for our futures—dreams that either match or complement each other. Eventually I come to feel as if I have bared my soul to her. We end the call with a promise I will fly out for the weekend with no plans other than for the two of us to try to gain deeper understanding of where we have been, both in our recent experiences and in a past we have only had flashes of.

When I watch Katherine's phone number fade as the call disconnects, emotions swirl through me in such a flurry it is hard to appreciate every single one. My God, could anything be more wondrous? My heart feels as if all of the good in the universe has flooded in. Now I am so grateful that I let myself explore what I could not understand. If I had fought my feelings and suspicions, if I had surrendered to what most people would think was happening, I would have missed out on the power of something incredible.

In the past few weeks the whole universe has opened before me and let its secrets escape—our bodies are limited to the now, souls transcend time, we can meet each other time and again, and most amazing of all, just because our souls get confined to our bodies, it does not mean they can't reach out in ways that boggle our minds. There was proof in that call, and soon that proof will be before me. Without a doubt, this journey has only begun.

Heaven

Brandon

It is bewildering how different my circumstances are over the last time I was in this airport. Katherine and I have spent countless hours chatting on the phone, yet today will be the first time we are face-to-face without any secrets. Will our meeting hold a heart-stopping moment of bliss? Will it be like old friends reuniting? Should I shake her hand? Should I hug her? After all the conversations we have had, not to mention our crazy connection, a hug sounds safe. A nice, not too long, not too clingy, but impassioned hug.

That wouldn't be weird, right? I don't want to come off as creepy.

Shoot, when we spoke yesterday, she was nearly bursting over how she felt she was about to be reunited with a long lost love. Given that, a hug is definitely warranted.

Before entering the baggage claim I force myself to take a few deep breaths. For a moment I feel centered, yet my eyes dart all over in search of her. Will she look like her natural self, or will she look like Ms. Hollywood?

God, those speckled eyes. I hope I get to see her without her contacts. Does she have any idea how beautiful she is without all that makeup? I want to spend my night getting lost in those eyes I have dared to let myself think are reserved for me. If for some unimaginable reason I tire of that, I want to count those adorable freckles.

Katherine is nowhere in sight, but a dark-skinned woman holding a sign with my name grabs my attention. The lady tells me Katherine is detained at work. By the time she is free not only will we have missed our reservation, but also all of the nice restaurants will be closed. I may be willing to come all this way to take her to a drive-thru, but I hoped for something better—especially since I have to fly out tomorrow afternoon. There is no way my boss can keep covering for me. Since I barely have enough money to make it home, I also can't afford to get canned.

No, I can do better than a drive-thru, and I will. I'm Batman, and if there is one thing Batman does, it is use his resources wisely.

I should have gotten candles. I had them in my hand.

Nah, I made the right decision. I want her to feel appreciated, not like I am trying to score. The flowers are more than enough, though I am not sure I got the right ones. Roses screamed ulterior motives. Carnations were too simple. The mixed bouquet felt manufactured—as if anyone could have them. Still, was buying three different bunches to make my own combination too much? This is the problem with getting to know someone over the phone. A woman can tell you what she fancies, but that doesn't let you see what puts sparks into her eyes. If this is the woman I am to spend my life with, I want to fill her eyes with light each and every day.

Thank God I thought to bring some of her favorite peanut butter. It makes this impromptu picnic seem less makeshift. It may not be the nice dinner I planned, but it is as romantic as our circumstances dictate it should be. I will not hesitate to let her see the real me. However, I have to question if a mellow hair band hit parade was the right selection. But if this is the music she loves, it is the music she will get.

The *creak* of the door causes my heart to race. A faint bit of light slips into the trailer before Katherine enters. Seeing her touches my heart as if she were an angel. Her tall boots, tight, black jeans, Jem and The Holograms Misfits T-shirt, and makeup that screams starlet remind me of how Saleena always looked like a punk fashion model. My being takes pause. Pieces that have long been scattered seem to come together, bringing the release of the tension my mind has held since before my life went to hell years ago. Merely being in the presence of this woman brings peace to my soul.

Katherine

My clammy hands turn the knob of the trailer door, and I feel Brandon will hear my throbbing heart before I finish stepping inside. This must be what it is like for people who meet online and spend months exploring their emotions before meeting in person. Our situation is so much more complex though. If I believe what seems to be the logical explanation for what has happened, this is my soul mate. That just might be true, because how my breath locks at the sight of him makes me feel I have found a lost love. It's hard to believe I feel such emotions when the last time I saw this guy, I was tossing him out of a taxi.

The tender sound of Warrant's "Heaven" glides through the air, yet it is the unique bouquet that catches my attention. The flowers look handpicked and tell me someone wanted to give me something special, not a cliché.

The man who has heard my words like an angel hears prayers sits on the floor, right in the middle of a tablecloth, a bottle of wine, and paper plates with sandwiches. Despite where we are dining, he has bothered to wear pressed pants and a black, fitted shirt with silver studs on the collar and sleeves. The top buttons are open and connected by a silver chain. The polished combat boots sell it. Somehow he manages to look cutting edge, retro, hard core, and softhearted all at the same time. It slays me.

Him doing all of this on such short notice makes my blood turn into one of those bubble lights my family puts on the Christmas tree. It also reminds me of what I first thought when I saw Brandon at the taxi stand: he looks sweet.

How he stands with hesitation is endearing. After all we have talked about—music, movies, philosophy, and the crazy connection we share—I was afraid he would act as if entitled to own me. Instead, he is as unsure what to do next as I am. Thing is, given all we have said, along with how we have connected over the phone and on Skype, I just want to curl into his arms.

We close the distance between us and simple hellos are exchanged. Our eyes go to the other's arms—both of us not knowing what to do and smiling over how the next action is obvious. It's not long until his warmth is against me, and I am overwhelmed by sizzling comfort that conveys my other half is searing back on. I don't want to let go, and judging by the cling of the hug and the grip of his hand in my hair, neither does he.

Energy slinks in, and my muscles feel freshly massaged— like after years of emotional loss I am getting my mojo back. The sensation is so overwhelming I become short on air, and my heart thanks God for helping me see who I am and what really matters.

Emotion races to my eyes, and I grip him tighter. This is how it feels to be held by someone who wants to appreciate you for who you are, because he has seen into your soul. Now I know there is nothing to fear.

Eventually we pull back as if accepting fate has brought us together and that is how we will stay. "Hungry?" he asks.

"Starved."

We take seats on the tablecloth, and he blows my mind by handing me a sandwich with double peanut butter and seedless, raspberry jam. I remember talking about the type of peanut butter I love on a talk show once, but I'm pretty sure I never got specific about how I make my sandwiches. Did he just know?

A bite puts me into bliss. Leaning back against the sofa, I kick off my shoes and let the stress of the day fall off. I'd go for a sip of wine, but that would require moving. I want to let my body melt into the floor.

"Tough day?" Brandon asks. His slip of a smile not only tugs at my heart, it also brings back memories of a dream I had—a dream he has me believing was a memory from another life. Is he really the same man?

My shoulders drop, and my head dips back as I groan. My

eyes turn to him, and we both laugh. "Well, let's see. The reason we ran so late is because the harness broke when they hoisted me up on a crane to fly me across the room."

Brandon's eyes go wide. He's so quick to try to swallow and ask if I am okay I am afraid he will choke. It's sweet.

"I'm fine. Fortunately, I was only two feet up when it happened. However, I did land flat on my face and get a nosebleed. Not only did I have to get checked out, we needed to get a new harness, file an accident report, and get an equipment inspection. Then I had to do a brief love scene with Evan. Despite how we play it to the press, he and I have things we are fonder of than each other, such as eating live spiders. When I dropped my towel we discovered that the body makeup artist hadn't properly covered the huge birthmark I have on my ribs for the lighting we were using. There it was, popping out at everyone and saying, 'Hello, sailor!' Worse, Evan thought it would be cute to bust out with, 'Hey, Katherine, have you been eating chocolate?' So not amusing!"

Brandon chuckles and hands me a glass of wine. "You have more than earned this. Are you sure you are okay?"

I darn near choke on my sip. Did I really tell him about my birthmark? Nobody knows about it except for the few guys I have been with. I even kept it under wraps from them for as long as I could. "Yeah, I'm fine. My ego is more vandalized than anything else." At least I think I am fine. I am getting a bit of a headache. Must be the stress of the day. Lord knows there has been plenty.

"Evan should have shown you some respect. Not only do you have feelings, he is a co-worker, which is a type of partner. Every partner needs the other to succeed."

Brandon takes a bite of his sandwich and leans back against the sofa, totally oblivious to the power of what he said. Communication and support such as this are gold.

Pain zips its way across my head. Why is he being so casual? Doesn't he care I am hurting?

Whoa! Where did that PMS-like flash of unreasonableness

come from? I also have not said a word about this ache attacking the right side of my brain. I try to massage it away.

"You okay?" Brandon asks. True concern blankets his face. His caress of my temple feels electric, and I want to melt under it. This is exactly the type of response I've always wanted from a man. "Did you land on this side of your face? Maybe we should get you to a doctor."

"No, I landed on my left, and it wasn't very hard."

"Still." Brandon starts to stand. "Let's err on the side of caution. Don't they keep doctors on call here?"

I grab his arm and nudge him back down. "I'm fine. Not having eaten recently is the bigger deal."

His eyes look firmly into mine. "Are you sure? I wouldn't mind taking you to the hospital."

God, those gorgeous eyes remind me of autumn leaves. His lashes alone could make him a star. "Yeah, I'm sure."

This moment is perfect. Not only is Brandon genuinely concerned, he's done all he could to make this night special. I'm glad we couldn't go out.

We spend nearly every moment of his whirlwind visit chatting, sharing, and dreaming. When we arrive at the airport for his return flight the pull of whatever it is we share keeps me tucked in his arms, clinging and praying time magically stops so we can stay this way.

I've spent hours fighting the urge to rush into something that promises to be the lead-in to a lifetime of happiness. While our relationship already seems quick by man's standards, our souls scream that a few hours of hugs and simple kisses that have put my head in a tailspin were too reserved. He raises my chin, and the kiss we share sends my mind soaring in a myriad of directions—praying for a future, knowing there has been a past, and embracing the present.

As Brandon walks away, I ask myself why I am not tossing everything and running off with him. Is it because I'm under contract with my job? Because I just got out of another relationship? Because the press would criticize it? It's all of those ridiculous things that don't matter, and none of them reflect my free spirit. All I know is when I see him again, I won't hesitate to let us be whatever we want to be.

Brandon

I turn to catch another glimpse of the woman I have shared hours of bliss with, and she blows me a kiss. Her eyes seem to reflect what my heart feels—we spend our lives chasing rainbows, yet when we find the pot of gold we stop to climb trees.

Why should we hesitate jumping in? This is our chance to go back and get what people want most. Katherine and I have been granted a magical chance to turn back the clock and right everything. All we need to do is not ignore this opportunity the universe has blessed us with.

I enter the airport, because as much as I want to return to her, a small part of me is running away. We've talked about so much, yet we have managed to avoid something important. Can I continue to be open with her about everything, yet conceal the fact the Saleena and Johnny died because of me?

Punk Rock Girl

Katherine

My fingers wildly tap on my legs, mirroring a familiar guitar lick. The chorus breaks in, and I sing along. This is it. This is the song that has been stuck in my head. There is no possible way I have heard it before, yet I know it like the back of my hand.

The song ends, and the recording engineer asks Saleena for another take. The voice that agrees sounds like a chipmunk yet sings like a bulldozer. Could that actually be me? How else would I know this song?

The posters lining Brandon's room make me feel a part of me has come home from battle. The whole concept of once being part of an underground music movement seems so odd compared to the life I have now, yet when I dig deep into who I am, it all makes sense. I got into acting because I wanted to be a rock star. I couldn't sing, so I jumped on another bandwagon to stardom.

Brandon thinks this was recorded around nineteen seventy-eight. That was right when the San Francisco punk scene was beginning to boom. He sees it as making Saleena a Bay Area punk pioneer. However, my gut tells me she saw punk as the right bandwagon to jump on. The more I learn about her, the more I see how we are partners in reaching for fame. It would be a lot harder to convince me we are different people than it is we are the same person.

My attention comes off of the room and onto the man rewinding the tape. How much I have missed Brandon over the past week is ridiculous considering how little I know him. I nudge him to lean back against the bed so I can tuck my head into his shoulder. I am at peace with this man; far unlike I ever was with Jason. And through our phone conversations and Skype sessions, Brandon already knows everything—that is, except for my darkest secret. So much has come to the surface you'd think sharing it would be easy, yet I continue to cower from it.

I pick up the box the tape came in and chuckle at the name, Negative Fate. How wrong was it that Saleena died right when fame was in reach?

Fame—it is hell to get, and it can slip away in a heartbeat. I've lost so much along the way ...

"I'm trying to hunt the other girls down," Brandon says, "but since one went by a stage name and the other got married, I keep hitting road blocks. Julie's sister responded in a forum the other day about a poster someone found for a show at Mubuhay Gardens when the band opened for The Dead Kennedys, so I sent her a bunch of questions. Hopefully, she will respond. There are a lot of blanks I need to fill in." Brandon's voice trails off, and I notice he looks a little ill. My heart droops for him. He told me Saleena and her boyfriend died in an accident, similar to his ex-fiancée.

Brandon closes his eyes as if he is watching an image build, and then rattles his head to shake it away. Through Jason, I have already seen how hard it can be to face each day when you have lost someone you love.

My jaw tightens. Sudden pain shoots through the right side of my head and across my brow, bringing me to scrunch it as if the action will press out whatever is trying to bore its way inside. It doesn't bring relief, nor does it silence whatever is screaming Brandon is lying about something.

My irrational feelings must be caused by transferring how upset I am at Jason for his deceit. Jason's lack of a spine kept him from being honest, so why do I suddenly feel anger toward Brandon? Brandon has never been anything short of a gentleman, and he doesn't need to know Jason still pisses me off. I keep my head dipped into his chest until the bulk of the pain passes.

When I do look up, I find a smile on Brandon's face so warm and bursting with the love of life I can't help but share it. "Hey, the weather is perfect," he says. "You up for a walk on the beach?"

I look to the window and chuckle at the grey sky. "It's totally overcast. It'll be freezing."

His gaze drops, and I can swear he is blushing. "That's kind of the point." He peers up and gives me the most adorable, puppy dog look. "Someone will need to keep you warm." His thumb caresses my cheek, and it is as if I have awoken from a dream. My soaring spirit sends my headache running for its life. "Thing is, as much as I would love to show you the beauty of Paris and the glories of Rome, I'm broke. At least here I can show you the beauty God gave the ocean while I stare at the beauty He gave you. I can't think of a sight more incredible to behold."

He's perfect. Absolutely perfect.

State Of Emergency

Brandon

Even though I am in my second home, Katherine's smile is all that has my attention. A smile crosses my face simply because she loves me.

She looks so sweet while wandering among the rows, flipping through bin after bin in search of treasures. However, this woman who spent her former life longing to be a rock star also looks like a fawn staring down a set of headlights.

I step up from behind and slip my arms around her waist, nuzzling my chin into her shoulder, and feeling I am the most fortunate person in the world because she lets me. The nuzzle is returned with the added bonus of a giggle.

A giggle! My girl giggles! Damn, that's cute.

"Looking for anything special?" I ask.

"You know, back when I had the time to buy records, I didn't have the money. Now that I have the money, I never have the time. After lunch, I'm coming back and loading up. This place is insane."

I peek at the bin to see what she is perusing—The Germs. Cool. She stops and taps on a copy of *Germicide*. "I need to make sure I grab this later."

I nod in hearty approval of her taste. "Give it here. Shane will stash it until you are ready."

"Thanks." I get a kiss on the cheek before she spins around and takes in the vastness of the store again. With a bite to her nail, she ponders her next move before checking out Black Flag and then moving on to The Slits. There it is. The same gleam in her eyes that I saw in Saleena. Katherine may think she is only driven by fame, but there is so much more. She and Saleena didn't jump on bandwagons; they knew what they wanted. "Hmm," I muse. "All killer punk bands either composed of, or who at some point had, female members."

Her fingers halt mid-flip. What I pointed out seems to be messing with her mind. "How have I missed that I am a fan of Saleena's contemporaries? Weird."

"Not weird at all. She's not only a part of you; she *is* you. Just because that career wasn't in this life doesn't mean you didn't have it or it wasn't valued. Passions get ingrained, kind of like a disease some of us can't shake."

Her face contorts in question as my words seem to seep into her. I've hit on something. She shakes it off with a laugh. "So, you are saying your music obsession means you are sick?"

"Fatally."

She smiles at my truthful, deadpan delivery, and my heart soars. All along I have thought I only want to give to her and get nothing in return, but the flight of my heart proves I want her to give me the gift of her smile, time and again.

The shop bell rings. Low and behold it's the skater kid with the pants that will someday cost him his life. "This may get interesting. Shane played savior the other day. This kid is either coming back to church for another dose or will test Shane's patience in an epic display of comedy."

"Shane? That seemingly mild-mannered nerd? I've only been here ten minutes, but I have seen enough to know a bomb may not get his eyes off of that ancient issue of *Teen Magazine*. How can he get riled? And why is he so into Pat Boone?"

God, seriously? *That* is what has his attention so locked? You'd think he would at least be reading about Gene Vincent or Dion. I so don't get my friends. "Trust me; Shane can get riled. When he does, he reminds me of a Muppet on PCP. He got into it with this kid over if Green Day is punk or not."

"Green Day? Like, Billy Joe Green Day? Rock and Roll Hall Of Run By Clueless People Who Should Know Better Green Day? The guys who own two *edgy* restaurants?" She scoffs. "So not punk, but they sure own a couple of pretty killer restaurants."

Ah! Music to my ears! I kiss her forehead in an overt display of admiration. "Thank God for you."

"Hey," the kid says to Shane.

"Hey," Shane returns. Of course his eyes stay on the article.

"So um …"

Shane sets down the magazine and waits while the kid searches for words. Finally, he gives him a break by asking, "Did you find something you liked?"

The kid snickers. "Yeah, a lot of stuff. I was reading about those MC5 guys, and the article not only talked about The Kinks, it said something about Iggy Pop being in a band called The Stooges. Got any?"

Yes! He found it! This kid found his passion!

My fists fly up in a double pump. It's all I can do to keep from yelling score at the top of my lungs. The news makes me so damn happy I start dancing to the tune of "We Are The Champions" as it plays in my head. Shane did it! I want a chance to play savior too.

I grab a copy of *The Stooges* and race over. "Here, this one is on me. Hold on!" I toss in a copy of Stiff Little Fingers' *Inflammable Material*. "This is the *punk* band Green Day sounds like! They were one of their biggest influencers."

"Sweet. Thanks, man! I owe you guys." The kid takes off, jumps on his skateboard, and whizzes down the street.

"Yes, someone gets it! An entire generation may now be saved."

"Probably not," Shane says with a grumble. "At least we turned one. That makes me a tiny bit less likely to pull out that *No Posers Allowed* sign I always threaten to put up."

"Our conversion rate is far too slow. Think there is a way we can create some sort of mill to churn 'em out faster?"

Shane actually looks up to answer. "You mean like a school? I kind of dig it."

Katherine's laugh-laced voice travels across the room. "Oh. My. Gawd! Where is Jack Black?"

We look at her, blankly, until Shane chimes in, "Probably

running around in his underwear while half-baked."

I can't tell if Katherine is on the verge of laughter or of strangling us. "You guys have seen *High Fidelity*, right?"

Shockingly, Shane sets down the magazine to take a good look at the person who can't process the obvious. He then makes a sweeping motion at the room and baulks at her. I add the words that match his visual. "Um, yeah. We kind of live it."

"Well, boys, I mean it in the sweetest possible way when I remind you of the scene where the customer, lovingly, tells the guys they are elitists who look down on everyone who knows less than they do. After spending the last few days with Brandon and now seeing Shane in action, I can testify that is pretty much everyone."

We don't even try to get defensive. "Yep," Shane says, "She's got our number." His eyes go back to his magazine.

My head drops. Why do people bust us for being awesome? "The truth of that scene shames every music dork in existence."

Katherine rubs my back. It sounds as if she should be patting my head. "At least you admit your shortcomings."

God, it is such a relief to be open with someone about who I am. I love how Katherine changes me into a better person without changing who I am. She's perfect.

Katherine

Brandon's shamed puppy eyes are so cute. The way they turn mischievous makes me want to skip lunch with Bailey in exchange for something a little more appetizing.

"I know what you are thinking," he says.

My belly flutters at the thought. "Don't tell me you can hear me again," I whisper.

"With a look like that, I don't have to." His caress of my cheek has me swooning, but his intense gaze has me ready to drag him off to the back room.

A female voice clears her throat and crashes my thoughts. Bailey waves to us, and I settle for giving Brandon a peck on the cheek. "Gotta go. Have fun with the boys." As I slip away, his hand runs down my arm, stopping at the wrist with a tug. The adoration in his smile beckons me in for another kiss, and I gladly surrender to the charge it brings me.

When I accept that I need to break away I grab Bailey who has gotten distracted in the jazz section. Lord, please, it's going to be hard enough to follow Brandon's conversations. The last thing I need is the same problem with her.

We make our way to the door as Shane rings up Brandon. Before he finishes, he tacks on an extra fifteen bucks and slips a plain, brown paper bag into the store-branded one. "Advance copy of the Raspberries CD I pointed out the other day," he whispers.

Brandon smiles and he—

I stop dead in my tracks. Oh my God! Did he just bite his lip? He reminds me of a schoolgirl who has heard the boy she likes wants to make out with her under the bleachers. That is ridiculous. I may be discreet about my love of poser metal but that was damned adorable.

Bailey grabs my arm and yanks me out the door. "So. Lunch. Z Café? It's only about a block away."

"Yes! Heavenly tasting health food it is. How is it tempeh always taste like cardboard, yet there it's delicious? Keep me away from the chocolate cake though. Dear God! How do they make it taste *so* good?"

Bailey snickers. "What's wrong? Is Brandon the junk food king?"

I look down at my gut. "Not in the least, but I think I've been wined, dined, and peanut butter and jelly sandwiched into gaining five pounds."

"I thought you achieved self-control with those last year."

"I did. Then I met Brandon and found getting out of bed to make breakfast is unusually hard."

"That good, huh?"

"More like that connected. Something about us takes intimacy to a whole new level." On the night we had dinner in my trailer I felt a puzzle had been put together. The more time I spend with him, the more I feel the cracks between the pieces are being filled in. I would gladly tell Bailey, except there is a monkey wrench hidden in there, and I don't know how to express that.

Bailey checks out my ass as I walk through the cafe door and head for the counter to place an order. "Yeah, you've gotten totally huge," she says, tossing up her hands. "What the hell are you talking about? Actresses—I swear! At worst you have gained two ounces."

Gah! Non-Hollywood types! "Okay, new subject. Any word from Carlouse?"

"Not a one!" she says with a fist pump. "I've no idea if he mooched the rent money, crawled back to his parents, or is on a friend's sofa. Knowing him, he's probably already shacked up with another sucker. But here is the real question; have you heard from Jason, and does he know about you and Brandon?"

In some ways the question doesn't bother me in the least. In other ways it stings. I hate how I was involved in something so toxic. "Not a word other than an email saying all of his stuff is out, and no, not that I know of. However, it hit the rags I was seen with someone, and they are speculating I left Jason for another man, which totally looks true."

After placing our order, we grab the stand with our number and head outside. I'm sure to grab a seat that allows me to people watch. However, Bailey's eyes are locked on me. "Are you really okay with all of this?"

My shrug comes without a thought. "Yeah, all except the part that looks like I left Jason for someone else, but the rag sheets are going to say what they want, true or not."

"Aren't you even a little upset Jason is going down without a fight?"

Why won't Bailey let up? "I'm relieved he isn't trying to get me back. Even if it meant being alone forever I think we both see how being together is a rotten idea."

Bailey gives me the look girlfriends do when they know you are full of it. "No, you aren't fine at all."

Dammit, I'm an actress; I should be able to pull off a lie. I must really need to face this. "No, something weird is going on, but it has nothing to do with Jason."

"From what you told me about how you met Brandon I would think the weird part had long passed."

"It's not him. Actually, it might be, or it could be all my fault." If I can't level with Bailey, I can't level with anyone. She already knows the weird stuff, so this should be nothing. "Some of the things Jason said got to me. He pointed out how driven I am, like way more so than I ever imagined, and it makes me be someone I don't like. It may also be the cause of something that is freaking me out, though I don't know for sure."

"Which is ... "

My sigh sounds more like I want to zonk out than I am frazzled. Even this conversation doesn't get my feathers all that ruffled. "I'm getting so angry lately—as in, I-want-to-rip-someone-a-new-one kind of angry. Usually I can rationalize why I am stressed, but this is a whole new game."

Bailey's head jerks back. "You? Anger issues? When you found out about Jason's lies, you held it together for days so you could think the situation through. When he proposed, look at the restraint you used in waiting until you got into the limo to chew him out. Above anyone I have ever seen, you know there is a time and a place for anger. "

"Not lately. For the last few weeks, I've been getting headaches, and then I get angry. It only happens when I am around Brandon. I don't get it."

Bailey is quick to jump to a higher level of concern, and it's totally sweet. "Did he do something to—"

I put out my hand to halt her. "No. He's the gentlest man I've ever met." I clear my throat. The smile that crosses my face is coated in smut. "Sometimes a little too gentle."

Bailey's smirk implies she could use a little gentle right now, yet her concern comes right back. "Does it happen only when you discuss a certain topic, such as, politics?"

"Nope. It's random. The other day we were talking about

music, and totally out of the blue, I wanted to call him a liar. I've replayed the moment in my head a thousand times and couldn't find a reason in the world."

Bailey looks as perplexed as I feel. "That's not like you at all. Could it be Jason's lies have gotten to you? Do you have any reason to suspect you can't trust Brandon?"

I shake my head. "No, but the Jason part could be right. The first time I met Brandon I thought Jason sent him to sway me to marrying him. But why would that still affect me?"

"Have you mentioned this to Brandon?"

"No, because this can't possibly be his fault."

"Sounds as if there is a closure issue. For the sake of you and Brandon, you need to find out what it is."

Maybe she's right. I may just need to let Jason have it.

Our food arrives, and I purposely change the subject. We spend our time chatting about the changes she is making. It's inspiring, and I can't wait to see where her new attitude gets her. Something tells me her world is only beginning to open up.

I Will Always See Your Face

Brandon

Cuddling on the sofa with Katherine curled in my arms is true bliss. It makes me want to bear my soul to her, and to pray she will do the same so I can see her spirit in all of its glory. I want to learn her fears so I can alleviate them—to know her dreams so I can do whatever she will allow to help make them come true. The first week of her trip has already flown by. While I cannot wait to see what the rest of her hiatus brings, I cringe every time the clock ticks, knowing she is a second closer to leaving.

My stomach lightly squeezes and then lets out a rumble. I'm starved. I also, almost, don't care. I am far too comfortable to think about anything other than the happiness we have found.

"Hmm … We should eat," Katherine says, yet she fails to move. "Other than a spoonful of peanut butter this morning, neither of us has had a bite since yesterday."

Again my stomach speaks up. This time it sounds more like a roar. I slip an eye open in search of my phone, which is all the way across the room. So much for ordering a pizza.

My stomach pinches. Even though I can't hear it, Katherine must because she sits up and says, "That's it. We're going shopping. All that is left around here is ice, beer, and cereal. And no, we are not scraping together any more peanut butter and jelly sandwiches. My ankles are bigger."

I laugh. "What? Your ankles! Geez! Where? Besides, who would notice that?"

"Everyone. You only notice your ankles chunking up when you start ballooning."

I pull her back down on top of me. "You are *not*

ballooning. And you look perfect. However, in the interest of full disclosure I feel the need to state you would look perfect to me even if you gained a hundred pounds, your skin turned purple, and you sprouted warts. All I care about is your heart, and I pray to God it never changes."

Katherine pops up, and I get a death glare that nearly sends darts through me. What did I say? I told her she is perfect, and that she would be no matter what happens to her body. I also meant it. That is exactly what I am supposed to do, right?

I sit, looking like a deer in the headlights, waiting. When she fails to respond I raise my brows and cock my head, silently asking what I did wrong. Either she doesn't understand the body language or she is deciding the best way to chop off my head so it sits nicely on a platter. Seriously, what did I say?

She shakes her head as if she is rattling away whatever bothered her. "Sorry, we should get to the store before your stomach gets so twisted it eats itself."

What is a guy supposed to do in this situation? If I continue to keep my mouth shut, I can't say anything wrong. Still, I want to know what I said so I won't do it again. I touch her arm and stop her from getting up. "Hey, I hope I didn't offend you. I meant what I said about you being perfect no matter what, okay? I'm also pretty sure you haven't gained an ounce."

She nods, forces a quick smile, and then turns away. Why am I being blown off? Should I let this die, or will that leave it to bite me in the ass later?

I get up and grab my wallet, keys, and our coats. As I help her with hers, her eyes go in any direction but on me. "Hey," I say. "How about we grab something fast and take it to the beach or a park or something? We have been cooped up here a lot lately."

Needless to say, how she flutters her eyes and then closes them as if shutting me out is not the reaction I expected. "Fine." She starts for the door, and I reach for her.

"Please tell me what is wrong. Seriously, I have no idea

what I said."

She tosses her hands up and rattles them at me. "I know! I know you only spoke genuine words not intended to hurt me. I know that! Okay?"

I slowly nod while not daring to say a word. I'm lost.

Katherine shakes her head, looking both exasperated with herself and me. "What you said was perfectly fine, but what I heard was I am fat, just not ballooning." I start to interject, but she cuts me off. "I know! You did not intend for it to come out that way, but that is how I felt it. When you suggested grabbing something fast to eat, all I envisioned was me chomping on a bunch of fried jalapeños while my chubby cheeks bounced."

"I'm sorry. I didn't mean to disrespect your body in any way."

Katherine turns indignant, reminding me of how she was in the cab on the night we met. "My body? Are you implying I have body issues? God!"

She has me bewildered. Not once in the weeks I have known her has food been a source of discussion other than how we would rather stay in bed and eat peanut butter and jelly sandwiches than go shopping.

Katherine grabs her head at the sides and sits on the floor. At first she reminds me of a child throwing a tantrum, but then I see she is actually crumbling under pain. I am quick to kneel next to her. When I raise her chin, I find tears. "I'm sorry," she says. "So, so sorry. I tried, but I can't live this way anymore."

Dear God, what did I do to hurt this woman I have come to love so dearly? "Honey, what is wrong? Please tell me what I did so I can fix it."

She shakes her head with her hands over her ears, making me feel she is beside herself with emotions she can't understand. "Sometimes I get so angry when I am around you."

My lips part in disbelief. How have I hurt her? Memories flood my mind as I review every moment we have shared, yet

I come up empty handed as to what I could have done. My thumb wipes away her tears, and she cradles her head into my hand. If I truly make her angry, why is she curling into my touch?

"I know I am being irrational. Call it chemistry, call it whatever, it exists. I thought I could handle it, but obviously I can't."

My stomach crashes when Katherine heads for the closet and pulls out her suitcase. "Honey, please tell me what I am doing wrong."

She shakes her head with tiny motions. "Normally everything is perfect, but every now and then anger builds out of nowhere. I get a horrible headache that feels like someone is smacking me with a warning sign and then tossing me into another one. My subconscious is trying to tell me something, and I need to figure out what before I fall any deeper for you than I have."

Katherine heads for the bathroom and grabs her things. I want to beg her to stop, but I force myself to stay calm and try to find the source of the problem so we can fix it. This could not all be over her thinking I implied she put on a few pounds. There has to be more. I try to grab her shoulders as non-threateningly as possible. "Honey, what is it I do that upsets you? Are you afraid I will pull a stunt like Jason did? Is it really me you are mad at?"

She sets her things down, and my mind stops spiraling. But the moment she looks at me her brow crumbles and the tears return, sending my senses back into misery. "I wish I knew. Time and again I have tried to lay a finger on it, but I can't. I love you, but sometimes I get a sneaking feeling something is wrong."

My ability to breathe disappears. That's the first time I've heard those words from her, yet somehow I have always known they were meant. Our feelings grew like wildfire, and that may be the problem. The force of my hand threw Katherine and me together, not fate. Maybe it wasn't supposed to happen now—maybe not ever in this lifetime. Is this the repercussion of messing with the universe? I thought taking fate into your hands was a good thing.

"Hey, did you hear what you just said? I love you, too. Can we please talk about this?" She nods. We are on our way to sit on the bed when she lets go of my hand and rubs her head with it, starting on her right temple and moving to her forehead. "What's going on with your head?"

"It's been hurting off and on since the day you came to have dinner with me in Toronto."

I can't help but notice how she phrases it as if I have something to do with the problem. "You mean since the day you fell from that crane," I remind her. "Can we please take you to a doctor?" I cup her head in my hands. I have so much concern over her health and our future that I could not hold back the falling water from my eyes if I had to. "Please, honey. Let me take care of you, okay?"

Katherine nods, and we head off to the nearest emergency room.

The doctor's assurance that Katherine is perfectly fine brings limited relief. Our drive home is silent as we both search to find what is causing her emotions that rip at our hearts.

When I pull into the driveway of my apartment complex Katherine stops me from getting out of the car with the touch of her hand. "I need to tell you something." Her dire look conveys she is about to break me. "So much has happened lately, starting with Jason's lies, going through the strange things that have happened to us, and now this. I have never, ever had anger issues, and I certainly don't have a reason to feel anger towards you. I can only guess there is still something I need to settle with Jason. Staying here is not going to fix the problem. I need to do some serious soul searching."

My heart crashes, and my body feels such a jolt I nearly reach out of my seat to grab her. I know damn well she is not talking about going to a hotel for a night; she's going home, to another country, thousands of miles away, to flee from me. I foolishly dare uttering the question I fear getting an answer to. "You are leaving my life, aren't you?"

My stomach bottoms out when her eyes go to the floor. "Maybe. I don't know. I've been a toxic person before, and I can't let it happen again. Even though things are often so perfect with you, I can't be around someone who brings out the worst in me. If we don't so much as talk for a few weeks, and it goes away, then I'll know."

A few weeks? How can I survive waiting that long until she tells me if we will ever be happy again? But the sight of her pain tears at my heart. I can't fight her. I love her too much to make her suffer.

"Please," she says, "when we get inside, let me pack and leave." I start to ask her if I can take her somewhere, but she halts me. "I'm a big girl. I'll be fine." And then the tears fall for both of us. Dear Lord, how did we get here? This isn't fair. I've done nothing wrong. "That look in your eyes right now, the one telling me I mean more to you than anything, it's the only thing that has kept me going this long. I can't hurt you anymore."

And I can't hurt her, which is why I have to fight every bit of my being and not beg her to stay.

My shattered heart leaves pieces behind as we walk up the path. In a few minutes, she will walk this way again, crushing those pieces when she leaves. Losing Amber was hell, but she is no longer on this Earth. Katherine will remain alive and popping up on TV screens around the world. I'll never be able to risk looking at a TV for fear of seeing her and knowing the happiness I fought to find, only to lose it over doing something so terrible it drove her away—yet I may never know what it was.

It takes all I have not to stop her from packing or to keep me from dropping to my knees and begging. This can't possibly be my fault. It just can't.

Suggesting she talk to Jason might be throwing her back into his arms. But I love her, and that means I want her to find what she needs. "You've told me a lot about the horrible things you went through with Jason. Maybe your anger is really fear I'll do the same to you. Have you truly closed out all of the pain you need to with him?"

She speaks so softly I can hardly make out her words. "You always want what is best for me. That's another thing to love about you, and more proof you deserve better from someone than anger."

Katherine closes her suitcase and looks to Saleena's reel-to-reel sitting on the dresser. Come on, Katherine. Look at all we have been. Think about all we could be. Are you going to throw that away?

She swallows back pain as she caresses the box. "After going through so much, I can't believe I am doing this to us." With a wipe of her eyes, she heads for the door. The beat of each footstep plunges the knife deeper into my heart. God, please have her turn around and let me dry those tears.

She stops when she reaches the door, but she doesn't look back. "If I don't say the word I don't want to say, maybe this isn't really over. Think of this as me hitting the pause button on that tape recorder."

She heads off into the night, leaving me destroyed.

All night long I stare at my phone—willing it to ring, checking Facebook and Twitter, and searching email. Whenever I can bear to look away, I close my eyes and hope to hear Katherine's voice, but all that does is bring back the memory of her leaving. I'm trying to honor her wishes and let her be, but I wish she would at least let me know she got to a hotel safely.

God, I am such an ass. I should have insisted on driving or called a cab and watched from the porch while she waited. No wonder why she is angry with me.

I place a call even though I know I am a fool for pushing her. It goes straight to voicemail and rips my wounds open for another dose of salt. How did I fail?

Standing off to the side of the entrance and peering through the glass door leading into the lobby of Endeara Candies makes me feel like a stalker all over again. Since I haven't been able to get the red out of my eyes, I don't want to be seen let alone have to dodge a conversation.

Come on, phone. You need to ring and distract Darla so I can slip in.

I wait, yet she keeps typing away. Doesn't she need coffee or something?

That's right. Bailey is here. Either she or Darla will be at that desk until someone fills in for them at lunch. I should have called in sick. No, I should have emailed in my resignation.

Half way back to my car I realize how weak I have become. My world was shattered when I lost my fiancée. I have since learned I killed someone in another life and carry a rock in my pocket reminding me of that fact. I got the love of my existence back only to lose her for unexplainable reasons. After all I have survived, am I going to let fear of talking to Darla stop me from going about my day like a normal human being?

I suck it up and head for the entrance—feet steady, resolve firm, eyes locked on the door—only to side step at the last second and enter the building through the loading dock.

As soon as I reach my office, I check all the usual places for a message from Katherine. The last time I checked was when I parked my car. I'm surprised I was able to hold off doing it again this long.

No calls. No Facebook posts. She hasn't been on Twitter or Instagram for days. Seeing there isn't a peep from her via email stomps on my soul, but I also find something else that smears it along the ground. What should be a wave of excitement comes through as gut-churning irony when I see an email from Janet, the sister of Julie, Saleena's old bandmate. She thinks I am a relative of Johnny's who is looking for answers. I had big hopes that once I got this email, I could find a way to come clean with Katherine and let her know how Saleena came to no longer exist. Now I am not so sure it matters.

Hi Brandon,

I talked to my sister regarding your suspicions around Saleena's death. She was shocked anyone remembered the band existed. She was also thrown by the rumor you heard regarding Johnny's suicide. For years she has kept quiet and asked no one talk about it. I'm not sure if she wants the whole mess to go away, or if she doesn't want to further smear the reputations of her friends. Anyone who saw Saleena on her last night pretty much knows the score anyway. Julie finally agreed the truth should come out because, in our eyes, the wrong person has been blamed—somewhat.

I'll never forget the night Saleena died. The girls had been the opening act and we were all partying backstage with a guy who claimed to be with Posh Boy Records. It was getting late, and the club owner kicked us out because we should have left hours before. We were all wasted—so much so that we were too far gone to notice how far gone we were. Johnny tried to keep things cool so we could wait it out, but the manager kept freaking. Since the Posh Boy guy actually had a business card, Saleena was quick to chase after him.

What people need to know about Johnny is he always did everything he could to respect Saleena's wishes and ideas. He wanted to call a cab and meet the guy later, but Saleena was concerned she would miss her big break and goaded Johnny into driving. So while Johnny drove while wasted, the story doesn't end there.

Here's what no one ever got straight. A friend of my aunt was a trauma nurse in the ER on the night of the accident. According to her, the right side of Saleena's head smacked into the front window because she wasn't wearing her seatbelt. The hit was so hard that had it been to the glass and not the bar that goes across the top, she would have gone through it. Then she hit the back of her head on the passenger window and got tossed into Johnny. If he hadn't already gotten the car to a near stop, she might have taken him out too.

Johnny was blamed for Saleena's death because he was behind the wheel, but it was as much her fault for pushing him into driving and for not wearing her seatbelt. Please make sure your family knows the truth. Your cousin was a good guy with a lot going for him. It wasn't only the pain of being behind the wheel when she died that broke him; it was the pain of missing the person he would do anything for, which he proved by going against his nature and driving while knowing better. Not a day goes by my sister and I don't miss them both.

Thank you for the .mp3 of the recording. Getting it is a miracle. We will cherish it forever.

Janet

P.S. Saleena wrote the lyrics to the song you sent right after she and Johnny had a huge blow out. She was very driven, and Johnny often had to shove her into keeping the rest of her life in check. That song is as much a testament to him as it is to her.

My fist slams onto my desk. The intensity of my thoughts sends my hands gripping my hair and me burying my head.

Dammit, Saleena! Why didn't you put on your seatbelt? So much could have been different. You and Johnny might still be here. I never would have met Amber, and maybe she would have been someplace else on the night of her accident—some place where ice cream was already in the freezer. How much would have been different if I refused to drive, or if you had worn your seatbelt?

I pull Johnny's rock out of my pocket and ask why. Why did we drive that night? Because of love? How stupid! We killed her and risked the lives of others when the worst that could have happened by not doing so was losing out on a recording contract. There wasn't a single guarantee she would have gotten one anyway. Hell, maybe a better offer would have come along.

Again I bury my head while my mind swims with what-ifs. If Johnny hadn't driven her, would she have hopped in that guy's car? Then what would have happened to her? Would fate have been the same?

Tears form as I see that a lifetime later consequences continue to haunt me.

"Nice try." The soft sounds of Darla's voice and her setting a box onto the ground pull me back into the present. "You okay?"

I turn my face away from her view. Why did she have to check on me? Why couldn't she be someone who doesn't give a crap about anyone else and let me wallow? Sometimes suffering is easier when no one cares.

Though her words sound like those of the woman I am used to, the tender tone in her voice conveys a side of her rarely seen. "I'd ask why you are avoiding me, but I think I know."

This is not a good time for reminders of how much my life sucks.

"Aren't you going to ask me *how* I know?"

Sweet and understanding or not, I don't need this right now. I find myself putting my head onto my desk as if trying to hide.

"Hey, come on. Talk to me," she says as she begins to massage my shoulders. I wish I knew how to respond, but I just don't. That letter made everything harder to process.

The massaging stops with a sigh. "Okay, new tactic." She snaps her fingers in my ear. "Earth to Brandon Wayne," comes through in her normal tone.

She is not going to let up. "Fine! *How* do you know Katherine bailed on me in the middle of the night, and for all I know, was mugged and is dead in a ditch?"

"I can't say. However, if you think about it, there is only one way I could know Katherine bailed on you, *for a really lame reason*. Where would she go?" She touches a finger to her chin and muses. "Hmm … Have you seen Bailey today?"

God, why won't she get on with it? "Your point?"

"Dude! For a guy whose last name is Wayne you suck at detective work. I came up here so you could stop worrying. Also, one of the guys in the warehouse found that box of old packaging samples. He didn't know what to do with it, so in true Endeara Candies fashion, instead of bringing it directly to you, he left it on my desk."

God, I am so lame! Katherine ran to Bailey last night. Thank God she is safe.

I pop up and narrow the space between Darla and I. In an odd way the closer I am to her, the closer I am to Katherine. "What did she say? Am I totally screwed?"

Darla goes back to musing at the air. "You know, Brandon Wayne sounds a lot like Bruce Wayne, but you remind me more of John Cusack than Batman." She leans back and sizes me up. "Yeah, certainly not Thor. Captain America? Ooh! Maybe The Flash. How fast can you run?"

I toss my hands up and rattle them, similar to what I want to do to her throat. "Dammit, Darla!"

"Yeah, definitely more like John Cusack. Look, I can't tell you anything, but for what it is worth, we all know Katherine is being ridiculous—me especially. You may be a little nuts around the edges, but there isn't a thing in the world any woman could ever be angry with you about."

I plop back down into my chair with my head in my hands. "Man," Darla says, "you can't grab a clue to save your life. Screw it, I promised Katherine I'd keep my mouth shut, but Bailey clammed up. If Bailey wanted me to stay silent, she would have backed Katherine. Katherine is confused. Hell, I'm confused by your story and you would be amazed by some of the wacky stuff I have heard. Katherine needs to figure out the reason why she is turning into a brat, and then all will be hunky dory. She's flying out tonight to go to her parent's place. That is where she clears her head."

I'm up from my seat in a blink. "No! She can't leave. I've got to stop her."

Darla pushes me back into my chair. Damn, for a trim girl she is as strong as a cement roadblock. "Sit! Panicking will make this worse, not to mention *it is best if you get a woman to come to you or meet you halfway.*"

I hate that she is right. Man, this also reminds me of when

Jennifer said, 'A loved horse is one not forced to drink.' God, I want to beat my head against the wall. I toss my head back in hopes it will hit something, and the contents of the box Darla set on the ground catches my eye. Sitting on top is a red, heart-shaped candy box that happens to have a pink rose attached to it. Why all the pink roses lately?

The universe seems to smack me in the face. How could I have been so oblivious?

Amber! She is the one who led this horse to water, which was by letting me hear Katherine's voice so I would track her down. 'Partners work together, but a loved horse is one that is not forced to drink' is about how Amber and I made all decisions together, but what happens with Katherine and I is something we have to decide on our own. Jennifer also said not hearing Katherine any more didn't mean I am not loved, or in other words, guided. 'Be Batman' means to follow Amber's Bat Signal. Pink roses appear at moments when I need to pay attention—like to Katherine on the first night I heard her voice and to Jennifer when she said to be Batman. They even turn up in conversation, such as when Darla inadvertently guided me to Toronto. If I want things to work out with Katherine, I need to pay attention.

"Personally," Darla says, "I blame Jason for being a prick. She probably heard something to make her transfer that anger. That has to be what is causing her headaches."

Her head …

"Do you think those things are unrelated? Maybe your cologne gives her a headache and triggers a bad memory. You know how on *The Brady Bunch,* Tiger's flea powder made Jan sick? Maybe your cologne—"

I smack my palm to my head both in a gesture of saying duh and to emphasize how I understand the problem. "I know why she is angry!"

"I was kidding about your cologne smelling like flea powder."

I smack a kiss onto Darla's forehead. "You are brilliant!" Swiping up my keys, I make for the door.

"Brandon, do not ambush her," Darla says while chasing me down the hall. "She needs space, and if you go bursting in like Batman, she'll get defensive and won't listen to a word you say."

Screw Batman! I'm someone better.

I'm John Cusack!

The Chain

Brandon

My brain races as fast as my engine. I should slow down. I should think about what to say.

I should have a boom box.

After skidding to a halt in front of Darla's fourplex, I attach my iPod to the radio and a raging guitar rattles my speakers. With the thing cranked, I get out of my car and make toward Darla's apartment. The blasted song doesn't seem loud enough to make it through the window.

Dammit, Darla! Why do you have to live all the way up on the second floor? She'll never hear this.

When I try to boost the volume by turning up the iPod, the difference is minimal, if not imagined.

Crap! I need a boombox like Cusack so I can get up against the side of the building—right next to the one rose bush that is in bloom.

Son of a ... Those are Amber Pink roses.

There is no mistaking what I need to do next.

"I'm sorry, lawn. You don't deserve your fate. Then again, most don't."

Within a moment, I've backed down the street, hit the gas, popped my poor baby onto the curb and across the lawn, and then stop so close to the bush that the nose of my car touches a branch, causing pink petals to fall on my hood. Weight locks in my throat, and I take a moment to blow a kiss toward Heaven. "Thanks, Amber—for everything."

Even with the song cranked, it doesn't seem loud enough, so I jump on the hood of the car. Why do I think this will help? I've not a clue in the world, but hey, what about any of this madness with Katherine has made sense?

I want to shout, but I am supposed to let her come to me. However, I've driven up on the lawn to right under her window. If she's here, she has to hear this.

Come on, Katherine! Hear this!

Katherine slides open the screen and sticks her head out. The way her hair whips in the breeze is like watching living poetry. As horrible as it is to say, her puffy, red eyes fill me with relief. She must be as torn up as I am. "Why are you blasting my song?" she yells.

"It's not *your* song; it's *our* song. We have always been a team, and I can't let you break us up." I hold up my phone with the email from Janet open, even though I know darn well she can't tell what I am showing her. "You need to read this."

Why does she look exasperated?

Come on, honey. Don't give up hope!

Bailey sticks her head out the window while I continue to shout to Katherine. "It's the key to why you get those headaches around me, and why you need to be as angry with yourself as you are me." Her face contorts in question, and I motion her to come down. "Saleena, it's the answer!"

Bailey turns to her and then points to me. I can clearly read her lips demand, "Get your ass down there!" She reminds me of Darla. That balls-to-the-wall attitude must be genetic.

As Katherine slips from my view, Bailey gives me two thumbs up and bounces like a pre-teen. "Darla knew you could fix it!"

"Yeah, but she is going to kill me when she sees the lawn."

Bailey's encouragement builds my self-esteem to the point where I feel invincible. I jump off of the hood to race to Katherine. Two steps in I stop, wait for her to exit the building, and then match her pace, meeting her halfway. Being next to her enlivens me as if I have been reborn. If all that has happened wasn't proof enough, this feeling confirms she is the other half of me.

Her eyes peer up enough to catch mine when she says, "Hi." They go back to the ground in embarrassment for the nonsensical emotions she hasn't been able to control. In an effort to show her it's all going to be okay, I duck my head under hers and let the soaring of my heart show the smile on my face as I return the greeting. I damn near cheer when she smiles back.

"You need to see this," I say, handing her the phone. "I wasn't honest regarding everything I know about Saleena. Remember how I was in contact with Julie's sister? Turns out she was there the night Saleena died. I, actually Johnny, played a part in Saleena's death, which is why you get angry with me. But read about how she died and why. It will explain those headaches."

Her eyes scan the email. When she gets to the part about the accident, her bottom lip drops. A few lines later her eyes pop up toward me, and it all seems to sink in. "I'm not mad at you; I'm mad at Johnny."

"In a way it's the same thing. Keep reading."

"This matches where I get the pain in my head. Oh God, this makes so much sense." Though she hands me back the phone, her eyes stay locked on the message in awe of its explanation. "So you think I am actually mad at Johnny for letting me be stupid?"

"Yeah, but remember, he was stupid too."

"Oh, God. I feel the world has been lifted off of my shoulders." And now it starts to happen. I see that look, that beautiful, glorious look a person only gets when they gaze into the eyes of someone they have fallen for. Her voice flows out like a gentle stream of hope. "I'd say this is the craziest thing I have ever heard but …"

I can't, and would not dare try to, hide the tears that come to my eyes. "I've heard crazier. I can't blame you for being angry, and I won't ask you not to be. But can you please see why and accept we are angry with Johnny for something we were both at fault for? I can't even let myself get beyond tipsy, let alone wasted. Now I know why."

I'm unsure how delicately I should handle the situation, but this is my partner, and I am going to treat her that way. With that in mind, I take her hands. "Katherine, you and I were a team once. We probably were before that, too. Do you think we can ever get past what happened a lifetime ago so we can enjoy the gift we have in each other now?"

She looks to the sky with a smile that is almost a laugh. "This is so insane. I knew my anger was irrational, and there had to be some explanation, but this takes the cake." Her sudden radiance convinces me everything is going to be all right. Lord, I want to put this glow on her face every day, but for much better reasons. "Do you think this is why people who just met instantly feel a strong connection of love or hate?" she asks.

"Yeah. I never thought about it before, but I get it now. Can you forgive Johnny for risking your life?"

I sort of expect her to chuckle because my question is ridiculous on so many levels, yet we both get how serious it is. "I'll make it happen. I promise. Can Brandon forgive me for being an irrational ass?"

"Given the circumstances, I think I kind of owe you."

As if all we have discovered has not been enough proof, the sizzle of the kiss we share as it fuses our souls back together reinforces all I have come to believe. If you are willing to hop on to the crazy train, the universe will give you one hell of a ride!

Trust Your Heart

Katherine

The glow of the clouds as the sun dips below the horizon tint Brandon's bedroom gold. Though the scene brings about a sense of peace, the growing shadows remind me of a hidden truth, putting a part of me at war.

Brandon mutes a sigh as he slips his arms around my waist, and rests his chin on my shoulder. The longer he stands here, staring with me at the sunset, the more I feel he is waiting for me to burst out with whatever I am holding back. Then again, I may only think he is able to sense my guilt.

"You don't have to give away any secrets," he says, "but can you assure me that whatever keeps weighing your mind isn't something that will send me searching for answers in an effort to save us again?"

I can't get anything past this guy. Sometimes I swear he can still hear me. "We are fine," I promise. "Ever since you showed me that email last week, I've never been happier."

"Then why am I so worried about you?"

If I learned one thing about myself while I was with Jason, it's that I need to come out of the shadows of my past mistake. I can only do that by facing Brandon along with myself. I break away to take a seat on the bed, pulling him behind as I go. "You know how you have pain in your past with Amber?" He nods and sits next to me. "Well, I guess everyone has some kind of story that follows them. I'm no exception."

While Brandon's tender touch on my knee brings comfort, it is the concern beaming from his eyes that calms my soul. Some of my tension vanishes as I see I am the only one here who will have a hard time accepting my situation.

"I was a few months shy of finishing two years of junior college when both the excitement and the stress of knowing I was moving out to go to a major university was hitting me. At the same time, it suddenly seemed none of my clothes fit anymore. First I thought I was bloated because my period was due. Then I realized how late I was and … well, later that afternoon, a test proved the jitters that kept hitting me had little to do with going off to school."

Brandon reaches for my quivering hands. His slightly open mouth makes him look so worried I feel he is the one who needs consoling.

"I'll speed this up by saying eight months later I gave birth to a little girl I never got to see, let alone hold." My voice locks on the words, and I sniffle back the sorrow that weighs my heart. Still, I press on. No matter how he reacts, I have to come to terms with this.

"I hate myself for what I did. There's no excuse, but I have come to face wanting to be in the spotlight drove me. I was all set to move to Detroit, but then the whole setback, plus feeling I owed it to her to be successful, spiraled me into moving to Los Angeles and bailing on school."

Brandon's head snaps toward me. "You were supposed to go to school in Detroit? Which one and when?"

"University of Detroit, about nine years ago."

His disbelieving stare probably looks like mine did when I discovered someone was actually hearing my voice. "That's where I went. That's also about when I went back after Amber died." His voice softens as if he can't believe the words he utters are true. "I was always meant to meet you."

How incredible would it have been to meet Brandon sooner? But thank God I have found a silver lining. In fact, I have found two, and they make my burden a bit lighter. "I'm glad that didn't happen. Not only would we not have such a crazy story, but also chances are I wouldn't have made it to LA, so I wouldn't have gotten my job. Giving up on school paid off." It's about time I saw things worked out somehow.

Why is Brandon shaking his head?

"No," he says. "The show started four years ago. You would have long graduated, so we would have already moved here."

Oh, no. He can't derail me now. "How can you say that with such certainty? There is no way of knowing what we would have done."

"The past has already shown I would never let you give up on your dreams. Besides, I didn't plan to move to LA, so maybe I was meant to be here all along." How his words raced out flatten my newfound comfort. However, now Brandon's voice grows distant. "I never gave it much thought, but the way I got my job felt more like a summoning than an offer. Why do I now feel I am here for a reason? I wonder what it is."

I constantly put myself in a bubble of excuses, but it has again popped. There's no way my fate would have been the same if I made different choices. There just can't be. "You think we would have gotten together, even if I had a kid?"

Brandon tosses his hands up as if the answer is a no-brainer. "I know we would have."

My chest feels so dull—so heavy my lungs aren't filling; yet I have no need to gasp. I have to go stare out the window because I can't face him anymore. God, please show me I am wrong. "So there was no reason for me to make her feel unloved? I could have left her with my parents, finished school, and met you? We would have come out here anyway?" No, this can't be right. There must be something that doesn't fit the picture, and I have to find it. "But then I never would have been able to audition for the part, let alone take the job."

"Why not? Besides, something tells me you make enough where we could have hired a nanny. Shoot, I could have been a stay-at-home dad." He snickers, and I think I need to puke. "I've always dreamed of owning a record store and having my kid help out. How awesome would it be to watch customers get outwitted by a six-year-old?"

He can't do this to me. For years the feeling I am a terrible person who abandons people to get what she wants has chased me. Now he is tackling me with the reality that it didn't have to be a one or the other situation. My arms curl over my head for fear of catching my reflection in a mirror. I don't even want to see my own shadow. "Oh God, I could not have screwed up more."

Brandon offers his embrace, but there is no comforting me. When it comes to this, there never has been. "Honey, I don't see it that way."

He doesn't have to. This is my pain. I have a right to feel it. "A *person*, Brandon! I gave away a *person*, and I did it in exchange for a crapshoot at a career that may fail because Jason is about to tank the entire show. God, how can he do that to everyone?" I feel so buried in emotions I can't see how I can ever get out from under. No amount of prayer has put an end to this nightmare.

"Honey, you gave a child to someone who wanted one."

My words scream out at him. He's pushed me over the line, and he needs to stop. I can't face this anymore. "Because I didn't want to be bothered! What kind of person does that make me?"

Brandon halts as if my words have slapped him. Everything about him takes pause and then … softens. With a look to Heaven he releases a breath, and I feel he has pulled a bit of the stress out of my body and sent it into the ether. His words remind me of a prayer filled with awe. "It makes you an extension of God."

"What? How can you claim what I did put me anywhere near being a deity?"

The calm in his voice continues to prevail. "Do you believe some things are so incredible the only way to explain them is by the existence of a greater power?"

Him taking my hands in his steals my vision. There is no doubt in my heart that I have to listen. "Yeah, so."

"So do a lot of others, and some of those people have been told their dream of having a family is impossible. One of those families adopted your daughter. They were given a blessing— a gift from God—therefore making you an extension of something greater."

Brandon's crazy, and I don't want to face him anymore,

yet the insistence in his eyes draws my gaze back to him.

"We didn't meet as intended because a greater purpose came along. You brought joy into another couple's life. Now I am grateful for the time I spent waiting for you because I know why it had to happen. If that couple is half as thrilled as I would be, it was worth every bit of my suffering. I hope you can find it was worth yours too."

Tingles ripple through my body, making it difficult to breathe. Others have told me I did something beautiful, and I have tried saying it to myself, but something in this man's words makes him sound like a messenger—as if the words come from a higher source. "Why didn't you have an abortion?" he asks.

Those words bring heat to my eyes. The answer to that has never been simple or even clear. "I could never decide how I felt about it."

Brandon raises my chin, drawing my eyes into his. His sincerity reminds me of all those paintings you see of saints addressing one who is suffering. "So instead you chose to sacrifice part of your life to bring joy into the world. In other words, you got the honor of playing God by responding to two people who prayed for a miracle. Don't you think they see you as a means by which prayers were answered?"

I want to tell him he is wrong—that no man could ever understand what it is like to carry a child, not only in his body but also in his soul, only to never get to hold her in his arms. But as much as I want to scream he is clueless, he has me stopped dead in my tracks. Brandon's words have hit my soul.

The big picture becomes clear. I could have had an abortion and saved myself the horror of people congratulating me on my pregnancy and telling me how wonderful my life was about to become—only for me to have to hide my tears of truth. I've now come to learn I could have had the baby and possibly had my career and Brandon anyway. But in neither of those scenarios does the true gift present itself. For years that family prayed like crazy for a baby. Jason reminded me they used the word miracle, but it never held meaning until now.

The tears streaming down my cheeks are because I have come to see one miracle, but another puts a rock in my throat. This man has shown me the light; much like my gut tells me he tried to do with Saleena decades before. Now I truly understand what she meant when she wrote, "*Are you the one who dares to stand in my way? For if you are, I just may be saved.*"

My little girl's new family may see me as their savior, but this man is mine. That, in and of itself, is a miracle.

Starting Over

Brandon

The noon rays of the California sun shine down as I walk in the path of my tire tracks that are still impressed on Darla's lawn. Though life now seems perfect, one nightmare will always haunt me. I want it to, because I don't think I could stand myself if it didn't.

The Amber Pink rose bush is now as sparsely flowered as its neighbors. I take a seat before it and pull the symbol of Johnny's burden out of my shirt pocket that sits over my heart. This rock used to seem so jagged and heavy, but accepting its existence and bringing Johnny into my life has taken away the harshest edges and given it a touch of sheen. I want to find the forgiveness our soul craves, but I can't let myself be at peace, nor can I forgive the driver who took Amber's life.

People make foolish mistakes every day. Most of the time the consequences are minor. Sometimes lives are altered. The driver that killed Amber never meant to hurt her, just like Johnny only wanted to give Saleena everything he could. However, it doesn't change the fact that his actions killed her, or that their friends and families continue to hurt. Johnny's cross is mine to bear.

I look up to the bush and focus on the last rose that seems full of life. Love pours out of my heart as if the woman it reminds me of were before me. "Amber, you've done so much for me, and in some ways I feel this is a horrible request, but I need you to ask the angels to hold onto Johnny's burden. I can't let something I would handle so differently rule me, so ask them to keep his pain concealed so I can live my life. But if I am ever about to put someone in harms way again, please have them remind me it is here. Thanks, honey. Thank you for looking out for me."

With regret for my past actions in my heart, I bore a hole into the ground and bury the pebble along with as much pain as my heart can release. In life Amber showed me a new world, but long after she has gone she has given me a precious gift I honestly never felt she could. My voice cracks as the words from my heart surface, and I see more than ever why we worked as a team and why I loved her. "Thank you for helping me see who I truly am and who I was. Thank you for loving me so much that you wanted me to adore and feel passion for someone again. May the angels always carry you on their wings, just as I will always carry you in my heart."

Tears fall from my eyes as I stand and bring my nose to the lovely bloom. The aroma sends a whiff of peace to my soul, further easing my load. With a smile to Heaven, I head back to my car, ready to return to work and the life I have built.

Silver, Blue & Gold

Katherine

There is a certain charm to Mulligan's, the favorite watering hole of Brandon and his friends. While I totally get why they like having a place to hang out, relax, and share stories, I also couldn't quite grasp the exasperation in his voice when he told me, "Yeah, it's a special party to celebrate Bailey's arrival and Darla's departure from Endeara. Of course, that means we are going to Mulligan's, you know, the place we *always* go." I've also become so fond of these Cherry Lemon Drops I may have finished my first one a little quicker than I should have and thus find myself at the bar, eager to try another one of their new concoctions.

With my Strawberry Basil Margarita in hand, I head off to join Bailey in our booth. However, when I catch sight of the look on her face, I stop dead in my tracks.

Bailey's eyes are locked on a tall man who is exactly her type—a man with dark skin, short, black, slicked-back hair with a classic wave in it, and eyes deep as sin. Dale tries to conceal how he can't stop looking at her by taking a sip out of his highball glass. Interesting. Dale has yet to strike me as shy. Right now, if he were a cat, I think his tail would be spiked.

Dale takes a couple of steps towards her, only to stop a few feet away as if asking permission to approach. It's so damn sweet, and there is no way I am interrupting it. Before Dale can see me, I detour and slip into the booth next to them.

Softly, he clears his throat. "Hi. I'm Dale."

"Hi. I'm Bailey."

The chuckle he lets out seems driven by nerves. "I'm sorry," he says, "I have absolutely no idea what to say that doesn't sound like a terrible pick up line. Got any suggestions?"

God, that sounds sweet.

"Not really," Bailey says with a slight laugh. How she sounds as nervous as he does causes my skin to tingle with excitement.

"Are you a ... Are you here by yourself?"

"For the moment. I am supposed to meet a group of friends."

He lets out another small chuckle. "Boy, you're not making this easy, are you?"

Man, I wish I could see this. From her tone, I can tell he has her blindsided. "I am sorry," she says, "but I'm enjoying how sweetly you are approaching this. Care to join me for a few minutes?"

Yes!

Brandon heads in, and I'm barely able to wait for Dale to sit so I can slip out of the booth and catch Brandon before he accidentally crashes their party. My finger flies over my mouth, asking him to keep quiet. "What?" he mouths.

I dash up and nudge him to the bar. Once there, I stick my hand up so no one else can see I am pointing in Bailey's direction. "Check that out!"

Brandon's eyes go huge. "Wow!" Those autumnal orbs land on me, and my heart gets swept up to heaven. However, it's his tender touch to my chin, drawing our lips together, that nearly melts me into a puddle of honey.

I'd love nothing more than to sit here and stare into those eyes all night, but after all I have heard from Brandon about Dale—the once womanizer who is supposedly looking for something real—I am both apprehensive and hopeful. Bailey is attracted to strong men, but part of the byproduct of that was how Carlos was a womanizer. However, Carlos has yet to learn his lesson. Could it be someone who has those same qualities yet is willing to cast them aside and settle down, could be her perfect match? "Do you think Dale and Bailey have a chance? She's been through a lot, and I'd hate to see her hurt."

Brandon's eyes narrow in concern. He leans back with an elbow on the bar and scratches his head at the base. Slowly, a smile builds, and he nods.

"Hmm ... Dale and Bailey ..." Brandon grabs my hand, and nudges me to walk over and join them. "You know, if this meeting happened a few weeks ago, I would go over there, boot him out to get us drinks, warn Bailey to run for her life, and then send Darla after him with a Taser and tell her to aim for his balls. Now, after learning the score, Dale getting to know a nice girl may be a slice of heaven for all of us."

"Then why are we headed over to interrupt them?"

"Although I am pretty confident Dale is not the scumbag I once thought he was, I've also become rather fond of Bailey. If Dale hasn't truly mended his ways, my arrival will send him running. If he stays, especially after the bomb I am about to drop on him, he's serious about keeping up the good behavior."

"The bomb?"

Brandon winks. "Just wait for his expression." We step up to the booth, and Brandon is quick to chime in. "Wow, Bailey," he says while looking at Dale. "You sure know how to pick them."

Dale turns to Bailey. "Remember that friend I told you about? The one whom without I would be in Chicago and probably miserable? I forgot to mention he is annoying."

"You also failed to mention I know him," she replies.

How Brandon addressed Bailey by name dawns on Dale. "Dare I ask?"

"Dale," Brandon says, "meet Bailey, *Darla's sister* and my new co-worker."

I can't help but chime in, "Not to mention my best friend and the greatest beauty makeup artist ever." My grip on Brandon's hand tightens. Seeing love bloom reminds me of how lucky I am and how I have come to learn Brandon is the man I never want to let go of. Maybe Bailey and Dale will find our happiness contagious.

"Wait," Dale says. He turns to Bailey while looking like he

has been popped into a state of shock. I swear the hair on the back of his neck is prickling. "*You* are Darla's sister? Peacock-haired woman? Lord, help us all! How did you get to be so normal?"

Brandon rolls his eyes at Dale, and then clears his throat and motions for him to sit next to Bailey. As Dale slides out, Brandon gives him a look that warms him to be on his best behavior. Dale responds by asking Bailey's permission to sit next her, and then returns Brandon's glare with an expression saying he's the one who should know better. It's comforting to see I have found a man who not only looks out for me but also for my friends. But Brandon is so much more than a great guy; he helps me find the parts of myself I have overlooked because I either didn't want to face or didn't understand them. That is why I have news that is going to rock the socks off of Bailey.

After Brandon got me to see the light regarding my past decisions, I took a step back and really heard some of the things he had been saying all along. He reminded me that Saleena's passions were also my own. Saleena loved the music she played, which is why I am so drawn to it now. For me, what began as a desire for fame grew into a love of the true craft of acting. Desires are fine, but passions are what feed a person's soul.

We slip into the booth, and I'm quick to reach across the table and grab Bailey's arm. I'm so excited by my news that it bursts out. "I handed in my notice this morning."

Bailey's expression freezes so quickly I fear her heart may have been stunned into stopping. "You ..." she swallows hard, "You what?"

"I told the producers this is my last season."

Bailey's eyes enliven. "Did you land a big movie like Jason did?"

My smile is so heartfelt my cheeks warm. "No, I've been so wrapped up in succeeding I forgot the real goal. *Vampires Undercover* isn't what I want to be known for. If the last few months have shown me anything, it is that taking a risk isn't as scary as I think. After all, every time we go to sleep there is a chance we won't wake up, yet it is during the peace we achieve right before slumber that our prayers are heard." I turn to Brandon and see the glimmer of water in his eyes as if he feels my passion and wants me to embrace it. "Brandon being in my life is proof you have to listen to your inner voice. Mine is telling me to grow."

Bailey's eyes turn watery. "I've always known there would come a day when you would say to hell with strategizing and start living."

"You mean that passion would take over?"

She nods, and tears fall. Mine fall right along with them. "That's exactly what I mean." She dabs at the tears and sniffles. Her hand flies to her mouth and she gasps. Her words race out. "Does this mean you are moving back to LA?"

"Yep! That is, unless the right thing comes along elsewhere. I want to focus on movies though, which means I need a home base. I'll be packing my bags in a few months."

Bailey tosses her head back and screams, "Yes!" Just like her, I couldn't be happier.

Brandon

I'm with Bailey. I don't think life could possibly be turning out any better. I feel so fulfilled, not only in whom I am but also by what I see in Katherine. The whole world is opening for her because she gave herself the gift of finding true passion. Day after day we face what life hands us. Some days there is little we can control; however, if we embrace the things that make our hearts sing, life will never let us down. I want that kind of happiness for everyone, be they the people I love or a cocky kid who is learning about life.

Dale's eyes are locked on Bailey as if he is gazing upon destiny. We all seem to be finding our way, yet I have to wonder; is Katherine's decision an act of fate or is she creating a new path?

There is no denying Amber and I were in love. Love is supposed to be all that matters, but we were opposite in so many ways. We always said fate brought us together. Fate is supposed to serve purpose. Was the purpose of our relationship to heal my heart after what happened with Johnny and Saleena, or was it something I'll never see?

Life is a chain of events leading to fate. One broken link and all of the pretty trinkets fall off. But we are the ones who add the trinkets—pretty or otherwise—and chains can be repaired. Did the chain that led me to Katherine get fixed, or was it never broken in the first place?

A few weeks ago I walked into a record store—the same record store I have been in hundreds of times—and was given the key to my past. That night I sat in this very bar where I saw a face on a TV. Both of those simple events presented me the key to my future.

I've always believed music holds magic. Maybe Warped Records and Mulligan's do too.

Find out what happened behind the scenes with Bailey and Carlos, along with why Dale went to see a psychic in *Moonlight Serenade*.

Playlist

"Voices Carry" - 'Till Tuesday
"I Can Remember" - The Raspberries
"New York Groove" - The Sweet
"Round And Round" - RATT
"It'll Be Alright" - Bullet Proof Lovers
"Voices Green And Purple" - The Bees
"Paranoia Is Freedom" - UXA
"Searching For Something" - Joey Ramone
"Dream Police" - Cheap Trick
"Destination Unknown" - Missing Persons
"One Way Or Another" - Blondie
"... And I Will Be With You" - Mr. T. Experience
"Where I Am Today" - Redd Kross
"Crawling From The Wreckage" - Connection
"I Wanna Talk To You" - The Absolute
"Institutionalized" - Suicidal Tendencies
"Instant Replay" - Dan Hartman
"Surrender" - Cheap Trick
"Rat Trap" - Boomtown Rats
"Second Hand News" - Fleetwood Mac
"Our Love Will Last Forever" - Mr. T. Experience
"It's All Over Now, Baby Blue" - Chocolate Watchband
"Strength To Endure" - Ramones
"Crazy World" - Redd Kross
"Heaven" - Warrant
"Punk Rock Girl" - Dead Milkmen
"State Of Emergency" - Stiff Little Fingers
"I Will Always See Your Face" - Love
"The Chain" - Fleetwood Mac
"Trust Your Heart" - The Kinks
"Starting Over" - The Raspberries
"Silver, Blue & Gold" - Bad Company

More by Diane Rinella

The Rock and Roll Fantasy Collection
Scary Modsters…and Creepy Freaks
It's A Marshmallow World
Queen Midas in Reverse
Voices Carry
Moonlight Serenade

Something to Dream On

The Forbidden Flower Series
Love's Forbidden Flower
Time's Forbidden Flower

About the Author

Enjoying San Francisco as a backdrop, the ghosts in USA Today Bestselling Author Diane Rinella's one hundred and fifty-year old Victorian home augment the chorus in her head. With insomnia as their catalyst, these voices have become multifarious characters that haunt her well into the sun's crowning hours, refusing to let go until they have manipulated her into succumbing to their whims. Her experiences as an actress, business owner, artisan cake designer, software project manager, Internet radio disc jockey, vintage rock n' roll journalist/fan girl, and lover of dark and quirky personalities influence her idiosyncratic writing.

You can visit her website at www.dianerinellaauthor.com and on Facebook at https://www.facebook.com/DianeRinellaAuthor/